DEATH OF A SHADOW

A BARBARA O'GRADY MYSTERY

SHARON ROWSE

THREE CEDARS PRESS

DEATH OF A SHADOW
A Barbara O'Grady Mystery
By Sharon Rowse

ISBN: 978-1-998037—18-9

ALSO BY SHARON ROWSE

The Barbara O'Grady Series: (in order)

Death of a Secret

Death of a Threat

Death of a Promise

Death of a Shadow

Death of a Lie

Death of a Dream

Death of a Chance

The John Granville & Emily Turner Historical Mystery Series: (in order)

The Silk Train Murder

The Lost Mine Murders

The Missing Heir Murders

The Terminal City Murders

The Cannery Row Murders

The Hidden City Murders

The Dockside Murders

For details on these and upcoming books or to sign up for her mailing list, visit Sharon's website at: www.sharonrowse.com

She burst into my office late one afternoon, eyes wild. "My sister's missing. You have to find her."

I looked across my cluttered desk and recognized an impossible case, complete with spiky hair and a pierced eyebrow. I seemed to have been specializing in impossible cases lately, and I was sick of them.

But I had a hunch that turning down this client was going to take careful handling. "Sit down and tell me about it."

"She hasn't come home." My would-be client thumped down into the vintage burgundy client chair across from me.

For a moment it was my own sister's patrician features and pinched mouth I saw across the desk, and I felt that familiar twinge of responsibility. I knew all about sisterly histrionics, thanks to some of the stunts Susanna's pulled over the years. Stunts I'd ended up rescuing her from.

"How long has she been gone?" The neutral tone took effort.

"Since this morning," the young woman said, and chewed on a fingernail.

She wore trainers and bike shorts, carried a helmet. The flat afternoon light painted dappled shadows on her pale face. My eyes kept straying to the dark metal hoop through one corner of her left eyebrow, my stomach muscles clenching at the thought of the needle going through.

"It's too soon to be worrying about her," I said.

She jumped up and put both hands on the desk, leaning her face close to mine. "You don't understand. She went to meet that creep. And she hasn't come back."

"What creep?"

"Some guy she met through a dating service. Can you help?"

In her desolate tones I heard echoes of a seven-year old Susanna, holding out a doll without a head. "She broke. Fix her, Barbara, please. I know you can."

A shaky movement from my client jerked me back to the present. "Why don't you sit down, and let's start with some facts," I said. "What is your sister's name?"

She scowled, straggly brows meeting, but sat. "Celeste. Celeste Deslauriers."

"And how old is Celeste?"

"She's thirty-two, no, thirty-three. Nine years older than me."

And a year younger than I was. I hoped Celeste—wherever she was—was considerably more stable than her excitable younger sister. "Have you reported her missing?"

She nodded. "Yeah. They took all the information, but I could tell they didn't think it was urgent."

"Does your sister have any disabilities? Addictions?"

"No!"

Then she was right. Her case wouldn't be considered urgent yet. "Have you called the hospitals?"

"Yeah."

"When did you see her last?"

"I told you, this morning. Around nine. We had a fight."

"About what?"

"I didn't think she should meet this guy. And she wouldn't even tell me his name."

Sounded like a smart move on Celeste's part. "What time was her date?"

"Ten. She was only planning to meet him for coffee. Playing it safe, y'know?"

It was barely four now. "Maybe the date is going really well," I said.

"But it's Sunday."

What was I missing? "And?"

"Sundays we always invite people over for dinner. Celeste starts cooking by one. And she's always on schedule."

"Maybe she decided to bring home takeout for once."

"Not Celeste. She's compulsive. Like anal, y'know?"

Lucky Celeste, to have her younger sister sum her up so easily. "You two live together?"

"Yeah," she said with a grimace. Then remembered why she was here. "She wouldn't just not show up. Not Celeste. Something's happened to her, I know it."

"Hmmm." I made some meaningless scribbles in my notebook. Celeste hadn't been gone long enough for anyone to panic. But how to convince her sister?

Watching that frantic face, I wished my own sister had showed such concern for me, even once. I softened, momentarily forgot that this was another impossible case. "Look, I'll see if I can find out who this guy is, and where Celeste went after their date. But I can't do much until she's been missing at least overnight."

The words were out. It was too late to call them back.

"But that's too long. What if she's in danger? She doesn't know this guy!"

She was over-reacting. Her sister was an adult, had been missing less than a day. "Is there something you're not telling me?"

She shook her head. "If you knew Celeste, you'd understand. Please!"

Clearly she'd been reading too many thrillers. But I couldn't ignore the fear in her voice. "I'll do some preliminary work, see what I can find," I said. "But don't expect too much. She'll probably just come home later. Now, what's your name?"

"Marie Deslauriers."

"Address?"

She gave it to me. Just off Fraser Street, on Vancouver's east side.

"Which dating service did she use?"

"Two Hearts. Downtown."

Who names these places? "And where was Celeste meeting this man?"

"Starbucks. The one at Kits Beach. Across from the water."

"At ten this morning?"

"Yeah."

"Did she drive there?"

"Yeah."

And she handed over a snapshot of a woman standing proudly in front of a bright red mini Cooper. The year and license number were written on the back.

Despite her panic, Marie was pretty organized. "Do you have a better photo of Celeste?"

She nodded, pulled out a close-up of the two of them, obviously dressed to go out. Marie wore fringed layers of scarlet and purple that clashed hideously. Celeste was an elegant contrast in basic black, a sheath dress that suited her slim figure.

Marie's bright red hair spiked straight up. Celeste's hair was a much paler red, drawn back up in a smooth chignon. Marie's face was excited, Celeste's was calm, her cool green gaze turned inward.

"Is this recent?"

"Yeah. Two months ago. We were at Lido."

Vancouver's newest nightspot. Celeste couldn't be all that anal. "I'll need to keep the photo for a bit."

"Keep it. It's just a copy." Marie jumped up and put a hand on my arm. "You will find her, won't you? Before he kills her?"

"Kills her?" Where had that come from?

"He could be a killer." Defensive now.

I looked down at her ragged fingernails. "I'll do my best. I'm sure she's fine."

I watched the look of relief pass over Marie's piquant features and hoped I was right.

————

AN HOUR later I stood in line at the Starbucks counter. I glanced through the plate glass windows that looked across Cornwall to the beach. Traffic was bumper to bumper as harried shoppers swarmed over the Burrard Street Bridge to homes in and Point Gray.

In contrast to the craziness was the serenity of the park, trees just leafing out and the ocean still and calm. Two weeks of non-stop drizzle had given way to a warm sunshine that felt more like July than May. The beach was littered with bodies soaking up the last rays of the day.

And I was working. What was the matter with me?

Inside the coffee shop, trendy beach-goers were ordering mocha frappuccinos and grande non-fat vanilla lattes. "Grande cappuccino," I said when I finally reached the counter.

I handed the bearded youth a five. "And I'm looking for someone who was working here this morning. Around ten?"

He scribbled on a cup, rang it in. "I wasn't on. Tanya was, though."

I dropped some change in the tip jar. "Which one is Tanya?"

"Thanks. Over there, with the beans?"

Tanya, a short redhead with a blue Celtic pattern tattooed around one wrist, was holding two brightly colored half kilo coffee packages, and chattering away to her customer. She was a talker. Good.

I inhaled the rich coffee aromas, drank some of my cappuccino. Okay, maybe taking this case wasn't so bad. I'd needed a break anyway.

And the sight of those beans reminded me I needed to restock my office supply. I sauntered over.

Tanya handed over the pouch of coffee and turned to me. "What can I get you?"

"Half-kilo of Sumatra, please."

She nodded. "These just came in, so they're really fresh." Reaching behind her, she picked up the bright foil pouch.

I waited until she turned back, then leaned towards her. "I was told you were working this morning."

"Yeah?"

"A friend of mine was in around ten. She was meeting this new guy, only she wouldn't tell me anything about him. I thought it'd be pretty funny if I could describe him, like before she did."

Tanya grinned. "That'd be good. What did she look like?"

I showed her the photo Marie had given me.

"Yeah, I remember her. She's pretty, but she looked real anxious for a while there. Till he turned up."

"He was late?"

"Guess so. He got there about fifteen minutes after she did. I noticed, cause like I said, she sat there by herself, kind of playing with her coffee. I was watching her cause I figured she was waiting for a guy, and I wondered if he'd be worth it."

"And was he?"

"He was kinda cute. Not my type, but yeah, probably worth waiting for."

"What did he look like?"

"He wasn't too tall, maybe five eleven or so, medium build, early thirties. Brown hair, mid-brown, you know, but shiny, nice cut. Could have used some spiking, but looked cute. His face was squarish, nothing special, but he had a nice smile, kinda tilted up on one side. I notice smiles," she said, giving me another grin.

So did I. "Did you notice what color his eyes were?"

She shrugged. "Something light. Blue maybe, or gray. I had a customer just then, so I stopped watching."

"Did you notice anything else?"

Delicate eyebrows drew together. "Yeah," she said. "When they left, he held the door for her, and his right arm moved sort of funny."

"Funny how?"

"I'm not sure. It just looked awkward, as though he'd pulled a muscle or something."

I filed that away. "When did they leave?"

"They weren't here more than ten minutes. It was pretty noisy, and they seemed to be trying to talk. He got a couple of coffees to go, and they headed towards the beach."

"Do you remember who served him?"

"Cheryl, I think. But she's off shift."

"No matter. Tanya, thanks so much. I can't wait to see my friend's face when I describe him," I said.

Well, at least I knew Celeste had made it this far, and had met the guy, whoever he was.

CHAPTER TWO

I waited for the light, then crossed Cornwall with the hordes. Last week's Gore-tex had given way to cotton and Spandex, with bare flesh everywhere. I watched a group of giggling bare midriffs scoot by, wondered what their tan lines looked like.

As I strode down to the beach, taking in deep breaths of salt-laden air, the blush of green on the chestnut trees overhead caught my eye. How would I capture that? Sap green with a hint of chrome yellow, against eggplant and sienna mixed with burnt umber for the trunk.

I was suddenly desperate for a paintbrush.

An in-line skater whirred by, missing me by centimeters. "Damn."

Why was I doing this? No more impossible cases, I'd said. More time for painting.

But investigating paid for canvases.

I wasn't about to admit the impact of Marie's pleading eyes.

Besides, there was no guarantee the gallery show Margaret Courtland had conned me into putting together for September would pay one red cent—I might not sell a single painting.

On that cheerful thought I sat on the middle bench, stared at the ocean and sipped my coffee, letting my gaze follow the curve of beach. Where would Celeste Deslauriers and her date have gone? And who might have seen them?

It was a glorious day—blue ocean, blue sky, warm sunshine, fresh breeze. A perfect day to be outside, to stroll along with your coffee, or just sit and watch the world go by.

The big saltwater pool wasn't open yet, it was too early in the year. The concession was doing good business, but my missing pair already had coffees. The cyclists, the skaters, the dog walkers, the lovers strolling hand in hand—all were too transitory to have seen Celeste and her "kinda cute" date, much less remember them.

So how to track them?

They'd just met, maybe they're attracted, but it would be awkward. They'd come down here, sit, sip their coffee, watch the water, chat a little. Marie said that Celeste was reserved. She wouldn't have wanted to sit still for long, it's easier to keep moving while they talked.

But which way? Left? No, nothing to see and the path ended too soon.

They'd go right. Stroll around the Point, chatting about how glad they were it wasn't raining, or about whether Cornwall should be closed to traffic, whatever. Maybe they stopped for a bit to watch the kite flyers by the Maritime Museum.

It's a nice day, they're getting to know each other. They had plenty of time. They'd probably head for the market on Granville Island.

I stood and dropped my empty cup in the nearest bin, and headed for my car.

———

GRANVILLE ISLAND WAS BUSY, the stalls packed with off-duty office workers picking up fresh salmon, pasta, maybe some asparagus. I drew in a breath laden with rich baking, garlic and fresh herbs. I loved this place—the colors, the bustle.

I'd even done a couple of paintings here, years ago. Not that they ever captured the feel of the Island. Maybe if I tried an abstract?

"Later, Barbara," I said out loud, earning an amused glance from the man who ran the organic herb stand.

I looked around. There were too many stalls to ask each one if they'd seen a woman I didn't think was really missing. No way anyone here would remember one couple in this mayhem, anyway. So if they'd walked this far, where would they have gone next?

It would be close to noon when they got here, so if things were going really well, maybe they'd go for lunch. Again, there were a too many options within easy walking distance, but only a half dozen or so with a "date" ambiance.

I checked them all, from the pub, to the wine bar, to the patio restaurant at the small hotel to the "cool" spot to the trendy bistro to the seafood place, showing Celeste's photo to a succession of hostesses and waiters. Nothing.

When I checked my watch, it was nearly half past four. She'd met her beau at ten. Where had they been all these hours? I glanced at a young couple who'd stopped to kiss, and grinned. Celeste and her date were probably back at his place, having wild afternoon sex.

Exiting the market, I looked across False Creek, eyeing the rows of upscale condominiums thronging the shore. If he lived there, they could have taken one of the little ferries back.

But then where was her car? I hadn't spotted it earlier, but on a sunny weekend, parking near the beach is a challenge. It could be anywhere.

Or maybe they hadn't bothered with Kits Beach, had gone straight to his place—she could have followed him home.

Which didn't fit with what Marie had told me about her sister.

Time to see what I could pry out of the dating service. If I could find it.

———

TWO HEARTS DATING AGENCY turned out to be easy to find. Their website popped up first in my search, and it was detailed—all about the magic of finding your soul mate. Please. As if people really expect to find their soul mates on a website.

I shook my head and punched in the numbers.

"Two Hearts," a sultry voice said.

"I need to speak with the manager, please."

"May I say what this is in regard to?"

"It's a personal matter."

She left me listening to a full strings version of the theme from *Titanic*.

"Isabella Marten here."

"My name is Barbara O'Grady. I'm a private investigator, and I've been hired to find a woman by the name of Celeste Deslauriers, who apparently went missing after a date with someone she met through your firm. I need to know the name of the man she met."

There was a short silence, but Ms. Marten was a professional. She didn't ask questions and her reply was calm. "I'm sorry, I don't know which of the men we introduced her to she would have dated most recently."

"This guy was about five eleven, brown hair, medium build, early thirties."

I could hear keys clicking. "That description fits all three men."

It did? Celeste must have very specific tastes in men. "If you give me their names, it will help me find her faster."

"I'm afraid that won't be possible. We have a confidentiality policy."

Not surprising. I doubt clients wanted their search for a soul mate broadcast. But I needed answers.

"Celeste is missing," I said. "Her life may be in danger and time is of the essence. You do understand that?"

"I understand, but I'm afraid our policy is firm. We only give that information to the police."

"That won't happen today. She only met him this morning."

"Exactly."

It had been a long shot anyway. "Could you at least call the three guys, ask if they saw her and when?"

"You do know what you're asking?"

"Maybe you could frame it as quality control? Her sister is frantic with worry. She says this is totally out of character for Celeste."

A pause. "Very well," she said at last, still sounding professional. "Where can I reach you?"

"I'll hold." Three seconds later, listening to an orchestral version of *The Way We Were*, I was regretting my words.

Eventually she returned. "Your luck was in. All three were home, but two say they haven't met her yet and the third says they met for coffee last weekend and haven't spoken since. He's annoyed, requesting another match."

"None of them met with her today?"

"That's what they say."

"So one of them is lying," Or Celeste had lied to her sister about who she was meeting, but I saw no point in complicating matters for Ms. Marten.

"Possibly."

"And you still won't tell me who these men are?"

"I've stretched our privacy rules as far as I'm going to, Ms. O'Grady. My clients were not pleased to hear from me on a Sunday."

"I'm sorry." And I was. She had a business to run, just as I did, even if I didn't think much of the business she was in. But if there was even a remote possibility Celeste's life was in danger...

"Look, I won't tell anyone where I got their names. Someone is lying and I need to find out why before it's too late."

"I'm afraid I can't give you the names," Isabella Martin said. "I'm sorry. I hope Celeste turns up."

"Yeah."

———

AS SOON AS I DISCONNECTED, the phone rang. Marie. I filled her in on what I'd found so far.

"So what am I supposed to do now?" she wailed.

I wished there were something I could suggest. Action of any kind, even futile action, is easier than waiting. "Celeste may well come home later tonight, or call. She has to be at work tomorrow morning, right?"

"Yeah, at eight-thirty. But you have to do something now! You have to!"

I could hear the fear in her voice, but something she'd said earlier had been niggling at me. "Marie, how were you and your sister getting along?"

A hesitation. "Why do you ask?"

Uh oh. "You mentioned a fight this morning. Were there problems between you?"

"No! It's just, sometimes she wants everything her way."

I wondered what Celeste's view was. "Just how bad was this fight? Bad enough that she might not want to talk to you for a few hours?"

"She'd never leave me worried like this. I should have heard from her by now."

Maybe not, if she and Marie were at odds, and her date was really hot.

"You'll probably hear tonight," I said. "But if she doesn't show up for work, call me. We'll sort out where to go from there."

CHAPTER THREE

The following morning, I staggered into the living room, blinking against the light, and nearly stepped on Cat. Predictably, he was lying in a patch of sunlight in the middle of the room. When I cursed him, he opened one eye and looked at me as if wondering what I was doing there.

"That is the wrong question, cat."

He blinked, slowly.

Cat is an enormous orange striped cat who belongs to my downstairs neighbor, Mrs. Pinkton. He refuses to answer to his given name—not that I blame him, since she calls him Buttercup—and he's somewhat confused about the limits of his territory.

Basically, he thinks my entire apartment belongs to him. "Now move."

Cat yawned, showing every one of his sharply pointed teeth.

With a sigh, I stepped around him. I've lost every argument I've ever had with that cat. I don't know why I tolerate him.

Halfway through a toasted eight-grain bagel, I felt a paw against my leg. I looked down to find him staring at me.

"Mrrrt?" he said, and slightly flexed his claws, just enough to give me warning that he meant business.

"All right, you big lug. Here's yours," I said, breaking off a piece dripping with honey and holding it out for him. He took it delicately from my fingers. When he'd finished chewing, he polished his whiskers. I could swear he was smirking.

"Stupid cat."

———

WHEN I GOT to my office at eight-fifteen, the first thing I did was put on a pot of Italian Roast. I'd painted far too late last night, and I needed the caffeine. As I drank the first mouthful, there was a banging on my door.

Marie. Face blotchy. Eyes bloodshot. Hair uncombed.

"You haven't heard from her?"

She shook her head, pushed past me, paced. "No. I called her work. She's not there. Didn't call. She's never late for work."

Damn. Marie had been right. Her sister really was missing. "Have you called the hospitals today?"

She paled, but nodded. "Nothing."

I could hear the edge of hysteria in her voice. "Have you talked to the police again?"

"They'll do what they can. But they'll be too late." She took a choppy breath. "You have to find her, Barbara. You have to. I don't know what I'll do if he kills her."

Her voice rose with every word. I wasn't up to this. But looking into Marie's shock darkened eyes, hearing her fear for her sister, I couldn't just walk away.

"It'll be okay," I said. "Sit down. We'll find her. Want a coffee?"

"I don't drink the stuff. Do you know what it does to your body?"

I looked at the ring through her eyebrow, and had to bite my tongue. Now was not the time. But I wondered how she got through the day without coffee. "Some water?"

She nodded, and finally sat down.

"You told the police everything you know?" I asked as I handed her a glass of water.

Marie nodded again, her breathing still ragged.

So they weren't seeing this as a Stalker case, either. That was a relief. "Is Celeste's car still missing?"

"Yeah."

I made a note. "Where does she work?"

"Vancouver University."

"What department?"

"University Advancement. She's a fundraiser."

That explained the polish I'd seen. "I'll need a list of her colleagues, her boss's name, anything you can remember. I'll need to talk to them. You're okay with that?"

"Sure. Whatever."

"I'll also need a list of her friends. Is she dating anyone, other than this mystery date?"

"No. No-one. I tell her she's too picky, but she just laughs and says that unlike me, she has standards." Marie started to smile, then remembered and her face went blank.

I had a sense I'd like the missing Celeste. "Does Celeste have enemies?"

Marie's gaze shifted and she began to pick at a hangnail on her left thumb. "No."

I'd come back to that one, I decided, watching her face. "Did she owe anyone money?"

"Celeste? You've got to be kidding."

Okay. "She's single?"

"Yeah."

"Has she ever been married?"

Marie nodded. "Twice."

I hadn't seen that one coming. It didn't match the image I'd been forming. I wondered if one of the exes qualified as the enemy Marie didn't want to discuss.

"Are they in town?"

"One lives in Squamish. The other one's in West Van."

One lived in a small university town on the way to Whistler, the other in the priciest neighborhood in Vancouver. Interesting contrast. "How long had she been divorced?"

"She and Ben divorced nearly ten years ago. Callum left two years ago."

I noted her choice of verbs. "And Ben is?"

"Ben Oliver, the one in Squamish. And Callum McLaughlan's the West Van one. He's in banking," she added without my prompting.

"And Ben?"

"A lawyer. But he doesn't work for the big firms anymore. He's into eagles," she added, as if that explained everything.

And maybe it did. During the spring salmon runoff, Brackendale, a whistle-stop just outside Squamish, plays host to the largest gathering of bald eagles on the continent. "How did Celeste and Ben ever get together?"

"We'd just moved here. He was interning at one of the big downtown law firms. She was doing secretarial work for another. They met at a club, got married six months later."

She shrugged. "It lasted a couple of years. But it turned out they wanted different things. The last year they fought all the time."

The pieces fell into place. "You were living with them?"

"Yeah."

"You must have been..." I did a quick calculation. "Thirteen?"

"Fourteen."

My nephew's age. "Have you always lived with your sister?"

It didn't seem to occur to her to wonder at my questions. "Yeah, her and our Aunt Thea, ever since my Dad died. Mom died when I was born."

She hadn't mentioned the aunt before. "Is your aunt still alive?"

A head shake. "She died when I was eleven. That's when we moved to Vancouver."

When Celeste was barely twenty. They hadn't had it easy. My heart went out to them, two girls struggling to survive in a hostile city. "What about the other one?"

"Callum? He's a snob. I guess we just didn't fit in with his expectations."

"You and Celeste didn't?"

She dropped her eyes. "They mostly fought over me living with them."

Why had she? She must have been nearly twenty-two when Callum walked out.

"Does Celeste ever see either of them?"

"You're kidding, right? She vowed never to speak to Callum again, which is awkward 'cause he knows too many of their major donors. And she and Ben just don't have anything to talk about any more."

"So she wouldn't have seen either of them recently?"

"Not Ben, for sure. Callum she might have seen at some fundraising dinner or other, but they wouldn't have spoken."

I wondered again if Marie knew as much about her sister's inner life as she professed to. Somehow I doubted it, and it wasn't based just on the apparent differences between the two.

I think it came from having a younger sister of my own.

Even if we'd been as close as I sometimes wished we could be, I doubt I'd have told Susanna everything about my life. Some of it I'd hold back, even now, to protect a younger sibling. Some I'd keep back from the need to carve out parts of your life that belong to you alone, and not to your family.

"I'll need their phone numbers, addresses if you've got them, same for Celeste's friends."

"Shit," she muttered. "Celeste would have all this at the press of a key."

"She had a smartphone?"

"Yeah. She ever went anywhere without it."

"Did she have a computer at home?"

Marie shook her head. My hopes fell. "They gave her a laptop. She used that."

"Where is it?"

"I dunno."

"Look for it. It's important." If Celeste was as compulsive as Marie thought, surely she'd have backed up her data.

Still, if Marie's picture was entirely accurate, I wondered how Celeste had managed to misplace two husbands. "I also need a list of everything Celeste did over the last week, who she was with."

"Like she'd tell me everything."

I just looked at her. "Everything you know about, Marie."

She flushed, resumed picking at the hangnail. I couldn't stand to watch her. "Marie, do you want me to find Celeste?"

She looked up, stared at me. "Of course."

"Then you have to level with me. Did Celeste have enemies?"

"No, she didn't." Firm voice. Meeting my eyes.

She wasn't lying, but my gut said there was something she wasn't telling me. Just like all my other clients.

"You know I can't find your sister unless I know where to look, don't you?"

"I told you," she flared. "Look at him." There was venom in her tone, in her eyes.

"I thought you'd never met your sister's date?"

"I haven't."

"Then why are you so sure he's the reason she's missing?"

She dropped her gaze, fidgeted. Something was up. "Marie? What do you know about him?"

"Just what I told you yesterday."

She was lying. I let her words hang in the air. It was enough.

"Celeste told me he came from Brenton, where we grew up," she said in a low voice.

Brenton was a whistle-stop on the old Canyon highway a couple of hours north of Vancouver. "So?"

"So they didn't like us much in Brenton."

"Why not?"

She shrugged, wouldn't meet my gaze. "Dunno. I was too little."

It was a place to start.

———

AS SOON AS MARIE LEFT, I was back on the phone with Ms. Marten from Two Hearts. She was not happy to hear from me. "I thought you understood I've done all I can to help."

"Celeste is still missing. I'd like to talk to you about her."

"I won't release—about her?"

"Yes. If I'm to find her, I need to understand her. Do you know her?"

"Yes, she's a lovely woman. I'm sorry to hear she's still missing."

"Did she fill out a profile with Two Hearts?"

"Yes."

"Then we need to meet."

Despite her reluctance, Ms. Marten agreed to see me at ten. I thanked her, broke the connection and tried again.

"Detective Hawald."

"Morning, Jerry."

"Whadda ya want, O'Grady?"

"I need a favor."

"What is it this time?"

I grinned at his tone. "Nothing major. I want to talk to someone about a case I've just taken on. And I need an introduction."

"Why don't you ask that boyfriend of yours?"

"Wrong jurisdiction. Nick's RCMP, remember? Besides, he's tied up on that task force."

Which meant I hadn't seen him in two weeks. I didn't even have a number to call. I hated that.

And I wasn't too happy to find myself missing him, either.

Jerry's voice sobered. "The Stalker?"

"Yeah."

"They getting any closer?"

Like I'd know. "If they are, they aren't letting anyone know. You haven't heard anything?"

"Nothing."

"Yeah." A short silence fell between us.

"So, what's this case of yours?" he asked.

"I've got a woman missing since yesterday morning, when she met a date for coffee."

"You're sure you shouldn't be talking to Nick about this?"

"Pretty sure," I said, and filled him in on the details. "What do you think?"

"I think you're right. MO's off. And the one thing we know about this guy is he's incredibly careful not to be seen. It's like he's invisible."

"I know."

After a small silence, he gave me a name and number. "Cathy's good, and I'll let her know to expect your call."

"Thanks. Oh, one more thing?"

"Now what?"

"Celeste's car is still missing. Can you run the plates for me?"

Mention of the serial murders had made Jerry unusually cooperative. "Yeah, I can do that. What's the number?"

I told him, heard the clicking of keystrokes.

I waited. I was picturing the Stalker's victims, raped, strangled, a cross cut into their foreheads, then Celeste's face. I shuddered.

I didn't want to think about what details might not have been released to the public.

"There's no report on that license, or on the woman the car's registered to. Celeste Deslauriers? That's your missing person?"

At least it wasn't bad news. "That's her. Thank, Jerry. And keep me posted if her name—comes up, will you?"

"Will do, Babs."

"Don't call me that." But it was a half-hearted response.

I put in a call to his contact in Missing Persons contact, Cathy Yip. She wasn't in.

I left a message, then called the towing yards. None of them had her car.

So Celeste probably hadn't parked anywhere near the beach yesterday. If she had, she'd have been towed by now.

———

THE OFFICES of Two Hearts were polished and professional, very current, but low on personality. Ms. Marten matched her surroundings perfectly.

Leaning back in her executive leather chair, she steepled her manicured fingers and looked at me. "Celeste seemed very nice," she said in a non-committal tone.

Ms. Marten was very well put together, a few years younger than I was. Her blonde hair was pulled back into a complicated twist, and she wore a Jones New York suit in this year's orchid.

I recognized it because my best friend Andrea had dragged me shopping a couple of weeks ago and nearly bought the same outfit. She'd finally vetoed it because she said it made her feel like a grape popsicle.

It was way too much money to spend on something so uncomfortable, anyway, especially factoring in the panty hose requirement.

On Ms. Marten, the suit looked like armor—strong, deflecting. She wasn't nearly as confident as she'd like the world to believe. How to break through that front?

"Come on," I said, steepling my own fingers, but leaning forward a little. "In your line of business, you must have an insight into people."

"Well, yes." Her face didn't know whether to be pleased or remote. She leaned forward a little to match my pose without even realizing she'd done so.

It was a start.

"You must have a feel for Celeste, for what drove her," I said, laying it on. "And your insight might save her life."

That got to her. I watched her eyes darken, a small crease form between carefully shaped brows. "Celeste was—shadowed, I'd say. My read was she'd been hurt, badly, some time in the past."

"So why a dating service?"

"Safety. We'd already screened the matches."

"That was important to her?"

"Put it this way—I'd never before had a client who insisted on being walked through our screening process before she'd sign up. I'd say it was very important."

I nodded, wondering if it was the failed marriages that had burned her, or the family history Marie had alluded to. "What else was she concerned about?"

"How much control she'd have over when and where she met the matches. If she'd ever have to see them again."

She'd been wary, then. "And you told her?"

"That she had full control. She had their numbers, they didn't have hers. She could phone the guy, arrange to meet on neutral ground. I suggested she chose a place with a large picture window, tell him to sit by it, then get there a few minutes late. If she didn't like his looks, she didn't even have to go in."

Yet Celeste had gotten to Starbucks early, waited for whichever guy she was meeting to show up. Why?

Ms. Marten was watching me. "She didn't take precautions this time, did she?"

"No. She met him at a crowded coffee shop, but she got there first and stood up as soon as he came in. She told her sister she was meeting someone from Two Hearts."

"It seems out of character for Celeste."

I was beginning to see real possibilities in Ms. Marten. "Then either she was lying or they were. What would you bet?"

One eyebrow raised. "Do I look like a betting woman to you, Ms. O'Grady?" she asked in a haughty voice. Then she grinned.

I did like her. "Yes, actually. And it's Barbara."

"Barbara, then. And please call me Isabella." Her smile vanished. "Celeste didn't strike me as a liar. Not a plausible one, anyway. Of the men?" She cocked her head to one side. "All three seemed sincere. But I suspect all of them could lie smoothly if they had to. Sorry I can't be more help."

"Yet all three men passed your screening? No question marks on any of them?"

"After you called, I rechecked their files. They were clean." She hesitated, fingers toying with the stack of files on her desk. "But isn't it possible she's fine somewhere? Just—I don't know. Forgot the time. Developed amnesia."

"Anything is possible, but given everything I've learned so far about Celeste, it isn't seeming likely."

She nodded slowly. "Yes. What about…"

She didn't finish the sentence, just looked at me, but I knew what was on her mind, on the mind of every woman in the city since the Stalker's attacks began. Will I be next?

"They haven't found a body, which doesn't fit the pattern. And she disappeared yesterday morning. All of the Stalker's victims vanished late at night."

I waited a moment, watched the impact of that hit her. "Are you sure you can't give me their names? I promise it'll be kept confidential."

Isabella looked stricken, but she shook her head. "I can't. It's more than my job is worth. But I will release that info to the police."

"Have you heard from them?"

"Not yet." She stood up. "Barbara, I hope you'll excuse me, but there is a small matter I have to see to. I'll be back shortly."

I nodded. What was she up to? As she pushed her chair back and rose, her elbow dislodged several folders. She didn't stop to straighten them, just left the room, closing the door behind her.

I stared at the folders fanned across the desk. There were three of them. Three names, all male.

I reached for the first one. Kyle Hanlon. Match: Celeste Deslauriers. Thank you, Isabella. I reached for my phone.

I snapped scans of the pages in each folder, which included names, addresses and workplaces. I was careful to get clear pictures of the headshots each of them had so helpfully provided. Nice looking guys. All with brown hair, white smiles, good suits.

When Isabella finally returned, I was sitting relaxed in my chair.

"Sorry it took so long."

"Not a problem."

"I've forgotten, where were we?"

"I was just about to thank you for your time."

Her eyes strayed to the folders and a look that might have been relief crossed her face. "You will let me know if—when you find Celeste?"

"Yes, I'll do that." I held out my hand. "Thank you, Isabella."

As I walked back to my car, I called Marie.

"Have you found something?" she asked immediately.

"A couple of possible leads. Did Celeste ever mention any of these names?" I gave her the names Isabella had given me.

There was a long moment of silence. I wished I could see her face.

"No. No I don't think so."

I didn't need a visual to hear the despair in her voice. Had she hoped to hear a name she recognized? "We'll find her."

"How?"

"One lead at a time. I need to talk to Celeste's manager. Did you find out if Celeste's laptop is at her office?"

CHAPTER FOUR

I took the really long way back to my office, the one with a detour that goes across a bridge and along Kits Beach. My luck was in. I not only found parking, Tanya was on duty behind the Starbucks counter.

She glanced at the photos on my phone, frowned a little and went through them again. "They all look a little like the guy I saw," she said. "But I can't be sure any of them are him."

"But it's possible one of these three be the guy you saw?"

"Maybe. I mean, I noticed the hairstyle, the smile, the arm. I'm not seeing those in any of these pictures. But maybe one of these could've been him, if he'd completely changed his hairstyle and his clothes…"

She shrugged. "I don't look at them and say "this guy", but I can't say for sure. Best I can do, sorry."

It figured. And Tanya's insight had surprised me. Most people don't look beyond the surface of a professionally taken photo.

At least I'd got a grande French Roast out of my detour.

I BARELY MADE it back across downtown to the Vancouver University campus in time for my meeting with Alicia Chambers. She was tall, platinum blond and carefully made-up, dressed in an aqua sheath that skimmed a trim figure. Her smile gleamed, but I sensed a layer of ice running just below the surface.

"Have you any word on Celeste?" she asked, as she ushered me into her spacious office.

I shook my head. Just for a moment, our eyes met, acknowledging the fear that lay between us. The Stalker had done that to this city, particularly to the women.

"Her sister told me to expect you. We are all so worried for her. How can I help?"

"I need access to Celeste's computer, particularly her calendar and her address book. Her phone is missing. I'm hoping she backed up the data."

Alicia nodded. "We're restricting access to her personal dealings only. Her business dealings are confidential."

It was a start. "Fair enough."

She led me down a long narrow hallway with file cabinets stacked along one wall. At the far end, she opened a door and let me into an office with windows all along one side. The architecture and the hot water radiators dated the building to the fifties. A laptop computer and a twenty-four-inch monitor dominated the cleared desktop.

Alicia gestured me towards the chair. "Everything is turned on and I've signed you in. I had the technical staff move any non-personal data to the network, which you won't have access to, so I'll just leave you to it. Call if you need anything. I'm at extension 852."

"Thanks," I said. My attention was on the laptop.

Celeste was a busy woman—and very organized. Clearly she was a big fan of To Do lists. Flipping through electronic pages, I built a picture of a full life. Some very competent techie had managed to leave all her daily appointments but remove any details. Unfortunately.

I'd need time to go through this in detail, preferably in the privacy of my office. With a quick glance at the door, I pulled a jump drive from my shoulder bag. While I waited for the files to copy, I looked around me.

Pale beige walls, a couple of Toni Onley prints, a double spray of white dendrobium orchids blooming on a wide window ledge. Celeste had a hammered pewter business card holder and matching letter opener on the surface of the laminated oak desk, along with a small crystal clock bearing testimony to some service she'd performed for the United Way a couple of years ago.

Books—mostly on fundraising or positive thinking—were neatly lined up on a bookcase of the same oak laminate as the desk. I didn't see any personal photos or mementos.

When the computer had finished humming, I tucked the jump drive safely in my bag, and went looking for Alicia. She was on the phone, so I hovered in the hallway until she'd disconnected.

"I have a few more questions, if I may?" I said, sitting down in front of her massive desk.

"Of course."

What else could she say? "What can you tell me about Celeste Deslauriers?"

Alicia tucked a swath of hair behind a delicate ear and re-arranged the pen and pencil set lying on her pristine desktop. "I don't know her well," she said.

"But she reports to you?"

"Yes. But I know her only in a work context, though, not a social one." She sat straighter, resting her hands lightly on the desk-top. Her manicure was perfect.

"As an employee she is dedicated, professional and thorough. She meets her goals and the donors like her. As a person?" She gave me a firm look. "Surely you don't think there is some connection between her disappearance and the work she does?"

If her offended tone was supposed to deter me, it wasn't going to work. "Since I don't know why she disappeared, it's too soon to rule out anything. The more I know about Celeste's life before she disappeared, the better. What can you tell me about Celeste, about the work she does?"

"As a fundraiser, her work is about building relationships with those who support our university."

"With donations?"

"Primarily, but also through volunteering and through their own connections. Often our biggest donors have been introduced to us by someone who is passionate about the work our university does, without necessarily being a donor themselves."

"And how would Celeste go about building these relationships?"

"Well. Often the university's relationships with a particular donor are long term, and Celeste would be the fourth or fifth fundraiser to work with that particular donor."

"Often. But not always?"

"No. She is also responsible for building new relationships with people who have a past relationship with the university or an interest in something we do. For example, we had a very large donation to our library from a science graduate who has fond memories of time spent in the library in his own university years. Another donor gave to the Fine Arts department because of his love of art, even though his degrees were in business."

I was more interested in the first part of her statement. "Building new relationships? Is that like cold calling?"

"Not at all. Our job is not sales, but rather about finding connections or interests that already exist, and building on them."

Right. Sales. "So how would Celeste meet potential connections?"

"She has a genuine interest in people, and a passion for education. People respond to that. Often an existing donor would introduce her to a new connection."

"And if a new connection had something to do with her disappearance, how would I go about finding them?"

White lines appeared on both sides of her perfectly outlined mouth. "You wouldn't. It would be an unforgivable intrusion into the privacy of our donors."

"Even though Celeste's life may be in danger?"

"I very much hope that is not the case. If it is, however, I cannot believe it is related to anyone she met through her work here."

She pushed her chair back and stood. "And now I'm afraid I have another meeting."

CHAPTER FIVE

I was still fuming when I got back to my office, and it had nothing to do with the traffic, which had been its usual awful. I dumped my stuff on my desk and stomped through to the mini-kitchen put on a pot of Railtown Dark Roast. I wanted the good stuff.

Someone needed to convince Ms. Chambers that people's lives couldn't be risked for the sake of business relationships. While my coffee brewed, I punched in Cathy Yip's number in Missing Persons. It went straight through to voice mail.

Probably a good thing, at least until I calmed down. I disconnected, thought about calling Jerry. Decided I'd better see what I had first.

I downloaded the files Isabella from Two Hearts had given me and the ones I'd from Celeste's computer onto my computer, did a backup, then started reading. Celeste's calendar was packed with appointments and meetings, often stretching into the evening.

No wonder she'd joined a dating service. With a schedule like this she barely had time to date, much less search for the right someone.

I could hear Andrea chortling in my head—that was what she

usually said about me. I ignored the thought. Wasn't my fault Nick was out of town.

So when had Celeste joined Two Hearts? Six weeks ago. I flipped backwards through her calendar. There it was—a small notation marked TH.

I flipped forwards, found TH1 a few weeks later with a note. "Rising star. Boring." Poor guy, whoever he was.

Forward another couple of weeks, a little TH2. The note beside it said "Possibilities." Huh. Probably meant she'd see him again.

I flipped forward. Nothing before last Sunday. So either the guy she met wasn't from the dating service, or she hadn't made the entry here yet.

There was no sign of a TH3. Maybe they hadn't met yet. Maybe he was the guy she'd met on Sunday. But she'd definitely met with two of the three.

I checked my notes. Isabella told me only one had admitted meeting with Celeste. So who was lying?

I called Isabella at Two Hearts. She was in a meeting, so I left a message for her to call me, then opened Celeste's address book.

Looked like the techie had found a way to delete all the business contacts, and what remained didn't tell me much. I needed Marie's list of Celeste's friends. I did find listings for both of Celeste's ex-husbands, and made appointments with both.

I turned to Celeste's personal documents. Again, there was very little there. A couple of cryptic spreadsheets, some miscellaneous files.

I did find a copy of a letter to her lawyer requesting an urgent meeting, but no specifics. The letter intrigued me, not least because I knew the lawyer involved, Claire Chan, quite well, having worked with her on a number of cases. I called Claire's office and set up a meeting.

I turned to the files for Celeste's Two Hearts matches, and printed off the photos, pinning them on the bulletin board beside my desk. Reading through their files, I found nothing useful.

If any of them had ever lived in Brenton, it wasn't in their files.

If they had quirky hobbies, or bad luck with previous girlfriends, it wasn't in their files. I googled the three of them and got hits on two.

Kovicks was listed on his law firm's website.

Hanlon was listed at his brokerage, plus he had his own website. Skimming it, I was pretty sure I wouldn't trust him with my money. If I had any, that is.

I couldn't find personal information on either of them, and nothing that hinted at a connection to Brenton. I didn't find any sign of a previous connection to Celeste, either. I'd have to dig deeper.

I'd barely started when the ringing of the phone broke my concentration. I glanced at the number.

Susanna. Now what?

"What's up?" I asked.

"Barbara, I'm holding a dinner party on Saturday night, and I'd like you and Nick to be there."

A dinner party? Give me strength. I hated it when my sister went into her Perfect Hostess mode, and I couldn't stand her dinner parties. Everything was as formal and flawless as Susanna pretended to be, from the table setting to the conversation.

And Susanna's entertainments always had an underlying purpose—they were never just about good food and good company.

"I don't think we'll be able to make it. The Stalker task force is taking up all of Nick's time." It was the perfect excuse.

"Could you at least ask him?" Her voice held a brittle note I hadn't heard before.

"I think you should just count us out this time."

"Barbara, you're just using Nick's work as an excuse. When was the last time you actually went out in the evening?"

She might have a point. Between my job, painting, and Nick's lack of availability, my social life has been pretty non-existent for the last couple of months. "I'm in the middle of a case."

"You're always in the middle of a case. When was the last time you came over here?"

She had me there. "Okay, okay, count me in." It was only one night.

"And Nick?"

"I'm sure he'll come if he can, but please don't count on him."

She sighed. "When will you learn how much power the woman has in a relationship?"

Probably never. I don't like playing those kinds of games. And my sister's own history isn't exactly a testimony to that particular sentiment.

I wondered if she even believed what she'd said.

But by now, all my warning signals were going off. "Who have you invited to this dinner, Susanna?"

"Oh, no-one important. Bob Victor and his wife. The Hamiltons. The Marshalls."

Devon Marshall. An award-winning journalist always hungry for a story. "That's why you want Nick there, isn't it? You've promised Marshall a scoop. What has he promised you?"

My sister's laughter sounded forced to my skeptical ears. "Now, Barbara, don't be so cynical. Would I do that?"

Not normally, but in this economy, every business owner is feeling the pinch and Susanna's husband Godfrey is no exception. I wondered if Godfrey wanted publicity or hoped to avoid it, and what had gone wrong. I wondered why I didn't just hang up on her.

In my mind's eye, I pictured a very young Susanna, throwing her arms around my neck. "I do love you, Barbara."

That was why. Somewhere down inside, she was always my baby sister.

"Sorry, Susanna," I said through gritted teeth. "You'd better just assume we can't make it. I wouldn't want to throw your numbers off."

If she picked up on the sarcasm, she ignored it. "At least ask him."

That did it. I let out the frustration I'd been feeling. With her? With him? It didn't matter.

"Susanna, I haven't even seen Nick in nearly two weeks. If he is free this weekend, I'm not letting him out of this apartment."

"Oh." A silence. "Well, let me know if you change your mind."

I disconnected, shaking my head. Sometimes I can't believe we're related. Other times I wish we weren't.

Isabella chose that moment to return my call. "Barbara? Is something wrong?"

I disciplined my voice. "I wondered how Celeste would have gotten in touch with her dates from Two Hearts?"

"We e-mailed her copies of the summary sheets for each of the matches. For the ones she chose, we sent names and telephone numbers."

Right. So what had Celeste done with the e-mails? There had been nothing in her inbox related to Two Hearts. "And when did she go out with the guy who said they'd met?"

"What...? Oh, just a minute, I'll look," she said, sounding flustered. There was dead air for a moment, then she was back. "Friday, April 5th."

And Celeste's diary said she'd met with two of the men. I wondered which one two hadn't admitted to a meeting? "And he said they hadn't met again?"

"That's right."

"I'll need his name."

"But that information is..."

"Confidential. Yeah, I know. But she's missing, Isabella. After meeting with one of your guys. And every hour that passes lessens the chance that this will end well."

"I know."

"You've already given the police everything you have, right?"

Another pause. "Yes. They called earlier."

"Then what is the harm in giving me the name too?"

"I sorry, Barbara. You'll need to get it from the police." And she disconnected.

My iPhone beeped to let me know I had a text. Anonymous. I opened it to find a surname. Hanlon.

Thank you, Isabella.

So where had Mr. Hanlon been last Sunday morning? I was googling him when the phone rang again. Call display was blocked.

I hate that.

And with the way my day had been going it would be Marie. I answered anyway.

It was Nick. "I'm between meetings, so I only have a minute," he said. "You free tonight?"

I was now. "More to the point, are you?"

He laughed, the rich sound filling some part of me I hadn't known was empty. "Maybe."

"Then maybe I'm free."

"See you at your place at eight," he said huskily, and was gone.

I sat staring at the phone for a long moment, my heart racing. Then reality hit.

The last time I remembered grocery shopping was the Saturday before last. No matter. I had a decent bottle of red. If he was hungry, we'd order pizza.

I glanced over at the photos of the three guys from Two Hearts. GQ material, all three of them. In my opinion, Nick's dark hair and sexy grin had them all beat.

I studied the faces a moment longer. Which two had Celeste met with? And who hadn't admitted to a meeting?

I needed more information.

———

I PARKED in front of the house Celeste and Marie shared, and finished off my coffee. Since I was trekking across town anyway, I'd rewarded myself with a coffee from Calabria on Commercial, who make the most authentic cappuccinos in town.

Traffic had been one big snarl and parking was a nightmare, but the coffee was worth the hassle, rich and strong, with a caffeine bite that rushed to my nerve endings. Some days I wonder how coffee can still be legal. Not that I'm complaining.

If coffee was illegal, I'd probably go broke trying to keep up with my habit.

The house Celeste and Marie shared was a small bungalow, dating from the thirties but carefully restored. It gleamed a soft yellow with porch, windows and eaves picked out in white. I was willing to bet that the color choices had been Celeste's and not Marie's.

Marie met me at the door and led the way down a narrow hallway, and into an airy bedroom. "This is Celeste's room."

The floor was dark hardwood, but everything else, walls, furniture, curtains and linens, was white. The effect should have been bare and cold, but somehow Celeste had achieved an effect that was fresh and feminine.

As I looked more closely, I could see she had used a variety of shades of white, which had saved it from starkness. Everything was neat, which seemed to be Celeste's trademark. I began to see why Marie had called her anal, but there was something seductive about a room that was so orderly.

Part of the attraction might be that I live in a permanent state of what I prefer to call creative disorder and Susanna calls chaos.

There was no sign of papers anywhere. "Does Celeste have a home office?"

Marie pointed to one corner of the room, where a white French provincial desk and chair sat. They looked so fragile, I hadn't imagined real work was done there. I walked over, ran a hand over the cleared surface. "May I?"

At Marie's nod, I sad down and opened the first drawer. Pens, pencils, stamps, writing paper, all organized. I shuffled the writing paper, but it was exactly what it purported to be. The second drawer was no better.

"Does she keep files at home?"

A brief smile lit Marie's wan face. "You didn't spot them either? Celeste always said no-one would." She reached over and lifted the white skirt of the bedside table, revealing a two-drawer filing cabinet.

"Mind if I go through them?"

Marie was watching me intently. "Go ahead."

I flipped through files labeled Taxes, Insurance, Mortgage, Utilities, Bank Account, Charities. Nothing on Two Hearts. No sign of her matches.

I glanced at Marie. "I don't see anything on the dating agency. They must have sent paperwork. Where would she keep that?"

"Probably on her phone. It was where she kept most stuff."

Not this time. I nodded, turned my attention back to the files. Her tax return told me she lived within her income, but there wasn't much left over.

The bank still owned most of the house, but her car was paid off. She lived within her means, but there wasn't a lot left over for luxuries. Not a good candidate for kidnapping for ransom, then. Which left what?

I kept looking.

Towards the back of the second drawer I found a folder called Legal. On the top lay a copy of the letter I'd found on her computer. I handed the letter to Marie.

"Do you know what this is about?"

"I've no idea."

"Too bad." I flipped through the file. All of the correspondence was with Claire Chan. Most of it related to the purchase of this house. "Was Celeste worried about anything in the last couple of weeks?"

Marie shrugged. "Not that I noticed. But who could tell?"

"She kept things inside?"

"Yeah, you could say that."

"Did she mention anything about seeing Claire?"

"Claire?"

"Her lawyer"

"Oh. No, she didn't mention her. Why are you wasting time

with that? I told you that guy's got her. It's nothing to do with any lawyer."

This is why I hated having clients hanging over my shoulder.

"We still need his name," I said. "And it's too early to make assumptions. I need to follow up every lead, no matter how slim. That's why you hired me, remember?"

I turned back to the filing cabinet, but there was nothing else to find. "Is there anywhere else Celeste might have kept stuff? In the kitchen, living room?"

"No. Everything that was just hers Celeste kept in here."

I looked around. It wasn't much to represent a life. "Did your sister have any hobbies?"

"Sure. Golf, tennis. Anything outdoors."

"Where are her golf clubs?"

Marie led me to the tidiest storage area I'd ever seen. Celeste's clubs stood in a plaid golf bag leaning against the wall. I searched the pockets. Nothing.

"Who did she golf with?"

"I never kept track."

Obviously Marie wasn't a golfer. "Where are her jackets and coats?"

"In the hall closet. I'll show you."

Nothing in those pockets, either.

Marie was watching me as if waiting for me to pull out the solution. "I'll need that list of her friends," I told her.

"Yeah. I'll e-mail it to you. Anything else?"

I glanced around. "I think I've seen everything I need to see. I'll get in touch with you later. But call me if you hear from her."

"Yeah. Barbara, you have to find her!"

Like that was news.

CHAPTER SIX

It didn't take long to get to Claire's Eastside office. Her waiting room was crowded—Claire is very good at what she does. And I'd been lucky. When I'd told her why I needed to see her, she'd squeezed me in.

After a short wait, I was seated in Claire's tranquil office, sipping a cup of green tea.

"You're looking good, Barbara. How's the investigations business these days?" she said, as she poured a second cup of tea into a delicate cup.

She looked pretty good herself—dark hair cut in a sleek bob dramatic with a cream silk suit.

"Busier than I'd like," I said. "I've been trying to put together enough paintings for a show and I just can't find the time."

"You're painting again? Barbara, that's fabulous. Still abstracts?"

"No, I've gone back to landscapes and cityscapes, but with an abstract quality."

"I always liked your landscapes. Make sure you tell me when the show is."

I grimaced. "It's supposed to be September, but at the rate I'm going, it'll be never. But tell me how you're doing? How are the kids?"

"They're good. And Mary I-Chia is finally sleeping through the night. Mostly."

"I don't know how you do it." I really didn't. I'm always amazed by parents of young children—I don't know how any of them survive. And somehow the lack of sleep Claire must still be suffering from didn't show.

She laughed. "Sometimes I don't either. It's the price I pay for having children late." Leaning forward, she clasped her hands neatly on her desk. "Now, what can I do for you?"

I brought out a copy of Celeste's letter. "You can tell me what this is in regard to."

Claire looked at me, brown eyes serious. "Barbara, you know I can't do that."

"She's missing, Claire. Her sister hired me to find her."

"You told me on the phone. There's still nothing I can say."

I'd expected that. "Can you tell me if the letter refers to any situation you believe might have been dangerous for Celeste?"

Claire tilted her head to one side, then she nodded. "Yes, I can tell you that. And no, I don't believe this situation posed any danger to her."

"You're sure? No hurt feelings, or angry losers?"

"I'm sure."

"And nothing that might in any way be connected with her disappearance?"

"No, not in any way at all."

Good enough. "Do you recognize any of these names?" I handed her the list of Celeste's dates.

"Not in relation to Celeste, no."

She knew them? How? I bit back my questions. If they were clients, as her careful answer suggested, then she couldn't answer them anyway.

"Is there anything else you can tell me that might help me find Celeste?" I asked her.

She sipped her tea in silence, her gaze on the bamboo moving gently outside her window, then shook her head. "No, nothing. I'm sorry, Barbara."

Another dead end. And Celeste had now been missing for more than twenty-four hours. "Thanks anyway. If you do think of something, you'll call?"

"Of course. And promise you won't forget about that invitation to your opening."

If I ever got any of the paintings finished. "I promise."

As I left Claire's office, my thoughts switched back to the hours that had slid by since Celeste vanished. What had happened to her? On the surface, she was the least likely person to just disappear I'd ever heard of. But how real was that surface?

Time to find out what ex-husband number one had to say about his former wife. I glanced at my watch—I had plenty of time to make it to Brackendale for my meeting with Ben.

As long as traffic over the Lion's Gate co-operated, of course. Which it generally didn't.

———

THE BRIDGE GODS were good to me for once, and past the Lion's Gate, traffic was steady all the way to the turnoff. The Sea to Sky highway is my favorite road in the world, twisting from West Vancouver to Whistler in a series of S-curves with breathtaking views.

On my right, a heavy blanket of dark evergreens—pine, spruce and cedar—reminds me that the whole west coast is rain forest. Living in the city, it's easy to forget that. Out here, Mother Nature is busy trying to reclaim the landscape almost as fast as we can pave and patch it.

The view to the left is part of the reason we try so hard— nothing but ocean and mountains fading away into the distance. Today it was a symphony of grays and mist.

I felt my anxiety fade. One day I'll figure out how to paint this the way it feels.

In no time I was passing through Squamish, then making a left off the highway to Brackendale. Following the signs, I made for the Brackendale Art Gallery, official home of the eagle count. The art gallery shared space with the area's most famous teahouse, which was where I'd arranged to meet Ben.

In winter, the creek swarms with eagles and the town swarms with tourists by the busload. By now, they were all gone.

Glancing around the nearly empty parking lot, I hoped Ben was already here. I hadn't left myself a lot of time. As I walked closer, I examined the building's sloping roof and cedar walls. It had been updated since I was last here, and it looked good.

The interior was all cedar walls and local art and smelled of good coffee and wood smoke. My attention fixed on the man who was rising to greet me. Tall and lanky, with sandy blond hair and thick mustache, a beak of a nose and a firm chin.

He looked rugged, comfortable in his skin and trustworthy. The trustworthy part always worries me. "Ben Oliver?"

He grinned. "Sure am."

This guy used to be a corporate lawyer? I couldn't picture it. "I'm Barbara O'Grady."

"I figured."

If he was a lawyer, even a former lawyer, he had to be able to string together sentences of more than two words. "I want to talk to you about Celeste Deslauriers' disappearance."

"Yeah, you said that. Have a seat. Coffee?"

Maybe he was trustworthy, I decided, as he put a fragrant, steaming mug in front of me. "When's the last time you talked to Celeste?"

"Must be over a month now. Maybe two."

"You've been divorced how long?"

"Nearly six years. But we keep in touch."

"Why?" The question popped out.

I've never been married, but I've never managed to stay in touch with any of my former lovers. Except Jayson, of course, and that's more his doing than mine. He likes to show off.

"We married too young for our marriage to last," Ben Oliver was saying, "but we could always talk. I care about her."

His gaze met mine. His eyes were hazel, and worried.

"So what did you talk about when you last talked? Was it in person?"

"No, on the phone. It was the tail end of the eagle season, and I don't leave then."

"What is it you do?"

"I have a law practice in Squamish, but I'm also part of the team that makes sure the eagles are protected. It's needed work—Brackendale has become more and more of a tourist destination when the eagles are here. We also track them, where their nests are, note which ones return."

"You tag them?"

"Some of them."

I found the whole subject fascinating, but it wasn't what I was here for. "So what did you and Celeste talk about?"

He shrugged. "The usual. Her work, mine."

"Was she worried about anything?"

"Marie."

"Why Marie?"

"You may have noticed that Marie's a little wild?" he said with a quirk of long, narrow lips.

I nodded. "A little."

"Yeah. Well, she has yet to settle down, decide on a life path. Celeste worries about her."

A life path? Now he didn't sound like a lawyer or a conservationist. What was it about the people in Celeste's life? "Did Celeste talk at all about meeting someone from her old home town?"

"From Brenton? No. Why? Did she meet someone from there?"

"I think so." I filled him in on what I'd learned about the mystery man from Brenton. It was too soon to decide if Ben could be a suspect, but anything he knew about Celeste and Brenton might help.

He sighed. "I always had the feeling Celeste's obsession with Brenton would get her into trouble, but she'd never listen to me on the subject."

"Obsession?"

He glanced at me. "She was trying to make reparation, I think. But I think the strength of her own emotions blinded her to what the other person was feeling. Which is odd—Celeste is normally very empathetic. It's what makes her so special."

Wow. "Had this been a problem before? With someone from Brenton, I mean."

"Well—it was a long time ago."

"Anything might help, no matter how small it seems."

"Celeste and I had just married. We were all three—Celeste, Marie and myself—living in an apartment in Kits, over on Second, and Celeste and I liked to walk on the beach in the evening, just the two of us."

I nodded, oddly touched, more by the softness in his eyes than by his words.

"One evening we were walking when a young woman called out Celeste's name. Celeste looked uncertain, then her face lit up. The woman's name was Leanne something. They'd gone to school together, though Leanne had been a good bit younger."

"Leanne was from Brenton?"

He nodded. "Celeste was practically bubbling over, inviting Leanne for dinner, saying she'd have to join us for the theatre. She was so caught up she didn't notice Leanne's face changing. When Celeste paused for breath, Leanne gave her a look of pure venom, spat out a few words, then stormed off."

"What did she say?"

"To the effect that some people will never have the money to enjoy the finer things in life."

"Ouch. What did Celeste do?"

"She deflated. She was miserable for days afterward." He paused.

"She hadn't meant to insult Leanne, just to include her. As her guest, of course."

Somehow I didn't think Leanne had cared. "Can you recall Leanne's last name?"

He squinted his eyes, seemed to peer into the distance. "An—something. Antler? No, that's not right." He shook his head. "Maybe it'll come to me."

"Did Celeste have any enemies?"

"Celeste? None that I ever heard of."

"What about Callum McLaughlan?"

"My replacement?" Smile lines crinkled beside his eyes. "As far as I know they're still friendly."

"And what would he say about you?"

Ben grinned at that. "He never did like the fact that Celeste and I remained such good friends. She came up and stayed with me for a while last year."

"After her second divorce?"

"Yeah. Bet that really burned old Callum." He chuckled.

I could see why Celeste had remained friends with him. But there was one more question I had to ask. "Where were you last Sunday?"

I expected anger. To my surprise, he looked pleased. "I was working all day—you can check with my boss, Dan Patel, if you like."

He must have picked up on my surprise, because he grinned. "I'm a lawyer," he said. "I know the questions that should be asked. If you hadn't asked them, you wouldn't be doing your job, and Celeste needs—and deserves—the best."

Oh. I liked this guy. And for what it was worth, I believed him. I'd still be checking his alibi, though.

As he said, it was my job. "One last question."

"Shoot."

"If Celeste hadn't been kidnapped, if for some reason she just needed to get away, is there somewhere she would go?"

He was shaking his head. "She'd probably come here. And

before you ask, no, she isn't here, and I haven't heard from her. But you have to understand Celeste. There's no way she'd go off and worry everyone like this. Especially not Marie. No, whatever has happened, you can be sure it's not Celeste's choice."

THE DRIVE back to Vancouver felt longer than the drive to Squamish had. Maybe because I was growing more worried about Celeste with every person I talked to, rather than less worried.

I'd just turned off the freeway into West Van when my cell phone rang. Jerry. I pulled over and answered.

"O'Grady, we found her car."

I could tell from his tone this was not good news. "Celeste's?"

"Yeah."

"Where?"

"The Downtown Centre. Abandoned."

That's what I'd been dreading. The underground parkade at The Downtown Centre—a huge shopping mall in the center of downtown—was where the vehicles of two out of the three murdered women had been found. "Any signs of violence?"

"Nothing so far. We're still going over it."

It was small comfort, but it was the best I was going to get.

"Jerry, is there anything on the security cameras? Celeste's last known location was in Kits. Maybe she drove downtown, or maybe someone else did it for her."

"The light was wrong when the car drove in, and it's parked in one of the few blind spots in the lot."

"So no pictures."

"No pictures."

"What time did it drive in?"

"Just after three p.m. yesterday."

Before I started searching for it. "Thanks for letting me know, Jerry."

"I'm sorry, Barbara."

"Yeah." What was I going to tell Marie?

As I disconnected, I tried to convince myself that this could be positive. There had been no body. The Stalker has always left the body with the vehicle.

He didn't have her. Serial killers didn't change their patterns.

Maybe not, but they escalate and the violence increases, some small part of my brain whispered.

I was halfway back to my office before I remembered Nick would be coming by in less than an hour. And being on the task force, he'd be the best person to talk to about the Stalker and whether his MO was changing.

CHAPTER SEVEN

J ust over an hour later, I was chopping bok choi for a stir fry. I'd given up on the idea of pizza—I needed an outlet for the fears Jerry's words had raised, and chopping vegetables into very small pieces sounded right.

My cleaver is authentic raw steel, which tends to rust if I'm not careful, but it's solid and makes a lovely chunking sound as it chops. It can even be therapeutic—I just focus on the repetitive motion. And on not cutting my fingers off.

Not this time. I couldn't get Celeste out of my mind. Where was she? What was happening to her?

The sharp buzz of the intercom made me jump and I nearly took off the end of my thumb.

When I opened the door to Nick's wide smile, all thought of Celeste and everything else fled. His hazel eyes laughed at me. "Hey, beautiful lady."

"Hey yourself, stranger." Then his arms opened wide, I lifted up onto my toes and moved into his embrace.

Finally I broke out of his arms. "Come in," I said, breathless and laughing, holding the door open for him. "We're putting on a show for the neighbors."

He peered up and down the empty hall. "I don't see any neighbors."

"Trust me, they're there, all crouched behind their peepholes, watching us."

"What, they lie in wait to see you attacked by strange men in the hallway?"

"Not men, just you. And you're not that strange."

"Well, thank you, ma'am," he drawled.

"See, the jungle drums announce your imminent arrival, and they line up to see the show."

"Your apartment building has jungle drums?"

"Oh, yeah."

"Wow. I'm lucky if mine has running water. Nothing so exotic as jungle drums."

I grabbed his arm and dragged him into the apartment, closing the door behind us. "Come have some wine. Maybe it'll settle you down."

"When you're within touching distance? Not likely."

Boy, had I missed him. I led him into the kitchen and poured him some wine.

Nick looked at the mess I'd made. "What's wrong?"

I hadn't realized he knew me that well. And I didn't want to force him to think about his case right away—it was his first break in ages. "Nothing. I'll just finish putting this stir fry…"

He looked from the pile of pulverized bok choi on the counter to the cleaver I'd forgotten I was still clutching and raised an eyebrow. "We can eat later. Tell me what's worrying you."

Okay, then. Dumping the cleaver in the sink, I grabbed my glass of wine and led the way into the living room.

"I'm worried one of my new cases might be intersecting with yours," I said. "How's it going with the task force?"

His face tightened and in the new lines beside his mouth and around his eyes I could see the price he'd paid for the last few weeks. "Not well."

"You're still no closer to finding him?"

He shrugged. "Depends what you mean by closer. We have forensic evidence, MO, profiles…"

"You've had profiling done?"

"Yeah."

"What did it tell you?"

"Not much we didn't know. He's male, probably Caucasian, late twenties to mid-thirties, somewhat paranoid, hates and perhaps fears women. He's intelligent, but likely not socially adept, a loner."

"I haven't seen any of this on the news."

"We're trying to avoid releasing it. Our guy loves the attention, and we're trying to downplay everything for a bit, see if it cools him off."

"Won't he just escalate?"

"That's the risk."

I could see the conflict in him. "And is there any sign that he's changing his MO?"

"This is the intersection with your case?"

I nodded. "I've been hired to find a woman who's missing. There's no sign of her, but Jerry tells me they've found her car. Abandoned. At The Downtown Centre."

"Any bloodstains?" It was cop's eyes that looked back at me now, hard and assessing.

"No. And no body. Which is why I wanted to know if there's any hint of the Stalker abducting his victims."

Nick sighed. "No, not yet. When did your missing woman disappear?"

"Sometime on Sunday. Mid-morning to mid-afternoon."

"And our guy takes his victims late at night. It doesn't sound like they're related."

"Good. That's what I'd been thinking, but…"

"Yeah. But if there's ever any sign that it might be this guy, I want you out of it. This guy's bad news."

I could hear the concern for me in his voice, so I ignored the implied order. I don't take direction very well, never have. Susanna says I'm just stubborn, but Andrea, who knows me better than anyone, says I'm trying to compensate for the chaos I grew up with.

Whatever. What I do know is that I get defensive when someone tries to tell me what to do, and it's torpedoed more than one relationship. And Nick and I had a good thing going. I wanted to keep it that way.

"I don't think it's the same guy," I said. "For her sake, I hope it's not." And for mine.

"Yeah."

We sat quietly, sipping our wine. I was relishing the familiar but not yet taken for granted warmth of his arm draped over my shoulders.

Since my last attempt at live-in bliss with Jayson Ho, which seemed like another life, I'd been on my own. And I liked it.

Now it felt odd to have someone else around. But Nick was different—had been from the start.

After a while I stood up, poured us both another glass. "Time to order pizza? I don't think the stir fry was destined to be one of my better efforts."

He grinned. "The manager's special?"

"Hold the anchovies."

He nodded, and put the call through.

While we waited, I remembered my sister's call. "Nick, Susanna asked us for dinner on Thursday."

"We're putting in some pretty long days. I'll see what I can do, but I doubt I'll be able to make it. Sorry, Barbara."

"It's okay, I pretty much told Susanna that." I didn't tell him the rest, that she really wants us there so she can show off her connection to the task force.

Nick doesn't know Susanna well yet. He's only met her twice, and both times she was in her charming but unassuming society hostess role. I miss the mischievous, unaffected girl I grew up with.

Sometimes I get glimpses of her, but it's as if Susanna has poured layers of shellac over who she really is. It goes well beyond irritating me. Almost as much as it worries me.

But I couldn't say any of this to Nick. Families always sound crazy to those outside them. Especially mine.

"Want more wine?" I asked him instead.

"Yeah."

Both tired, both worried, we finished the pizza and the wine, then spent the rest of the evening distracting each other.

CHAPTER EIGHT

I slept well, and woke up feeling pretty good. Watching Nick trip over Cat had added a fillip of hilarity to a day that had already started out right.

At the office, I checked my messages, then glanced at the top folder in my urgent file.

Celeste. Damn. What was I going to do about Celeste?

I called Ms. Yip in Missing Persons, left another message, then called Jerry.

Who answered. I nearly fell off my chair.

"It's Barbara," I said. "I haven't been able to get in touch with Cathy Yip. Have you heard anything on my missing person's car?"

"Good morning to you, too. And so far the tests have come back clean. No sign of blood."

"Well, that's good news. Except that she's still missing."

"Yeah, except for that."

"Think Ms. Yip would tell me if she's checked her credit card and cell phone usage?"

"The sister's filed a missing persons report, right? Let me see what I can do."

"Thanks." I disconnected, frowning. I hadn't even told Marie they'd found Celeste's car.

At least the news was a little better than it had been yesterday—Celeste wasn't the Stalker's latest victim. Probably.

Marie hadn't given me Celeste's list of friends yet, either. I reached for the phone, which promptly rang.

I eyed it balefully. It was Susanna's number. As if I didn't have enough on my plate.

And I hadn't even had my second cup of coffee.

Resigned, I grabbed the phone. "Morning, Susanna."

"Barbara? I need your help."

"Don't worry, I haven't forgotten about your dinner party. Night after tomorrow, right?"

"I don't care about the stupid dinner party. I don't care if I ever have another one."

This from my determined, upwardly-mobile sister? "What's wrong?"

"It's Cory. His bed wasn't slept in last night."

"And you've just discovered this now?"

"I went to bed with a migraine. Godfrey was supposed to wait up for him."

Godfrey had probably decided boys would be boys and gone to bed.

I felt a clutch of panic in my stomach. Cory, my fourteen year old nephew, is a good kid, but right now he's testing limits, and my sister sets a lot of them for him to test. "Where did he go last night?"

"He was supposed to be at Jeff's, but when I phoned there, they hadn't seen him since nine or so."

"Do they know where he went?"

"Jeff's mother says Jeff doesn't know."

"Did you talk to Jeff directly?"

"No."

Mistake. "What about Gabby? Does she know anything?"

"She says not."

At fifteen, I wouldn't have admitted knowing where my younger sibling was, either. "Does she seem worried?"

"She seemed annoyed I was bothering her."

That was a good sign. "What time is his first class?"

"Nine."

"Have you called the school to see if he's there?"

"I didn't think of it. But he wouldn't have clean clothes."

Not enough to stop most teenage males. "Call them, then call me back."

"I can do that. Oh, Barbara, I hope he's there."

So did I. But I suspected he would be. I got up and put a pot of Italian Roast on to brew. When the phone rang, I dived on it. "Well?"

"He was there. Thank God."

I didn't want to think about how relieved I was, even though I'd been pretty sure he'd be there. "Have a talk with him when he gets home. Find out where he went, and why."

"I will, Barbara. And thanks."

"Sure."

"And you are coming on Thursday? You and Nick?"

"I'll be there, but Nick can't make it."

"He's always welcome, even at the last minute."

Uh huh. "I'll see you Thursday."

I disconnected, then considered Susanna and her kids. What was going on, that Cory would pull a stunt like that? Could be just the onrush of testosterone, but my gut said it was more than that.

Something was going wrong in his life, either at home or at school. What could I do to help? I doodled on a scratch pad while my thoughts went in circles, then I wrenched my mind back to Celeste.

Finding Cory had been a matter of knowing where to look. Was there an easy answer for Celeste that I'd missed? If she wanted to disappear for a bit, where would she go?

I reviewed the files I'd been looking at the day before, not sure what I was looking for. Nothing caught my eye. I'd just pulled out my notes and begun reviewing them when my door burst open.

Marie flung herself down in the chair opposite my desk. Today she was wearing black tights, a very short denim skirt with an oversize orange shirt over a tight citron T-shirt. There was a purple stone dangling from the ring through her eyebrow, matching the purple steaks that had sprouted in her hair. I met her eyes, held that angry gaze.

"What are you doing? It's been three days, and nothing!"

"It's two days," I said. "And the police found Celeste's car."

"Where?" It was almost a shriek.

"The Downtown Centre. But before you panic, there was no sign of blood or violence of any kind. Is there a reason she would have gone there?"

"No way! Celeste hates shopping in malls, and especially underground malls. She'd do anything to avoid them."

"If Celeste wanted to disappear for a while, is there anyone she'd go to?"

"I told you, he took her!"

Okay, wrong approach. "Calm down, Marie. I'm trying to help. I need that list of her friends. And does she have a close friend?"

"Yeah, well I'm sorry. But it's my sister who's missing, you know?" She handed me a crumpled list. "Here. Most of these are people she knows from work or has done volunteer work with. Celeste doesn't have anyone really close. Except maybe Jaimie."

"Jaimie?" I ran my eye down the list.

"Yeah, they get together sometimes. And she's not on the list."

Why not? "Last name?"

A faint line formed between brows that were tipped with purple. "Jaimie—something. I think she's the one who put Celeste onto that dating service."

Which meant I could find her. I made a note. "Is there anyone else Celeste was close to?"

"Not real close. Not that she'd tell stuff to."

It sounded awful. I'm a bit of a loner, but I'd be lost if I didn't have Andrea to talk to when things got tough.

Unless Marie didn't know nearly as much about her sister's life as she claimed. "What about her ex-husbands?"

"She never sees them."

Not quite the story I'd heard from ex-husband number one. "You mentioned a dinner party. Who was invited?"

"I didn't say Celeste didn't have friends. We socialize a lot. Just that there's no-one she really talks to."

Uh huh. "I'll need a list of the people that were invited on Sunday."

"Which Sunday?"

"Last Sunday. Why? Did you often have dinner parties on a Sunday?"

"Yeah. Most weeks."

The mind boggled. No wonder she'd been so convinced something had happened when Celeste didn't show up on Sunday afternoon.

I wondered if there was anything else she hadn't mentioned. "How many people were invited?"

"That week, six. Most weeks it was between six and eight people."

That was a huge amount of work. How had Celeste done it? And why?

But that was my own bias coming through. I think hosting dinner for six once every couple of months is too much work. It isn't the cooking, it's everything that goes with it—place settings and candles and light banter. Especially the light banter.

"Was it always the same people?"

She shook her head. "The guest list rotated."

Of course it did. "Can you give me a list of the guests for the last month. Or even two?"

"It'll take me a while. And I still think it's a waste of time."

I ignored that. "I need it as quickly as you can get it to me."

"Okay. But what are you doing to find Celeste?"

"I'll track down Jaimie, see if she recognizes any of Celeste's dates. Then…"

"Recognizes them? You mean you've got pictures?"

"I got them from Two Hearts yesterday? Why?"

"You only told me some names, not that you had photos."

What was I missing? Then the penny dropped and I reached for the file.

"You know what this guy looked like?" I asked as I spread copies in front of her. Marie leaned forward, eyes intent on the faces of Celeste's three matches. Her face fell.

"It isn't any of them," she said. "He doesn't look like this."

"How can you be sure? Did Celeste show you a photo?"

"No, she told me about him."

She expected to recognize a photo from a description? "What does he look like, then?"

Marie's eyes slid away from me. Was she hiding something? Or was my irritation showing?

"He looks a little like these guys," she said. "But they just aren't the guy Celeste told me about, that's all."

To my frustration, it was similar to what Tanya had said. "Celeste told you her date on Sunday was from Two Hearts?"

She nodded.

"And that he was from Brenton."

Another nod.

"But she wouldn't tell you his name."

"Right."

This was worse than useless. "Thanks. I'll be in touch. Please get those lists to me as soon as possible."

"You'll let me know? If you hear something?"

"Of course," I assured her, as I closed the door behind the impossible case I'd never intended to take on and now couldn't see a way out of.

As Marie's footsteps faded away, I slumped behind my desk and called Isabella at Two Hearts.

"Barbara! Any word on Celeste?"

"Nothing yet. I do have a question for you that might help find her."

"Shoot."

"I need the name of the woman who recommended Two Hearts to Celeste. Jaimie something. Do you have it on record?"

"We should have. Let me check."

This time I listened to the musak version of *Up Where We Belong* for thirty interminable seconds. Then Isabella was back. "Yes, I have it."

"Got a number?"

"I can't give it to you. Client confidentiality."

Right.

"But I can call her and ask her to contact you directly."

"That would be great. Thank you," I said, and gave her my cell phone number.

"You will let me know what happens?" Her voice was shaky now.

"I promise." I just hoped Jaimie decided to call me soon.

At least I had other leads. And I was seeing ex-husband number two at eleven.

CHAPTER NINE

I poured a cup of coffee and sat back at my desk, skimming the list Marie had given me. Cassie and Brian Stewart's names jumped out at me. Celeste knew them well enough to have their home number? I punched it in. Cassie herself answered.

"Cassie? It's Barbara O'Grady."

"Barbara? How are you?" I could hear the surprise in her voice. I'd helped her out on a previous case, and she'd been grateful, but I wouldn't normally call her at home. Oh well.

"I'm good, thanks. And you?"

"I am also well, thank you."

"Cassie, I'd like to ask you a few questions about Celeste Deslauriers. She seems to have disappeared, and her sister gave me your name. She's very concerned."

"Celeste has disappeared? That is truly terrible. I'm happy to help, but I don't know her well."

"How do you know her?"

"She worked for the United Way when I was a volunteer there. And we socialized occasionally when she was married to Callum McLaughlan, since Callum and Brian have occasionally done work together."

"Was their divorce amicable?"

"He seemed fine with it. I don't know how she took it. Some men are meant to stay single, if you know what I mean?"

My mind switched to Jayson, and his determined self-interest. I knew. "Do you know of anyone who might wish her ill?"

"Celeste? No. She's a lovely person."

I was starting to get that. "You'll give me a call if you think of anything?"

"Yes, I will. And Barbara, I hear you are painting again."

It took me a second to adjust to the change of subject. "How did you know?"

She laughed. "Oh, I have my sources in this town."

She certainly did. Cassie was connected both socially and politically, but through her own art collection and her seat on the Art Gallery board, she was a force to be reckoned with when it came to anything artistic.

"And I've always respected Margaret Courtland's eye for a good painter," she added. "If she says you're good, then you're good."

I felt a warm glow, followed by a rising panic. Margaret had made seeing two of my recent paintings the price for her help with a previous case. Now I've committed to producing seven more paintings for her for a September show.

Sometimes I think I've lost my mind. "Thank you."

"I'm looking forward to seeing your show," she finished.

"Technically it's not my show, since I won't be the only artist participating. I don't think I'm ready for a solo show yet."

A pause. "Ah. May I ask when you last talked to Margaret?"

Um. Margaret had left me a message on Saturday, asking me to call her. Which I'd been ignoring because I didn't have anything else finished. "It's been several weeks. Why?"

"I'd suggest you get back in touch with her. And Barbara? If Margaret thinks you are ready for a solo show, then you are ready."

A solo show? Me? But wait—that would mean at least sixteen paintings. I had two!

I swallowed hard. "I'm finding it challenging to finish the paintings I've already promised her," I admitted.

"You'll send me an invitation to the opening?"

"Absolutely." If Cassie Stewart wanted to come to my opening, assuming I had one, her invitation would be gold edged.

"And, Barbara—do whatever you have to in order to be ready for that show. The interest is there now."

"There's just the little matter of doubling the number of canvases I'd need to finish and frame," I said, trying to hide my shock.

"It is a matter deciding what you want, Barbara. If you want something badly enough, you will make it happen."

After we disconnected, I had to remind myself to breathe, then sat staring blindly at the opposite wall, thinking about the partially completed canvases stacked against my bedroom wall. A solo show? Me?

Painting and making a living from my work had been my dream my whole life, until I let Jayson and my own fears convince me it was a dream I could never achieve.

After six years of trying to bury that dream, I've finally admitted it's central to who I am. I need to paint. I've fought past my fears until I finally feel I'm beginning to do better work than I've ever done in my life.

When I can find the time, that is.

But Cassie was right. Am I going to make my dream happen? Or am I going to let circumstances pull it further and further away from me?

I was still wrestling with the commitment that question implied when the phone rang. "Hello?" I answered, forgetting where I was.

"Is this Barbara O'Grady?" A woman's voice, husky.

I snapped into work mode. "This is she," I said crisply, to counteract the un-businesslike greeting. "What can I do for you?"

"You asked Isabella from Two Hearts to get in touch with me? This is Jaimie, Jaimie Grandis."

"Thank you for calling back, Ms. Grandis."

"Please, call me Jaimie. And this is about Celeste—what else would I do? You're a private investigator?"

"Yes. I've been hired to look into Celeste's disappearance."

She didn't hesitate. "What can I tell you?"

"Have you heard from Celeste since Sunday?"

"Not a word."

I could hear the worry in her voice, but I asked anyway. "And is that unusual?"

"Yes. We talk most days."

And Marie didn't even know Jaimie's last name? I'd been right—Celeste had hidden large chunks of her life from her sister. "And you have no idea where she might have gone? Or why?"

"Celeste wasn't planning to go anywhere. She would have told me."

I noted she hadn't quite answered my question. "Do you know her ex-husbands?"

"I met Callum a few times. He didn't much like me."

"What did you think of him?"

"Under that thousand dollar suit is a little boy who still thinks love is expressed by how many toys you have."

"What about his relationship with Celeste?"

"She tried to heal him. He tried to turn her into a trophy."

Sounded like she didn't like him much, either. "And Ben Oliver?"

"I've never met him, but I liked how Celeste talked about him. They kept in touch."

Marie thought they didn't. "Was Celeste seeing anyone?"

"If you mean was she sleeping with anyone, the answer is no. Celeste is choosy. And usually very careful. That's why I've been so worried about her."

"Why?"

"Well, she was determined to meet that guy again. I told her not to."

"What guy?"

"Someone Two Hearts introduced her to."

Two Hearts again. "Was she planning on meeting him on Sunday? And are you sure he was from Two Hearts?"

"Yes, and yes. He…" She paused. "This is important, isn't it?"

I considered explaining, but I wanted her first impressions. "Yes, it's important."

"Okay." Another pause. "Celeste told me she met him through Two Hearts. I have no proof that she did."

Interesting. "Is there some reason she might lie to you about it?"

"I hope not. It would be totally contrary both to who Celeste is and to our friendship."

Huh. "Any chance you have his name?"

"Sorry, no. After I said she shouldn't meet him, Celeste wouldn't tell me his name."

"Why did you suggest she not meet him?"

"I didn't like the vibes I was getting."

Oh great. A flake. "The vibes? Did you meet him?"

"No, I didn't, but I could feel his energy through her. It wasn't a good combination, her vibes and his. They didn't mesh. As if he was overpowering her. It made her nervous, but she wouldn't admit it."

Hang on. "Had Celeste met this guy? In person? Before last Sunday, I mean?"

"Sure. They got together for coffee the previous Tuesday."

It hadn't been in her diary. "Marie didn't know?"

"Nope. Celeste told her she had to work late. There are lots of things Celeste doesn't tell Little Sister."

I was beginning to get that. "So when she met him for coffee on Sunday, it was a second date?"

"Yes. They were going to walk to Granville Island if it wasn't raining."

So I'd been right. And no wonder Celeste hadn't been worried about security—she'd already met him. "Do you know where they met on Tuesday?"

"I'm not sure, but I know Celeste likes Café Buzz. You know, out on Broadway? I'll bet they met there."

I'd check it out. "Did Celeste tell you anything specific about this guy?"

"She liked him, I think. And she felt sorry for him."

"Why?"

"She said he'd spent his whole life trying to get over what happened to his family when he was a boy. She could relate to that, and I think she felt guilty."

"Guilty?"

"Sure. Because of her father."

"What about her father?"

"Didn't Marie tell you?"

No, she hadn't. Why not? "Why don't you tell me."

"Okay, let's see if I can get it all straight. They were all from this small town, Brenton. It's on the Fraser Highway, the old Canyon route."

"I know it. Marie mentioned she and Celeste had grown up there."

"This guy did, too. Anyway, Celeste's father was the local bank manager, and because the town was so small, he handled everybody's investments as well."

Uh oh. I could see where this was going. "Go on."

"So anyway, the market crashed or something and everybody's money was gone. Her father committed suicide and everybody treated Celeste and Marie and their aunt like outcasts."

"You're sure this guy was from the same town?"

"Yes."

"Did his family lose money too?"

"I think so, but Celeste didn't say much. She carries so much guilt about what happened, parts of her aura are absolutely gray."

Oh no. "You're a psychic?"

"Yeah."

"How did you and Celeste become friends?" I tried to keep my tone non-judgmental, but I don't think I succeeded.

She laughed. "Nobody understands it. She seems so straight laced on the surface. But you don't grow up in the circumstances she did without some major damage. She's spent her life trying to make reparation and trying to heal."

"So where does this guy come into it? Part of the reparation?"

"That's it. I suspect you're a little psychic yourself, Ms. O'Grady."

Me, psychic? Yeah, right. Andrea would laugh her head off at the thought. "It's Barbara."

"Barbara, then," she said with a little smile. Then her voice sobered, darkened. "I'm afraid Celeste saw him as damaged like herself, and that she was trying to heal him."

Oh boy. But Ben had come to the same conclusion, so maybe Jaimie wasn't totally out to lunch. "And?"

"And I'm afraid he's more damaged than she knows. He's dangerous, and especially for her."

"Did you tell Celeste any of this?"

"She wouldn't listen. Said I was too protective of her and that if I met him, I'd see how genuinely sweet he was."

"Sweet?"

"Guy probably has a great cover story. Sociopaths usually do."

Whoa. What kind of psychic talks about sociopaths so casually? "You think he's a sociopath?"

"It's just a label, but a good one in this case, I think. I'm talking about a seriously damaged human being."

Now she was making me nervous. "You never told me what it is you do?"

"Besides being psychic you mean? I'm a psychologist."

Whoa. I hadn't expected that. "How does that work?"

She laughed. "Surprisingly well. It gives me a dual insight into people. Of course, I don't mention being psychic to my colleagues. Or my clients."

"I can imagine." But was I talking to the psychologist or the psychic? "What do you mean by damaged?"

"What I picked up from him was a need to impose his sense of how the world should be on everything around him. And the little

Celeste told me confirms it. But of course I'd have to meet him in person to be sure."

Uh huh. "We have to find him first."

"I know. If I get any feel for where they are, I'll let you know."

Right. Of course she would. "Then you think Celeste is alive?"

"I think I'd know if she was dead. Yes, I think she's alive."

Jaimie was one of the stranger people I'd talked to recently, but she was the only one Celeste seemed to confide in. I needed her.

"Thanks for the call, Jaimie," I said. "And please call me if you think of anything else that might be relevant."

"I will. And thank you, Barbara."

"For what?" I asked, surprised at the warmth in her tone.

"For caring." And she disconnected.

Leaving me staring at the dead phone, wondering why Celeste would lie about her date. Jaimie's fears tumbled over each other in my head, fueled by worry, mixing with what Cassie had said, until I wanted to scream.

Cassie's challenge pulled at me. Was she right? Was I letting the opportunity for a show slip away? But did I really have that option?

Gremlins of doubt niggled at me. I shoved them away. Unless I finished my canvases, I had no chance.

But with Celeste missing, how was I to find the time? I grew more worried about Celeste with every piece of information I uncovered.

"He's a sociopath." Jaimie's words echoed in my mind.

She might be a self-proclaimed psychic, but she was also a trained psychologist. Could she be right, even if she knew the guy only through what Celeste had told her?

The phone rang. Not a number I recognized. Now what? "O'Grady Investigations."

"Barbara."

His voice didn't sound right. "Nick. What's up?"

"We've got another one."

Oh no. "Redhead?"

"Brunette."

Not Celeste.

And the Stalker never took two so close together. "Not my client then. But how awful. Same MO?"

"Yes."

Not that he'd be able to tell me if it had changed. But he hadn't hesitated. Someone else had Celeste. "I'm so sorry."

"Yeah."

I could hear exhaustion in his voice. This ugly case was wearing him down. He was taking it personally that they just couldn't seem to catch the bastard.

"Barbara, I definitely won't be able to make your sister's dinner on Thursday. And I don't know when I'll be able to see you next. We're eating and sleeping this thing."

Well, at least it was one less demand on my time. I could concentrate on finding Celeste. And on painting. "Don't worry about it. Just get him."

A weary laugh. "We're trying."

"You'll get him, Nick. I know you will."

"Thanks for the vote of confidence. I wish I was that sure."

I hated the defeated note in his voice. "Look, Nick, if any time you can take a break, come over. Even if it's only for a few hours."

What was I saying? some part of me thought in panic. I'm already in a time conflict. I ignored it, deepening my voice and adding a campy Greta Garbo accent. "We have ways of distracting you."

At least it got a laugh.

"That's for sure," he said. "I might just take you up on that."

"I'll count on it." I disconnected, took a deep breath. I had to get out of the office, clear my head. Besides, I wasn't sure I could handle any more phone calls.

CHAPTER TEN

I was halfway around the seawall before the tension in my neck and shoulders began to release. It was a beautiful day, sunny and clear, with just enough breeze off the ocean to keep me from overheating. There were six freighters sitting at anchor in English Bay and I briefly wondered where each was going and what it carried.

As I passed the mermaid sculpture, I almost expected to see Nick running towards me. This was where I first talked to him, despite the fact that he'd been renting the office down the hall for months before that day. In his running gear Nick's truly magnificent shoulders had been on full display.

I smiled at the memory, suddenly missing him with an ache that took me by surprise. Jumbled together with that feeling was the confusion engendered by my conversation with Cassie.

When it came to Nick, I didn't know what I wanted, except that I wasn't ready for it to end.

When it came to painting, I knew I wanted to be a success. Or did I?

I hadn't even called Margaret Courtland back yet.

Was Cassie right? Was I putting off the possibility of restarting my painting career because I was afraid of failure? Or maybe afraid of success? It was an unsettling thought.

My feet pounded the asphalt as I remembered how it felt attending other artists's openings. How much I'd wanted to see my own paintings on a gallery wall.

I pictured one of Jayson's openings, when he'd been on the verge of breaking out, and we were still together. I could still see his gleeful smile, the pride that virtually rolled off of him, with me clamped possessively at his side.

I could hear that melodic voice. "This is what success looks like, Barbara. You can experience it through me—it doesn't matter that your own painting will never get you here."

The words had burnt like acid. Just remembering them hurt. I'd finally thrown Jayson out of my life six years ago, and managed not to remember that particular scene. Until now.

Was I still letting his words influence my actions? Or, in this case, my non-actions.

I did a slow simmer while I considered this thought, my feet pounding faster and faster. I was busy. I had no time to paint. But Cassie was right. If having my own show was important to me, and as the key to my dream, it had better be, then I'd make the time.

So why hadn't I?

Celeste. As I thought about her, I caught my toe on a bit of uneven pavement and nearly tripped. Catching my balance, shoving the sense of guilt back down, I ran on. I'd been procrastinating on my painting before Marie showed up in my office.

"But Celeste hasn't got long left. She needs every minute you can give her," my inner voice said. "And what about Nick? You know what he's going through. He needs you right now."

All true. All excuses. If it wasn't Celeste, it would be another case.

Someone would always need me. What about me? What did I need?

To paint. The answer came clearly, with no hesitation. It was what I had always needed, it had just taken a while to figure it out.

And I couldn't blame all of my fear on Jayson—much as I'd like to—he'd just added to the doubts about my abilities I'd held since I was a child.

So. Who was going to run my life? My fears?

Or me?

It was an easy question, with an obvious answer. It's just that answering the question wasn't enough. I was going to have to follow up with action. Not so easy.

That's why I hate this psycho-babble stuff. People spend all this time and all this pain digging into their psyches and feel proud when they come out with answers. Trouble is, that's when the real work begins.

It's not enough to have answers. You have to act on them.

I ran on, feeling each step, each breath, until I felt like a running machine with neither thought nor emotion. Then I focused on the case, on Celeste.

I couldn't shake the feeling she was running out of time.

At least now, after talking to Jaimie, I had another lead to follow. I was probably looking for a guy whose roots were in Brenton, which was what Marie had told me from the beginning.

Yet without the information on why people from Brenton "didn't like them much", Marie's information hadn't seemed as urgent as it did now. Why had she held back those critical details, when she was clearly so frantic about her missing sister? I had a few new questions for my client.

I zipped back to my place for a quick shower. For my meeting with ex-husband number two, I changed into my version of a power suit. Then tossed a clean set of running gear into a bag for the office.

Driving back downtown, I ignored the midmorning traffic and concentrated on what I wanted to ask Callum McLaughlan.

———

CALLUM MET me in the lobby with an outstretched hand and a polished smile. I saw what Jaimie meant about his suits—this one was deep slate and cut to fit beautifully. His tie was a pale mauve against a crisp white shirt.

He led me into an office as expensively furnished as he was and waved me into a deep chair before taking a seat behind his desk.

"Now, what can I do for you, Ms. O'Grady? I understand this has to do with Celeste DesLauriers?"

"With your ex-wife, yes. She's missing."

He nodded. "Marie called me. I'm sorry to hear it."

That's it? "When did you last see her?"

"Two or three weeks ago, I suppose." Warm, polished tones, eyes that seemed concerned yet watched me closely.

"Where?"

"A recognition dinner for the firm. At VU."

"Not since then?"

"No."

"And how did she seem?"

"As serene and beautiful as ever. And as remote."

"Remote?"

"Celeste is not a woman who is—emotionally available," he said, and something flickered in his eyes. Regret?

I would have said the problem was his, not hers, but now I wondered. Does anyone ever really know what goes on in someone else's relationship? "You knew she was dating again."

"Yes." Clipped tone.

"Did she ever talk to you about anyone she was seeing?"

"We didn't have that kind of relationship."

"What kind of relationship did you have?"

"We were—friendly acquaintances."

How could you treat someone you'd been married to, lived with, as an acquaintance? Was he really as unmoved by her disappearance as he seemed?

"Is Celeste the kind of person to leave town without telling anyone?" I asked.

"Definitely not. That is completely out of character for her. She is very careful about the social niceties."

And that was a very carefully worded comment. "Does Celeste have any enemies?"

"None that I ever heard of."

"You don't consider yourself her enemy?"

"Of course not." The eyes lit then, but what emotion fired them?

"Is there anyone you think I should talk to?"

"Rather than waste time talking to me, you should be talking to that eco-cowboy first husband of hers."

Eco-cowboy. I liked that. "Why do you suggest I talk to him?" I asked.

No point telling husband number two that I'd already met with husband number one.

"The heat hadn't gone out of that relationship, not by a long shot," Callum said. "And I don't think either of them knew whether it was love or hate they felt."

Which put a very interesting slant on Celeste's relationship with Callum.

I thanked Callum for his time and refrained from telling him I'd be back, though I was sure I would be.

CHAPTER ELEVEN

Thinking about how much I trust my instincts reminded me of someone else whose instincts about people I trust—Andrea. In addition to being my best friend, Andrea owns and runs the best temporary placement agency in the city. And she hears everything.

All three of my candidates from Two Hearts work in offices, so all of them probably hire or work with office temps from time to time. If anyone would know the gossip about the three men, she would.

I punched in her number.

"Trusted Temps. Andrea Fisher speaking."

"Hi, Andrea."

"Barbara. I haven't heard from you in days." She sounded annoyed.

"I've got a case."

"You've always got a case."

"This time the client's missing, maybe kidnapped and I don't think she's got a lot of time."

Her voice dropped. "Not the Stalker?"

"No, I don't think so."

"What did the ransom note say?"

It was a good question. What kind of kidnapper doesn't send a ransom note?

One where the victim doesn't ever come home, a little voice in my head answered. "We haven't got one."

"Then how do you know she was kidnapped?"

"Because she vanished on Sunday after a date, and her car was found abandoned. That's why I called you."

"Why?"

"She had three dates lined up through a dating service. I'm not sure which one she saw on Sunday, or if it was any of them. They're all professionals, and I thought you might have placed someone with one of them."

Now her tone was all business. "Names?"

I gave them, knowing she'd keep them confidential.

"I'll get back to you as soon as I can. And Barbara?"

"What?"

"Don't think you're getting off that easy. How long does a phone call take?"

I was left grimacing at a dial tone.

Truth is, with Andrea, a phone call can easily take an hour and a half. Time I didn't have.

I went back to my computer. This time I was looking for info about Brenton. I found a little.

The town was still there, but the population had shrunk to fewer than 300 souls from the 800 it had once held. There was still a bimonthly newspaper, a café and a general store. The school had closed—too few pupils—as had the bank, and there had never been a hospital.

When the four-lane Coquihalla Highway went through in the late '80's, it pulled most of the traffic—and most of the business—away from the aging, two-lane section of the Trans-Canada Highway running through the Fraser Canyon. Longer driving times, steep hills with sharp curves and steep drops into the Fraser River far below took care of the rest.

Towns all up and down the route had decayed or vanished entirely. Brenton was no exception. I wondered where the displaced population had gone. Vancouver, probably. Kelowna. Kamloops. Where the jobs were.

I checked my watch. Twenty minutes. Andrea is usually faster than that. I flipped through the notes I'd made about Brenton, thought about what Jaimie had said about the place, then picked up the phone and punched in Marie's number.

It was time she told me the truth about Brenton. The whole truth, not just the bits and pieces she'd given me so far.

Marie wasn't answering her cell. I disconnected, drummed my fingers on the desk. Got up and put on a pot of French Roast, extra strong, glanced out the window. Clouds were massing on the horizon, but the sun was shining on downtown, glinting off the windows in the building opposite me.

The phone rang. I glanced at the number displayed and grabbed it.

"Nick?"

"Barbara. I have an odd favor to ask."

"If I can do it, I will."

"Thanks." I could hear relief in his voice. "Are you free tonight?"

"I thought you were tied up?"

"I am.

Okay, then. "What kind of favor?"

"Can you and Andrea go to Mandino's for dinner? It's on me. I need your opinion of the place."

Mandino's was downtown-chic, and a real meat-market from what I'd heard. "I'll check if she's free. Anything particular you want my opinion on?"

He chuckled. "Anything that strikes you as odd."

"You really want me to go to a place known for attracting Vancouver's trendy few, and take note of anything I consider odd?"

He chuckled. "Anything that might be odd for a place like that," he clarified.

I was glad I'd made him laugh. "And this would be related to your current case?"

"Yeah."

"And you can't tell me why." It wasn't really a question. Besides, I already knew the answer.

Andrea and I were both single, in the age range of the Stalker's victims. Mandino's must have come up as a possible connection.

"Nope," he said. "But it won't be dangerous. "

Meaning they were watching the place. I quickly ran through my urgent list. I had to eat anyway. "Sure, I'll do it. How do I contact you?"

"I'll call you. And, Barbara?"

"Yeah?"

"Thanks. And I miss you." And he was gone.

While I was still thinking about what I would have said in return, the phone rang. Andrea. "You've got something?" I asked her.

"Uh huh. And believe it or not, we've done work for all three of them."

"Great. What can you tell me about them?"

"Not a thing."

Figured. "Nothing to tell?"

"Not yet, anyway. I still need to talk to the temp who worked for them. Oddly, one woman worked for all three, and I haven't been able to get hold of her."

"She's not a brunette, is she?" I said flippantly, then regretted my levity.

"Yes, as a matter of fact. Why?"

"Forget it. I was making a rather sick joke."

But Andrea is quick. "The Stalker's latest victim?"

"Yes. But please, forget I said anything. It's not likely to be her. How many brunettes are there in Vancouver?"

"You're right. But she usually leaves a message on a work day."

"Andrea, don't buy trouble."

"You're right." But I could hear the worry in her voice.

"Feel like going to Mandino's for dinner?" I asked.

"Wait a minute. An hour ago you were too busy to talk. Now you want to go out for dinner. What gives?"

I explained.

"It's a good thing you're my best friend," Andrea said darkly. "Or I might never forgive you. You have time to run Nick's errands, but no time for me."

"But you have to admit it's an intriguing errand. And if I can do anything that helps to catch the Stalker, I will."

"I agree," Andrea said.

Neither of us said anything for a moment. What was there to say?

Andrea broke the silence. "And Nick will undoubtedly make it worth your while," she said with a sly note in her voice.

"Andrea!"

She chortled. It's the only word for the sound that came down the phone line.

"I wish I could see your face right now, Barbara. But you can't tell me you aren't good together. I've seen your face after you've been with him."

She was right, we were great together. But I wasn't about to tell her that. She was already annoying enough on the subject of my love life. "So, are you up for dinner, or not?"

"Sure, but you're going to have to make it up to me. Maybe share some juicy details about Nick."

Not a chance. "Why don't I collect you at eight. Your place?"

"Eight's good, but I'll be working late. Look, it's walking distance from both our offices. Why don't we meet there?"

"I may be running a bit late. If that's a problem, I can pick you up?"

"No, I'll just order a drink and people-watch if you're late."

"Then I'll see you there." I disconnected and dialed Marie again. Still no answer.

———

THE RICH SMELL of freshly brewed coffee finally caught my attention. I got up, poured a cup, added cream, wandered to the window. I took a sip, staring at the sky, which was rapidly clouding over.

Cassie's words kept battering at the edges of my mind, demanding to be let in. "If not now, Barbara, when?"

I was no closer to finding Celeste. And I'd just committed tonight for Nick.

How was I going to find the time to paint?

How could I not?

I swallowed another mouthful of coffee. Did I really want a show?

It was a no-brainer. Yes, I wanted a show.

Okay, then I needed to make it happen.

Before I could change my mind, I dialed the Courtland Gallery.

"Margaret, it's Barbara O'Grady," I said when she came on the line. "You'd left a message to call you."

"Yes. I've been reviewing your work, and I think you're ready for a solo show. I like what I've seen so far—it's stronger than your previous work. And I may have several interested collectors."

Cassie must have called Margaret, bless her. Wait a minute. Where had the 'several' had come from? Or was Margaret exaggerating?

She was still talking. "You've agreed to provide seven more works in addition to the two I already have, but we'd need at least fifteen for a show. Sixteen would be even better. And I happen to have a hole in my schedule in October. We had a cancellation for health reasons. Can you be ready by then?"

Fourteen paintings? By October? It was only five months away—too soon. "Yes, I can do that," I said before I could talk myself out of it.

"Terrific. Come in the next day or so and we'll do the paperwork."

"I'll do that. Thank you, Margaret."

"You're welcome. And Barbara, I expect to do very well from your show. Just keep that in mind."

I'd rather not. Suddenly the idea of people buying my work was more terrifying than the thought of how much work I'd just committed myself to.

I poured another cup of coffee, but my stomach jumped and quivered at the first mouthful. Now I couldn't even drink coffee? Oh, I was in big trouble.

I glanced at my watch. Oh. I'd missed lunch. Food would probably help.

CHAPTER TWELVE

I closed my office door a little too firmly behind me, and grabbed a bottle of water from the mini fridge, to go with the chicken salad sandwich I'd picked up. It hadn't started raining, yet, despite the clouds, but it wasn't a day for eating in the park. Not that I had time, anyway.

Between bites, I called Two Hearts, then finished my lunch while I waited. When they finally connected me to Isabella, I told her what I was looking for.

"We'd have no reason to ask about their hometown, Barbara, and I doubt we have any records beyond their sign-up sheets," she said.

"Could you check anyway?"

"I'll get to it as quickly as I can, and get back to you."

Five minutes later the phone rang. "That was quick," I said.

"Glad you think so," Jerry said, sounding amused. I could just picture the smart-ass grin on his face.

I wasn't going to explain. "What's up?"

"We've got the final report back on your client's car. Nothing else suspicious."

"Anything on her credit cards or phone?"

"No activity at all. The missing squad is following up."

Not good. "Thanks, Jerry."

"Don't mention it, O'Grady. But this clears things, okay? I don't owe you any more info."

I sighed. He loves this game. "No, I owe you."

I disconnected and the phone shrilled. This time it was Isabella. "What did you find?" I asked her.

"We had no further information on two of them. The third guy wasn't from Brenton."

"Who was the third guy?"

"I'm sorry, I can't tell you that."

Which meant I could expect a text. "One more question. How thoroughly do you check their personal information?"

"We check current employment data and verify identity."

"So any of them could have lied about where they were from?"

"Why would anyone do that?"

"If one of them is our guy, he wouldn't have wanted his background easily traced."

"Oh. Yes, any of them could have lied."

I nodded, even thought she couldn't see me. "Okay. Thanks."

"You still haven't found anything, then?"

I couldn't keep the frustration from my voice, and didn't try. "Nothing definitive."

"If anyone can find her, I have a feeling it'll be you, Barbara."

Not another woman with 'feelings.' Which was hardly fair, given how much I rely on my own instincts.

And she was just trying to help. "Thanks, Isabella. I'll let you know if anything turns up."

I checked for texts. I had one from Isabella. It said, "Hanlon". Nothing else.

Interesting.

I went back to plotting my trip to Brenton. Without coffee, yet. The local paper, the *Brenton Bugle*, wasn't on line—and I was betting none of the libraries in Vancouver had back copies on film. A few clicks and I had my answer. Nope.

Looks like I needed to find time for a visit to Brenton, unless I could track down Celeste's mystery date first. If I cleared my schedule, I could go the following day.

The phone rang.

Marie. Finally.

"Marie, why didn't you tell me the full story about your father?" I asked before she could launch into yet another rant.

There was a telling silence. "Why would I?"

"Because you were worried about Celeste dating someone from Brenton, and you didn't tell me why." This was no time to be anything but brutally frank with her.

"Look Marie, if your sister has been kidnapped, she may not have much time left. You need to tell me everything that might be relevant."

There was a stifled sob on the line.

"Marie?"

No reply.

"Marie, I'm doing everything I can to find Celeste. But you have to work with me."

More silence.

"Marie, is there anything else I should know?"

"Yes." It came out defiant.

"What?" I was struggling to hold my irritation in check. Did she want her sister found, or not?

"I can't tell you over the phone. Can you meet me back at my place?"

"Is it really necessary?"

"Yes."

"I'll be there in twenty minutes. But Marie? No more games."

"Fine." And she disconnected.

At least she'd taken my mind off my October deadline. I'd known this was going to be an impossible case, and Marie an impossible client. I'm seldom wrong in my first impressions of clients.

So why do I keep taking these cases?

So you don't have to paint, a little voice whispered in my ear. I stopped dead, mug in hand. Was that it?

Then I laughed at myself, switched off the coffeemaker and grabbed my purse.

Yeah, right. Of course it had nothing to do with the fact that the only cases that came my way were the impossible ones.

And I still had bills to pay.

———

I SAT FACING Marie in a living room that was far less immaculate than the last time I'd seen it. Newspapers and fast food wrappers were spread on every surface. There was no doubt which sister was the neat one in this family.

Marie sat on a pale green love seat facing the ivory sofa where I sat. My client didn't match the décor. Worry lines creased her forehead and her mouth was pinched tight.

"We should have heard something by now, shouldn't we?"

I wasn't even going there. "What did you want to tell me?"

She stared at me for a moment. Her eyes were huge, the irises nearly vanishing. Had she taken something?

Then the words poured out. "I don't know what Jaimie told you, but our father was an idiot. He wasn't a crook. They made him so miserable that he killed himself, then they made our lives hell. Celeste still feels guilty—as if she had anything to do with it—but I don't. I'd like to see them all fry in hell."

Whew. I'd seen the anger in her, but hadn't guessed it ran this deep. "Who is 'them'?"

"Brenton."

"The whole town?"

"Yeah." Her voice was clipped now, as if each word hurt her.

"Why would your sister agree to meet someone from Brenton?"

A shrug. "Maybe she was always trying to make up for it, make it right."

Maybe Marie had a greater insight into her sister's character than I'd given her credit for. Fleetingly I wondered if Susanna knew me half so well. "What about you?"

"I don't think they'll ever forgive us."

"That's why you think your sister's in danger."

She didn't look up. "Yeah."

"And what do you know about the guy from Brenton that Celeste was seeing?"

"Celeste wouldn't tell me anything except where he was from—she knew how I felt about that place. But she wanted to fix the mess everyone thought Dad caused."

"How? Pay everyone back?"

Marie laughed. It was a bitter sound. "Hardly. She'd have to discover a diamond mine to afford that. No, she had this theory that the worst damage was not the lost money, it was the loss of trust."

"She wanted to heal them?" It was what Jaimie had said, too. And Ben.

"Yeah. She wanted to help him rediscover trust." She gave another little laugh, and this time it hurt my ears. "My God, she wanted to restore his faith in people, and he's probably going to kill her."

For a minute I didn't know what to say. "So why were you keeping all this from me?"

Marie grimaced. "I couldn't face it."

I wasn't buying that. "You have no choice. Tell me everything you've been holding back, or I'm off the case."

I let the silence stretch.

Marie looked down, picked at a ragged cuticle. "She started seeing him without telling me," she said, her voice barely audible. "Like she didn't trust me. So I spied on her."

"When?"

"Tuesday night. She said she'd be home late, and I guessed. So I followed her."

"To Café Buzz?"

"Yeah. But how did you know?"

"I'm a P. I. It's what I do."

"Oh."

"And what happened on Tuesday?"

"Don't you know?"

I didn't answer.

She colored a little, which surprised me. "I didn't recognize him, but Celeste did. She looked really happy to see him. And she called him Danny."

Marie had seen this guy, and this was the first I was hearing about it? What was wrong with her? "Don't you want your sister found?"

Her eyes got wet and she sniffed a couple of times and stared at her hands, twisting in her lap. "More than anything."

"Then why am I only hearing this now?"

"I—I thought you'd find him at Two Hearts."

Right. "What else do you know about this Danny? Did Celeste know his last name?"

"I—she didn't say. He looked kinda shocked, then glanced around as if he was nervous and hushed her right away. I figured maybe he wasn't using his real name."

Sounds like she was right. "Do you know a Danny?"

She shook her head. "But a lot of people lost everything and left town after our Dad—died. He could have been one of them."

"How old were you when he died?"

"Three."

So she wouldn't remember it. "And how old did this Danny look?"

"About Celeste's age."

"Would you recognize this guy again?"

"Yeah, I'd know him."

"What does he look like?"

"Medium height. So-so build. Brown hair."

"Eyes?"

"Probably blue, but I was too far away to be sure. I didn't want Celeste to spot me."

Her description matched what Tanya at Starbucks had told me.

Of course, it also matched with thousands of others in the city. I flipped back to my notes. Tanya had also said he held his arm awkwardly. "Marie, did this guy have anything wrong with his arm?"

She nodded. "Something about the way he held his shoulder."

"Which shoulder?"

"The left, no, the right one."

Bingo. It was the right arm Tanya had noticed. But she hadn't recognized any of the three photos from Two Hearts.

"What about the photos from Two Hearts I showed you before?" I asked, pulled out my phone again. "Are you positive none of them is Danny?"

She flipped through them twice. "Yes. They all look kind of like him, but they're much better looking. These guys are gorgeous. Danny is—generic."

Which meant that Two Hearts was a false trail, a waste of time. Time I couldn't afford to be wasting. It didn't matter who those guys were—they had nothing to do with Celeste's disappearance.

Wait a minute, though. "Marie, I thought Celeste had described the guy from Two Hearts she was dating."

Marie fidgeted. "I made that part up, so I could explain how I knew what he looked like."

Cursing silently, I took a deep breath. I didn't understand her. "You're the one telling me how critical it is I find your sister immediately. How could you hold this back?"

She chewed on her lip and didn't answer.

I'd recognized similarities to my relationship with Susanna, but maybe it had blinded me to something else. And I was beginning to suspect that something else might be critical to finding Celeste in time.

"Marie, you're the one who's so worried about finding your sister in time. What else haven't you told me?"

"Nothing." Defensive now.

"What really happened in Brenton?"

"I don't know!" She practically yelled it at me. "I get a migraine when I try to think about those years, and everything goes fuzzy."

What had gone on in that town, anyway? "Well, keep trying. I need anything you come up with if I'm going to find Celeste alive."

Marie's face went so white that her piercings looked like scars, and I almost felt bad for putting it in such harsh terms.

I couldn't let her keep lying to me, though, not with Celeste still missing. Which brought back Marie's first lie. "Marie, Celeste must have had photos of the three matches from the dating service. Did she ever show them to you?"

"No."

Maybe she'd kept everything on her phone. "I need some kind of photo of this Danny. Does Celeste have any photos or annuals from her school years that might have a photo of him in it?"

"Nothing from Brenton. Celeste keeps stuff like that, but my aunt wouldn't let her buy anything."

Great. The aunt sounded like a real horror show. Then I realized Marie was hesitating. "Marie? Is there still something you're not telling me?"

"I—might have something else."

She wouldn't meet my gaze. Now what? "Oh?"

She grabbed her messenger bag, slowly pulled out a folded sheet of paper with a ragged edge. Still not meeting my eyes, she held it out to me.

The quality of the heavy paper surprised me. It had probably been pulled out of an artist's sketchbook.

I unfolded the page to find an ink drawing of a man's face. It wasn't quite a portrait, more like a caricature, with certain features, especially the eyes, exaggerated for emphasis. The drawing was spare, but the use of line and shading, the way she'd caught expression and something of his character, were excellent.

"You did this?"

"Yeah. It's pretty quick, but I think it's like him. It might help?"

It would definitely help, especially if she'd caught him as accurately as the quality of this sketch suggested. "When did you do this?"

"Um. The day I saw them in the coffee shop."

She was definitely nervous about something. Not telling me earlier, maybe? Or was it showing her work?

"You're very good. Where did you study?"

She glared at me. "I didn't. This isn't anything, really."

I looked back at the drawing. It was definitely something—it was good. And it half-reminded me of work I'd seen before, though I couldn't think whose.

Marie reached up, swept her hair behind her ear. The small tattoo on her forearm, bared by the movement, caught my attention. It was a stylized mermaid, done in shades of aqua and green. It was beautiful. And the lines of it were similar to those in the drawing she'd just handed me.

"Did you design your tattoo?" I asked.

Her eyes followed mine, then she quickly pulled her sleeve down so the tattoo vanished. "Kinda. Raul, the tattoo guy fixed it up some."

"You're very talented."

She blushed a little, but her lips tightened. "This isn't helping us find my sister."

So the topic of art was out of bounds. Why?

And I wasn't lying. She did have talent, but apparently she didn't want to admit it. Or maybe just not to me. "If I can borrow this, there are a few people I want to show it to."

Her face looked more scared than pleased at the idea, but she nodded. "Okay. If it'll help."

"It will." It would have helped even more two days ago, when she first hired me, but there was no point ranting at her now.

I had work to do.

CHAPTER THIRTEEN

I was still fuming as I fought traffic heading east on Broadway. Why on earth hadn't Marie told me all this to start with? And why had I taken on this case? I knew better!

The more I thought about it, the madder I got. I would have called and fired her, except by now I felt I knew Celeste. I wanted to see her found safe.

Even if I did have to keep dealing with her infuriating sister.

The traffic ahead of me had come to yet another halt, in a screech of brakes and a smell of oil and diesel fumes. At least I now had a drawing of this guy. Now I needed a confirmation that Marie's drawing really did look like the man Celeste had met last Tuesday.

A last name would be nice, too.

By the time I reached Café Buzz I'd calmed down a little, but I was still annoyed with Marie. And with myself, which was worse.

The place was cozy, dimly lit and felt like a student hangout, heavy with the aromas of coffee and fresh cinnamon buns. The guy behind the counter was in his early twenties with the kind of build that said he worked out often. He brought my cappuccino quickly, but seemed disinclined to talk.

The hell with subtlety. I didn't have time for it.

I pulled out my investigator's license. "I'm investigating a disappearance."

Now he was interested. Ice-gray eyes lit up and he leaned forward. "How can I help?"

I nearly grinned, despite my worry. Pulled out Celeste's photo. "She was in last Tuesday with a guy. Did you see them?"

"Tuesday? What time?"

At least Marie had been able to fill in that blank. "Around five. Were you here?"

He nodded, peering at the photo.

"I see a lot of people come and go," he finally said. "I know most of the regulars, though. And I think she came in fairly often. Usually by herself. She'd sit in a corner, and write in a big notebook or something."

"Did you see her last Tuesday?"

"Yeah, guess I did. Not sure it was Tuesday, but she sat over there," waving to a table by the window. "And this guy joined her."

"Can you describe him?"

"Pretty much medium. Hair, build. Didn't look like he'd ever been to a gym."

"Hair color?"

"Brown."

"Ever seen him before?"

"Not to remember. He's not a regular, though."

I pulled out the drawing. "Is this the guy?"

He picked up the drawing and examined it closely. "Yeah, that's him. To the life."

"What about the two of them, as a couple, I mean. How did they seem together?"

"Looked like they were in an intense conversation most of the time. "

I nodded. "Hear any of it?"

"Nope, sorry."

"Anything else strike you about him?"

"Nah."

"Thanks." I dropped a ten in the tip jar, handed him my card. "Call me if you think of anything else. Anything at all."

That earned me a big smile. "Sure will."

Well, at least Marie's latest story held up, and the sketch was recognizable. It was more than I'd had that morning.

I checked my watch. I had time to swing by Isabella's office, see if she recognized the sketch.

———

ISABELLA'S OFFICE looked even more spartan than before, but she seemed flustered. "Barbara. This is a surprise."

After keeping me waiting nearly fifteen minutes, she didn't seem to want to meet my eyes. "The police were just here. A Ms. Yip."

Ah, the elusive Cathy. "And?"

"I told her everything I shared with you, but she didn't say much. Any idea how their investigation is going?"

"We're sharing information, but it gets harder after the first couple of days when someone vanishes. Especially when there's no sign of violence, and very little in the way of evidence. But I do have something I'd like you to look at."

I pulled out Marie's drawing and handed it to her. "Do you recognize this guy?"

"Um. No, I don't." She held the drawing away from her, squinted a little, as if trying to see him differently.

"Could he be one of Celeste's three matches? Maybe if he'd had a little work done?"

"No, definitely not."

"Could he be a client here?"

"I don't think so." A pause, then, "Wait a minute. I know this guy —I've seen him somewhere. Or at least I think I have."

"Where?"

"I don't know—it's more a feeling than a memory. As if I should know him."

"But he's not a client?"

"No. Definitely not. This feels—distant, somehow."

Or maybe she really, really didn't want it to be a client. It would reflect badly on Two Hearts. Which wasn't new. It would always have reflected badly on them.

So why was I thinking this now?

It was the first time I'd felt Isabella was worried about anything other than finding Celeste as quickly as possible. Was I overreacting to her having a bad day? Or had something changed?

"Thanks," I said, accepting the drawing back from her. "Call me if you think of anything else, will you?"

I left with her promises to call the minute anything occurred to her ringing in my ears. I hoped I could believe them.

It was raining lightly, so I dashed for the car, thinking about what I'd just learned.

The piece that really didn't fit was that Celeste seemed to have lied about Danny being one of her Two Hearts dates. Could Isabella be wrong?

Maybe Danny was a Two Hearts client, even one of Celeste's three matches, but had changed his name and altered his appearance.

Which might explain why the sketch was familiar but Isabella couldn't place him?

I didn't like the implications of that possibility at all. And without a last name for Danny, I had nowhere to start. Good thing I was going to Brenton tomorrow.

———

BEFORE STARTING THE ENGINE, I called Marie. "How well do you remember people from Brenton?"

"I told you, I never think about the place. I get a migraine every time I try."

There was a story here. "How old were you when you left?"

"Thirteen."

"That's when you came to Vancouver?"

"Yeah. Our aunt died, and Celeste was working for the United Way here."

"You lived with your aunt?"

"She moved in with us after my mother died when I was born. Except my dad died when I was three and Celeste went off to university when I was eight. Then it was just me."

That might explain her attitude. I wondered what the aunt had been like. "You lived with Celeste when you moved here?"

"In a crappy little studio apartment out on Kingsway. Our old house wasn't fancy, but at least I'd had my own space."

And sometimes attitude is just attitude. My admiration for Celeste rose. Twenty-two, with what was probably an entry job, and she's caring for her angry little sister and working full time, all from a cramped studio apartment that was probably in a pretty rough part of town.

It couldn't have been easy for her. I had to hand it to her for guts and style.

"When I talked to Ben, he mentioned he and Celeste ran into a woman from Brenton, someone named Leanne. Ring any bells?"

"No last name?"

"He couldn't remember."

"Figures."

So she was still mad at him too. I wondered how long she held grudges. "If I give you some names, can you tell me if their families ever lived in Brenton?"

"No. I told you, even if I try, I can't remember any of that stuff."

I was starting to feel empathy for my troublesome client. She hadn't had it easy.

But she wasn't exactly making my job easy, either.

CHAPTER FOURTEEN

Mandino's was too loud and too stark for my taste. My favorite black dress fit right in, but I didn't. I felt like I'd wandered onto a movie set, and any moment the lights would blaze on.

When I eat out, I prefer to focus on the food and the company, not on some trendy designer's concept of New York Style. Still, I'd heard the food was good.

Before the hostess swanned back from escorting the last couple, I spotted Andrea at the table Nick had reserved for us. I sauntered over, conscious of eyes following my progress. Probably wondering if I was 'someone'.

"Quite the place," I said to Andrea once we were seated.

She looked around, her eyes bright. "I don't think I'll be a regular, but I like the energy of it all."

"That's not energy, that's pretense. High-level posturing."

"Don't be so negative, Barbara. I'm glad we're here, I've been hearing about Mandino's for months. This is the place to see and be seen."

"That's what I mean."

"You're impossible."

"No, I'm not. I just know what I like."

"You do realize you're sounding like a crotchety stick-in-the-mud?"

"Stick-in-the-mud? Now who's sounding past it?"

"I'm serious, Barbara. I'm getting worried about you. You used to like going out, checking out the new restaurants, the new plays. Now all you do is work."

"That is not all I do."

"Okay, sometimes now you paint, which is a good thing. Only you've turned that into more work. It isn't good for you. You need to get out more. I think you've forgotten how to enjoy yourself."

"Hey, I'm dating Nick now, remember?"

"Which is terrific, except he's been out of town or unavailable so much, it doesn't help."

"Believe me, it helps," I said with a grin, thinking about our last night together.

Andrea gave me a shrewd look. "And did the two of you actually go out? Or did you cook and stay in?"

Andrea knew me too well. "What's that got to do with anything? I wasn't working, and that seems to be your main complaint."

"No, my main complaint is…"

Before she could finish telling me what was wrong with me, our waiter materialized at her elbow, hair spiked just so and notepad at the ready. "What would you like to drink?"

"I'll have another Cosmo, and Barbara? A glass of wine?"

"Burrowing Owl Cabernet, please." It was my current favorite, and hard to find, being made in limited quantities at one of the small estate wineries in the Okanagan.

"And are you ready to order?"

Andrea and I looked at our unopened menus. "We'll need a few minutes," I told him.

"We were catching up," she said, with a saucy smile.

"Sure, no problem, take your time," he said with an answering smile.

I've never met a man under ninety who could resist that smile of Andrea's. She's slain a legion of waiters with it. And we were assured of attentive service all night.

"I'll be right back with your drinks," he told her.

Andrea turned back to me. "You've always been driven, but lately you've forgotten how to live."

I looked at the partiers around us, then back at Andrea. "Oh, and this is living?"

"You know what I mean, Barbara."

I wasn't so sure I did know, but I was sure I didn't want to talk about it. "So what do you think of the place so far?"

She gave me a look that said we weren't done talking about my life, but obligingly looked around. "Since neither of us has been here before, it makes it tough to spot differences. Surely that hunk you're dating knows that."

Andrea had met Nick for the first time a few weeks previously. She'd approved of him. Always a good thing, given that she's my best friend, and he's my main guy. At least for now. "I think he knows. Which means we're looking for something not usual to this scene."

"Ah," said Andrea, then paused while our waiter put our drinks in front of us.

I noted that the table beside us, who'd arrived just before we did, were still waiting for their drinks. Andrea's charm strikes again.

I took a deep swallow of my Cabernet, which was amazing, as always, and looked across at my sometimes too perceptive friend. "Thanks, Andrea."

"For what? I know it can't be my comments on your life—you never thank me for those."

"Can you blame me? No, for the speedy arrival of our drinks."

She looked lost. I indicated our waiter. She grinned. "Oh, that. Don't mention it."

I took another, slower mouthful of wine, sat back and let my senses absorb the feel of Mandino's. All around me, people were talking, laughing and eating. The food smelled heavenly, but to my ears there was a brittle shrillness to the sounds around me, almost a desperate quality. Yes, it was a meat-market, but it wasn't that. What was it?

"Barbara, I think we'd better look at the menus, or I'm going to expire from hunger. Everything smells so good."

"Good point," I said, opening the oversized menu in front of me.

The entrees were trendy fusion and the prices were astronomical but the chef clearly knew what he was doing. Everything sounded good. I was torn between seared ahi tuna with wasabi and the filet mignon with brandied kumquats. "What are you having, Andrea?"

"Our research might take a while, right?" she asked.

I knew that tone. Now what was she up to? "It could."

"Did you see the tasting menu? I'm sure it would take hours to properly appreciate."

The best thing about a new restaurant was trying as many things as possible, while still leaving room for dessert. And the tasting menu included dessert. Plus it looked spectacular. Pricey, but spectacular.

Six appetizer-sized courses, starting with a lemon-grass spiked lobster bisque, followed by a goat cheese and cranberry salad, working through grilled wild boar with shiitake mushrooms, the ahi tuna and the filet mignon and ending with a rhubarb and Stilton cheesecake. I'd have to fit in a two-hour run tomorrow to make up for all that food, but it would be worth it.

"That looks good to me."

"Great." Andrea beckoned our waiter over. "We'll both have the tasting menu, and the wines that go with it."

"But…"

"Good choice," he said, and vanished in the direction of the kitchen.

Andrea looked pleased with herself.

"Don't you think that's a little much?"

"Why? We can cab it home. And when was the last time you just had fun? You know it'll be worth it."

Yes, I did. But I'd be paying for this one, not charging Nick for it. I glanced around, then turned to Andrea. "Back to why we're here. Any thoughts?"

She shook her head. "Not yet. Why don't we just enjoy ourselves, talk and eat, and see whether anything strikes us."

"Makes sense to me." A small commotion at the bar caught my eye and I glanced over.

A couple had just made their way to the far end of the bar. She was wearing a short but stunning dress and was lovely enough to cause a buzz even here. He stood with his back to me, wearing a beautifully cut suit. I couldn't see his face, just dark hair barbered to cup the elegant shape of his head, but he looked annoyingly familiar. Why?

Andrea sensed my interest and looked over at the bar, eyebrows raised slightly. "Ah, Callum," she said with an approving nod.

Callum? He turned around as if aware we were staring at him, and I was indeed looking at Celeste's second ex-husband.

He wasn't looking at us, though. All of his attention was focused on the very young, very long-legged blond beside him. Her dress was probably as expensive as his suit, even though there was a lot less of it. He didn't seem to mind, though.

"You know Callum?"

"Sure. He's a client from way back. What's more interesting is that you know him. C'mon, give."

I grinned at her. "Nice try. But it's business. He's the ex-husband in the case I was telling you about."

"Ex—Barbara, are you telling me that Celeste Deslauriers is the one who's missing? The one you're looking for?"

I very carefully hadn't told her that, but there was no point denying it now. And in any case, she was far too upset for quibbling over semantics. "Yes. I take it you know her?"

She nodded. "Not well, but we've worked together on a couple of United Way campaigns, and what I know I like. I met Callum through her."

"I don't suppose you've heard from her in the last week?"

"No. Is that how long she's been missing?"

"Since Sunday."

"So that's why I haven't heard from you. I'm sorry I made such a fuss. Finding her is more important. You have no leads?"

"Nothing concrete, at least."

"And the police haven't found anything?"

"No."

She nodded. "You'll find her, Barbara. You haven't failed me yet."

Oh, terrific. Apparently this case had just become another of Andrea's "you-can-solve-this-Barbara" projects. Just what I needed —more pressure. "What can you tell me about Celeste and Callum?"

"Surely you don't suspect him."

"You know me, I suspect everyone. But you know them better than I do. What do you think?"

She started to shake her head, then looked thoughtful. "I would have said he idolized her. They weren't right for each other, though."

"Why not?"

"A lot of little things. And the sister living with them didn't help."

I could imagine. "Go on."

"But I think the main thing is they had different values. Callum cares too much about all this," she said with a vague wave. "He cares about belonging here. Celeste doesn't."

"Why did they split up?"

A shrug. Andrea took a sip of her wine. "No-one really seemed to know. They just said they were better friends than partners."

"Not acrimonious, then."

"No. Not that anyone ever saw, anyway."

"And you call me a cynic."

She raised her wine glass in a mock toast. At that point the waiter brought the bisque and a smooth Viognier to go with it and we focused on the food for a moment.

"The odd thing is," Andrea said, soup spoon halfway to her mouth. "For all Callum's need to be a player, I didn't expect to see him with someone like her," and she tilted her head slightly towards Callum's luminous date.

"Why not?"

"He's more real than that. Or at least I thought he was. Maybe the divorce was harder than either of them let on."

Maybe. Or maybe Callum was a better actor than he looked. "Do you think he could have anything to do with Celeste's disappearance?"

"Callum? No." She sampled another spoonful of bisque. "Mmmm. But then, I didn't expect to see Callum dating twenty-year-olds, either."

I nodded, made a mental note. As the waiter cleared our plates and brought the next course, I glanced around the room, looking for whatever Nick hoped I'd see as well as keeping an eye on Callum. He and his date were still at the bar, drinking champagne. I wondered what they were celebrating.

I was just about to turn back to the salad course when I noticed a handsome brown-haired man had stopped to speak to Callum. He too looked familiar.

"Andrea," I hissed. "Who is that? Talking to Callum?"

"Who is what?" she said as she obligingly looked over. "Oh."

Her eyes had gone round.

"Don't keep looking," I said. "They'll know something's up, just from the look on your face. Who is it?"

But I had a sinking feeling I knew.

"Kyle Hanlon," she said, confirming what my intuition had already told me. "And isn't he…?"

"One of Celeste's supposed three dates," I said. "Who apparently had nothing to do with her disappearance. So why is he talking to Callum?"

"Well, he is an investment broker," Andrea said logically. "And since Callum's a corporate lawyer, it makes sense that they'd know each other."

And from the look of Kyle, Mandino's was probably his second home. "I wonder if he already knew Celeste? Or at least knew of her."

"You're not liking this case much, are you?"

"No. And I'm not getting anywhere in finding her."

"You will, Barbara. You always do. Have some more wine."

We talked and laughed our way through the next few courses, catching up and sharing horror stories. Amazing, exquisite taste combinations followed one after the other, each paired with the perfect wine. Between the great food and better company, I almost forgot Nick's assignment. Almost.

But I never lost sight of Callum and his date.

Kyle Hanlon hadn't stayed, he'd joined a larger party, none of whom Andrea or I recognized. Callum and his date had eventually moved to a discreet table for two along one wall, where I had glimpses of them enjoying the same meal we had.

Our very attentive waiter had just brought out the cheesecake, coffee and port when Andrea's cell phone buzzed. She glanced at the number.

"Sorry, Barbara, I have to take this."

"Not a problem," I mumbled, already savoring a mouthful of the best cheesecake I'd ever eaten.

I now understood why Mandino's was so popular. I'd just leaned back and was sipping my raspberry port when and exclamation from Andrea had me focusing on her.

She'd gone white. After a moment she said, "Thanks for letting me know," and disconnected.

"Andrea. What is it?"

She took a shaky breath, pressed her napkin to her mouth for a moment. "That—that was my assistant, Mary? My temp, the one I couldn't reach today? She's—she's just been identified as the Stalker's latest victim. Apparently it was on the late news."

Picking up her port glass, she downed half of it, put it down, looked at it, and downed the rest.

"I'm so sorry."

"Thanks. Can we leave?"

"Yes, of course. Why don't you finish your coffee and I'll get the bill."

She was too shocked even to protest. Once I'd settled up, I called a cab and had him drop Andrea off first. I offered to come in with her, but she didn't even want to talk.

"I need sleep, Barbara," she said. "But come morning, I need to talk to you. Come over for breakfast?"

"Sure. Call me when you wake up?"

She nodded, and was gone. It was a horrible end to what had been a pretty amazing evening.

All the way to my place I debated whether it was really a coincidence. The Stalker's latest victim is the only one of Andrea's temps that worked for all three of Celeste's proposed dates. And Nick had asked us to go to Mandino's for a reason, something connected to the Stalker, which was still not apparent to me.

Except that I'd seen both Callum McLaughlan and Kyle Hanlon there, both of them obviously regulars, both of them with links to Celeste Deslauriers. Was I missing something?

The headache that was building by the time I got home convinced me that Andrea was right. I couldn't make any sense of all of this tonight.

I'd talk to her and Nick in the morning.

CHAPTER FIFTEEN

Nick called early the following morning, and I filled him in on what little Andrea and I had picked up at Mandino's the night before. I couldn't tell if any of it helped, which was frustrating, but it was nothing compared to the frustration he must be feeling.

I did ask if either Callum McLaughlan or Kyle Hanlon were persons of interest to the task force. That he could tell me. No and no.

I also filled him in on Andrea's connection to the latest victim, which not only served to remind me how she was feeling, it also deepened Nick's frustrated anger at their seeming inability to catch this monster, whoever he was. Not a great way to start the day.

Breakfast with Andrea wasn't exactly a cheery event, either. The waffles were good, but they might as well have been plaster replicas for all the pleasure either of us took in them. Andrea was upset, and visibly grieving for her late employee, though she insisted she was fine. She planned to go into the office.

"I have to be there," she said. "It'll hit some of the others even harder than it's hitting me. I'm the one they'll turn to."

"Call me if you need anything."

"I thought you were going to Brenton today?"

"It's only a couple of hours away. And that's what cell phones are for."

"Never mind about me, I'll be fine. Just focus on finding Celeste. I can't deal with someone else I know being killed."

I nodded. I had my marching orders.

"And Barbara? Be careful."

"I always am."

She just shook her head at me. She knows me too well.

———

I WAS on the road to Brenton by seven-thirty. It was overcast, and fog clung to the highway. Not the best day for driving the old Canyon route, but at least I was going against traffic. Long lines of headlights rushed past me, heading for downtown. A glance in my rear view mirror showed ribbons of taillights strung along for miles, gleaming fuzzily through patches of fog.

Once I was past Hope, I had the road to myself except for the eighteen wheelers and the occasional pickup. I half listened to Miles Davis on the CD player, but mostly I ran through what I knew about Celeste and her life. I didn't have a full sense of her yet, but what I knew I liked. And none of it gave me any insight into why she'd disappeared.

She didn't seem to have any enemies, or at least none that weren't related to her father. Even that possibility was based only on Marie's opinion and what Jaimie had heard from Celeste, both of which could be questionable. Or not.

Which is why I was headed to Brenton at this ridiculous hour. I needed facts if I was to find Celeste, and I couldn't stifle the small, cold voice that said I'd need to be faster if I wanted to find her alive. The more I found out about her, the more I wanted to do just that.

I reached Brenton before ten, and turned into the small building with the big red "Café" sign towering over it. Six big trucks parked in the gravel lot out front told me the food would be plentiful and good and the coffee would be strong. Just what I needed.

If my luck was in, the gossip would be plentiful, too.

It was, though it took a while. First I ordered coffee, eggs and homemade biscuits, which came with lashings of butter and raspberry-rhubarb preserves. I was finishing my second cup of coffee by the time there was a lull in business. Aside from me and one trucker at the end of the counter, silently working his way through a plate three times as full as mine had been, the place was empty.

"More coffee, dear?" the pint-sized waitress asked, whisking my plate away. A blue plastic name tag pinned to her hot pink blouse read 'Bet'. "You must have enjoyed your food. Most don't get through this much."

"You have a good cook. The biscuits and preserves were amazing."

She beamed at me. "Why thank you. I'm kinda proud of them."

"You made them?'

Bet nodded. "I'm the baker and preserver. And my hubby's the cook."

"Between the two of you, it's no wonder the place was hopping earlier. I know I'll be stopping here anytime I'm up this way."

I could see the questions behind her eyes, but asking straight-out would take all the fun out of it.

"Not so many come this way, anymore," she said instead. "We're lucky to have so many loyal customers. Let me get you that coffee."

Moments later she was back, pouring a stream of dark, strong coffee into my cup. I always knew I'd found a genuine old-style diner when I found one that still served coffee in cups rather than mugs. This place was the real thing, the coffee alone enough to keep me going for hours. The good food was a bonus, and one especially welcome on such a damp, chilly morning.

"So, you just passing through?"

"No, I have business in Brenton."

"Oh?" With efficient motions, she refilled my creamer, made

sure the sugar dish was full, while waiting for me to satisfy her curiosity.

"I'm doing some research on what Brenton was like before the Coquihalla went through, and I gather that the *Bugle* has been in business for quite a few years. Where would I find them?"

"They're just down the road a bit, on the left. You can't miss them. And yes, they've been in business for more than forty years. Does Old Joe know you're coming?"

"No. I need to take a look at his archives, so I thought I'd just drop in. I figured he probably opens around ten?"

She shook her head. "That approach would have worked a few decades ago. Not now."

Now we were getting to it. "No?"

"Nope. Town isn't what it used to be. We can't support even a weekly anymore. Joe still publishes once a month or so, mostly 'cause he's too stubborn not to, but I can't see how he's even paying his bills."

"That's sad. What happened? Lack of jobs?"

"Partly. This used to be a big lumber town, and there was some mining, too. Copper, mostly. That's pretty much gone now. And the new highway taking most of the traffic didn't help much, either. None of that's the real cause though."

"No? So what did happen?"

"Scuse me, dear. I'll just top up everyone's coffee."

A true storyteller, Bet knew how to build suspense. She took her time refilling the cups, including one for herself, then slid into the booth opposite me. "Ah, that feels good. Now, where was I?"

"You were telling me why the town is dying."

"Right, right. Well, this was a thriving little town once upon a time. We even had a school that went right up to grade nine, before they had to bus into Hope. And the town was growing, partly because the kids were finding jobs here and staying. Then the bottom fell out."

"What happened?"

"The local mine failed. Those folk who had money invested

there, which was most of us, lost pretty much everything. A lot of folks had to leave town, cause they couldn't afford to start over, not working for themselves. It was a hard time. And it was damned hard to lose so many good neighbors. It pretty much took the heart out of those who were left."

"I can imagine."

She shook her too blonde head. "I doubt anyone could imagine who didn't live here," she said. "Not really. See, hard times can happen to anyone, but this was deliberate. The man who ran the local bank betrayed us."

Here it came. "What? How?"

"Being the bank manager, he knew exactly how many of us were scraping by. He helped us invest in mining stock we had no business investing in, made it easy to borrow the money to do it."

"So you invested."

"Yep. And for a while we all watched that stock go up, cheered it on. Looked like we'd make that bit more that made the difference between scraping by and living well. After a bit, neighbors were convincing each other that this was the best thing ever, and borrowing more. And Guy Deslauriers, that was our bank manager, he got promoted."

"Were you just investing in that one stock, or did you diversify?"

"We had the inside track, didn't we? The mine was in our backyard, and we knew the guys involved. It was supposed to be a sure thing." A shrewd look. "Sounds like you know something about the stock market."

I'd learned, because so many of my cases seemed to have a financial aspect. And because I like to know what is happening with my own money, what there is of it. "A bit."

"Uh huh. Well, we should have made sure we knew something, too, not just trusted Guy to advise us. But we didn't know that then, and it seemed too good to be true." She stirred a couple of packets of sugar into her coffee, drank. "It was."

Somehow this story was even sadder hearing it from one of the burned investors than Jaimie's version had been. "What happened?"

"Pretty much what we should have expected. The stock started falling fast, and there was suddenly no market for it. Seems there was rumors about there being no copper. Turned out it was more than rumors."

Ouch.

"Some of us tried to believe Guy was as deluded as the rest of us. That didn't last long, though. Not when he'd helped us into loans way bigger than we could manage. Next thing we knew, the bank had frozen our regular accounts, and none of us could get at our money. Word was they were investigating."

Not good. I wondered if Celeste knew any of the details, like why her father had approved such loans, let alone encouraged them. Marie certainly didn't seem to. "Then what happened?"

"They brought in a couple of men from Vancouver who talked to us. Treated us like idiots, too. A couple days later, the story ran in the *Bugle*. The bank had fired Guy. He killed himself that night."

"How awful." I tried to imagine the impact on his family, on the town. "What happened to those who'd had their accounts frozen? How did they survive?"

"Bank took everything to cover the loans. For some, all they could do was declare bankruptcy. We were lucky—we'd lost all our savings and some of our inventory money, but we didn't have any loans. We kept going. Just."

"Others weren't so lucky?"

"Nope. Town population fell nearly half."

"Did you know everyone that left?"

"Most of 'em were customers. And it was small even then, so yeah, I did."

"That must have been painful."

"Worst part was we couldn't even help them. We had too little left. Nearly didn't make it ourselves."

"Any of the ones who left keep in touch?"

She gave me an interested look.

"A few. Why?"

It was my turn. "It's why I was going to the newspaper archives.

I'm looking for information on three families." I debated how much to tell her. The sharp look in her dark eyes told me I couldn't put much by her.

"I'm a P. I., and my client was originally from here. She's lost both her parents, and is hoping to get in touch with former neighbors."

"Bet you can't tell me your client's name, either."

I laughed. "You'd win that one."

Bet nodded. "Fair enough. Which families are you looking for?"

"Kovicks. Hanlon. Stephanos."

She pursed her lips, took a sip of coffee, then slowly opened another packet of sugar and stirred it in. Another sip, a nod. "No, I don't recall anyone with those names around here."

"No-one?" I wasn't surprised, exactly, but I couldn't keep the disappointment out of my tone.

Bet didn't miss it, either. "It that important to your client?"

I nodded.

"My memory's still pretty good, mind, but it's possible I didn't know everyone, especially if they weren't here that long. And we had a few of those. You might want to check the school records, too."

"Thanks. Where would I find those?"

She told me. Gave me exact directions, too. "More coffee, hon?"

"Maybe one more cup. It's good coffee," I said as I finished writing down the directions she'd given me. "How many people left town then?"

"Maybe two dozen families within the year." She gulped down some coffee. "Not Deslauriers' family, though. The sister-in-law took the kids. And they stayed."

What was this? There was an edge to Bet's voice that I hadn't heard even when she was talking about financial ruin. "This was the mother's sister?"

"Yeah. Anthea Swan."

I knew that name. Anyone with even a remote interest in art in this country knows that name. "Wait a minute. Anthea Swan was from Brenton?"

A blank look. "Not originally. But I thought you knew. She took care of his kids after Deslauriers' wife died."

"Oh. No, I didn't know." And this changed things. Because I did know about Anthea Swan, at least as much as Vancouver's art world knew about her—the few facts and the endless gossip.

I remembered when she'd died, and we'd talked of nothing else for months. Marie was her niece? And had lived with her for what, a dozen years?

I needed coffee. Now.

Once I had a full cup steaming in front of me, I considered what Bet had said.

Anthea Swan was a very prolific artist who had painted in almost complete isolation for most of her life. Well, she was isolated from the artistic community, anyway.

When her work was finally discovered—she must have been in her forties by then—she was an overnight sensation. Two of the best galleries in Vancouver competed to offer her shows and exclusive partnerships.

Her shows always sold out on opening night.

Anthea Swan's world was strong, powerful and bleak. She had a clear artistic vision and had honed her message over the years so she could say exactly what she wanted to say in as few strokes, and as few colors, as possible.

As an artist, she was brilliant, if difficult to work with.

And the woman? I didn't know a lot about her life before she was discovered, except that whatever life she'd led had resulted in one of the bleakest outlooks on our world and its future I'd ever encountered in a traditional painter. And her suicide at the height of her success only served to emphasize that.

Then there was Marie's belligerence and her refusal to talk about her art. What had it been like for her, growing with the woman who had turned into Anthea Swan, the artist? Especially

between the ages of eight and thirteen, with both of Marie's
parents dead and Celeste away at university.

"Swan's work was very bleak," I said carefully. "Was it because of
the financial mess?"

"That one had money from somewhere. Or at least, after the
smoke cleared, she did."

"She didn't have money before?"

"He did, she didn't."

"Did the girls inherit something?" If so, Marie either hadn't
known about it or hadn't been honest with me.

A shrug. "Who knows? They didn't do any of their banking in
this town any more, did they? Not after all that mess."

Secrets piled on secrets. "So what was Swan's life here like?"

Another shrug. "You'd have to ask her nieces. She was never the
most forthcoming of women. Most days you were lucky to get a
nod or a "morning" from her."

"Did you ever see any of her work? Before her success, I mean?"

"Sure, she used to hang it here at the diner."

"What?"

"For years, she'd finish a painting, ugly things they were, and
hang it here for a couple of months. Called it her pre-exhibition." A
short laugh. "Course back then we never thought she'd amount to
anything."

"So why did you let her hang them here?"

"Brought in the customers, didn't they? Everyone had to see
them, comment on them, rail against her."

"Sounds like no-one liked them much."

"Nope."

"Why?"

"Because we were in them, the whole town."

Swan hadn't painted portraits. Just bleak, empty cityscapes and
landscapes. Harsh, barren. I used to feel cold just looking at them.
"How do you mean, you were in them?"

"She painted how Brenton felt."

Wow. I needed to go back and look at Swan's work. "That's pretty bleak."

Bet nodded, drew deep on her cigarette. "Yeah."

I was missing something about this town. "How did it get so bad?"

Bet shrugged. "Times were hard."

I could hear the sound of trucks pulling up outside, and knew I was about to lose her attention. "I have one more question."

"Shoot."

"I'm looking for two children who would have been about twelve when Guy Deslauriers died, but I only have first names. Any chance you might recognize them?"

"What are the names?"

"Danny and Leanne."

She sighed, put down the coffee pot. "No. Wish I had an answer for you, but to be honest, I didn't get much chance to keep the kids straight. It was the adults I dealt with, and even then I spent most of my time here."

"I can probably find them in the school records, then. What about the newspaper? How would I get to see the archives?"

"You'll have to find Joe and ask him. This time of day, he's either probably at home or at the tavern. Tell him I sent you," she said with a grin, and gave me very precise directions.

I thanked her just as the door opened on her next wave of customers. She gave me a smile and a wink. "Come see us for lunch," she said. "You'll probably have more questions by then."

I laughed, as I was meant to, and left an extra-large tip. Both the food and the information were well worth it. And I planned to be back for lunch.

CHAPTER SIXTEEN

My first stop was the small and tired-looking Brenton City Hall for the school records. I do love the Freedom of Information Act. Not that it got me very far.

There were no families named Kovicks, Hanlon or Stephanos that had children registered in the years I was interested in. I couldn't find a Leanne in any of the classes either.

Maybe Ben had the name wrong, or maybe she'd changed it? There was a Danny Deeping, in the same class as Celeste. The records showed his brother Aaron, two years younger, as well, though both vanished from the records when Danny was twelve. That fit the facts Marie had told me. Maybe she'd stopped lying to me.

I could hope.

I went back to the desk, to see if the very helpful clerk could suggest where I might find class photos. She was a woman of about Bet's age, but with nothing like her vitality.

This woman's hair was pale blonde and carefully coiffed. She wore the same pastels that on Cassie Stewart looked so elegant, but this woman just looked dusty, as if she'd been stuck on a shelf and forgotten for too many years. The bitter lines carved beside her mouth and across her forehead didn't help. Still, she was very help-ful, and her life in this dying town couldn't have been easy.

She unearthed the file showing class photos by year, and quickly found the right year, when Celeste and Danny were both twelve, and then the right class photo.

I wondered why she was being so helpful, but decided not to question my luck. Instead I asked if I could have a couple of copies, and she obligingly made them, on a mammoth copier that looked like it should be long dead, but which made surprisingly crisp copies.

I pointed out Danny Deeping. "Do you recognize this boy? The one with his arm in a sling?"

"Sure. I was the school secretary, I knew all the little ones. Now, that sling…"

She peered closer, glanced at the date on the photo, then nodded. "Yes, that's Danny Deeping. He fell off a retaining wall a few weeks before this was taken, banged up his shoulder pretty good. The photographer was annoyed, because it messed up his composition."

"Do you remember someone named Leanne?"

She frowned. "No-one by that name. What does she look like?"

I was winging it, but what did I have to lose? "A perky blonde."

Her finger tapped against her pursed lips for a moment. "Perky," she said softly. "Ah. That could be the Purvis girl. Now what was her name?"

She swung towards her computer screen, tapped briskly with long, pearlized nails. "Here we go. Elaine. Elaine Leanne Purvis. She was ten that year, in the same grade as Aaron, Danny's little brother."

I made a note. "And you knew all the parents too?"

"Of course."

"I was stunned when Bet told me that the artist Anthea Swan used to live here. I had no idea. Did you know her?"

Suddenly she didn't look so faded. "Oh yes, I knew her. Not well, of course. She made her opinion of all of us pretty clear."

"What do you mean?"

"She had as little to do with the rest of us as she could. And she was a nobody, back then. She kept that kid pretty close to home, too. I used to feel sorry for her."

"Kid?"

"Yes, the little red-headed kid. Was that her name? Marie, I think. Marie Deslauriers. Then Anthea died, and we never heard from the kid again. Nor from her sister. Not that we minded."

Poor Marie. "How long did Anthea Swan live in Brenton?"

"Moved here right after the mother died. Her only sister, apparently."

"Where did she move from?"

"I never knew. "

I'd find out. "So she was here what, ten years or so?"

"More like twelve. Didn't seem to suffer much from the hard times that hit the rest of us, either."

"No?"

"No. She didn't seem to need to work, for one thing. Barely looked after the girls, either. Just painted all the time."

"She must have had money from somewhere, to afford food and clothing as well as paint and canvas."

"Maybe she lived off the money the estate paid her to look after the two girls."

I'd have to check when Swan had started painting, and when the bulk of her output was done. "Estate? I'd heard the father lost everything, then committed suicide?"

Pale blond eyebrows went up. "Bet still loves to gossip, does she? Well, I suppose there must have been money somewhere."

The tone was casual, but I didn't buy it for a second. How this town must have hated seeing that family with any amount of money when they were broke.

I wondered why Swan had chosen to stay in Brenton. Maybe all that emotion made the town a good subject. It couldn't have been comfortable, though.

Or good for Celeste and Marie.

"We didn't see much of her. She sent one of the kids to do most of the shopping."

"What kind of guardian was she?"

"Well. She seldom attended school conferences, though she made sure the children went, of course. She had to do that much. She made sure they had food, clothes, attended school.

There were a lot of conferences about the young one, Marie. Rebellious, that one was. I don't believe Anthea Swan made it to any of the meetings about her. She seemed unable to make that girl study. Or she didn't bother trying."

Marie had been left with Anthea Swan while Celeste went to university and started to build a career. Had Celeste been escaping?

It must have been hard leaving her young sister in that kind of situation, but she probably hadn't had much choice. There were certainly no career options here. Maybe that explained why Marie was still living with Celeste now, though.

And I wondered how Marie felt about being left behind, stuck in a town that hated her family, with only Swan for companionship.

Had Marie gone to university?

Being a bike courier seemed to suit her restless, rebellious personality, but had it even been a choice? And why was she so hesitant about her artistic ability?

Some of Jayson's more cutting phrases ran through my mind.

I'd be willing to bet that Swan's bitterness hadn't been confined to the canvas.

I'd have to have a talk with my client when I got back. I thanked my informant, and escaped.

Back in my car, I cracked the window open, pulled out my smartphone and googled Danny Deeping.

Nothing on him, nothing on any of his family members. Nothing on Leanne Purvis by any combination of her names, either.

What, they'd all left Brenton and vanished? Or just changed their names?

What exactly had gone on in Brenton all those years ago?

———

THE ADDRESS BET had given me for Old Joe was on a pot-holed road that paralleled the highway. There were half a dozen smaller homes, weathered and sad-looking, and a few lots that were empty except for foundations, and in one case a half torn down fence. It spoke even more clearly than Bet had of the devastation that had overtaken this town.

Old Joe's was the fourth house down. Someone had made the effort to repaint the trim, and the moss that covered the other roofs had been kept at bay, or mostly so. The front porch sagged a little, but the steps were solid. I checked each one before I stepped on it, just to be sure.

I rapped on the door, and it echoed inside. It sounded like there was a long hall, with no carpets and little furniture. I waited, but there were no response. I knocked again. Still nothing.

With a shrug I headed back for the car and the other destination Bet had mentioned—the local bar. I didn't really expect it to be open yet, but it was far too early for lunch, and I wanted to see those back issues.

I had no plans to spend the night here—not that I'd seen anything that resembled a hotel—so the sooner I started digging into old newspapers, the better.

———

THE BROKEN ANTLER WAS OPEN, and most of the stools along the bar were already full. My first impression as I walked inside was that the place was well-named. Dim, crowded and too hot, with the smell of cheap beer and too many years of cigarette smoke, it reminded me of a place caught in a time warp. Looking at the faces that lined the bar, not a one of them under seventy, I could see the reason for that.

As my eyes adjusted to the light, I could see that the walls were lined with photos and posters. Again, all of them were old, but they held color and life that I hadn't seen anywhere else in town.

I had the feeling I was looking at Brenton in the Days Before, as Bet would have said. It was a sad contrast.

The seven pairs of eyes considering me weren't sad, though. They were thoughtful, and interested, and definitely alive.

"Help you?" asked the bartender, a tall, beefy man who had to be pushing seventy himself.

I glanced at the mugs in front of each of the patrons.

"Give me a pint of whatever's on tap," I said, and drew out the only free stool on my end of the bar. This was definitely a moment for "joining them."

Eyes turned back to their drinks and their neighbors, but it was pretty quiet in there until the bartender put my mug in front of me.

"Passing through?" he asked.

"I'm here to do some research in your newspaper archives," I said, hoping I was playing this right. "If the owner will agree to let me have access."

"So why're you here?"

"Bet at the diner said you might know where to find him."

"Huh."

A silence fell, with everyone keeping their eyes straight ahead, to give Old Joe time to decide if he wanted to deal with me or not. Luckily, curiosity won out, which is what I'd been counting on.

"What're you looking for?" asked the second man down from me. He looked to be the youngest one there, now that I took a better look at him, closer to sixty than seventy, though his hair was pure white.

Tall and rail-thin, he had gray eyes with thick dark brows that gave him a hawkish look. I suspected the intellect behind those eyes held a similar resemblance to a raptor. I was ready for him.

"I'm a P. I., working for a client whose sister has disappeared. She was last seen with someone who lived here more than twenty years ago. I'm looking for information on him or his family, anything that might help me trace him."

"He a suspect?"

"I don't have enough information to suspect anyone of anything. All I know for sure is that my client's sister has vanished, and I can find no record of the fellow she'd met with, other than in the school records. And he was twelve then."

A pause. "No other record at all?"

There was no emphasis behind his words, which oddly seemed to give them even greater impact. I glanced at the faces around him, which had also grown blank. "Nothing I can find. And I did my homework."

Again the exchange of glances.

"I'm Joe," the hawk said. "Who's your client?"

"Sorry, that's confidential."

Joe nodded, as if the information didn't surprise him. I couldn't think of him as Old Joe anymore, not with those eyes staring at me.

"Okay, then. Who's the guy?"

"Danny Deeping."

Joe kept his gaze on me, but I felt the shock run through the room. The name meant something to them. "Know him?"

"Knew his father. They left town a long time ago. Danny was just a kid then."

What weren't they saying? "Any idea where they went?"

"Nope."

"Anyone else who might know?" It was risky, asking questions in front of his buddies. Sometimes that encourages people to talk. Sometimes it has the opposite effect. I couldn't tell which kind Joe was, though I got the sense he wasn't intimidated by much.

"Nope." Not even a glance towards any of his fellow townsmen.

Right. "Any chance I can get a look at your news archives?"

"Sure, I can arrange that. You staying here tonight?"

"I wasn't planning on it."

"Then I guess we'd best finish up, so you can get some work

done while it's still light." He glanced at the bartender. "What do I owe you, Dan?"

"Let me get that one," I said. "It's the least I can do, for dragging you away like this."

He smiled at that, and suddenly looked approachable. "Well, thank you. I won't say no."

He waited while I took care of our bill, then held the door for me. "You can give me a lift," he said. "It's not far."

And it wasn't—maybe four blocks down the highway. He directed me to a mid-fifties concrete block building that stretched the full length of the block. Faded black letters in the closest storefront proclaimed the *Brenton Bugle*. On the far end, the other storefront was a dry cleaners, though it appeared closed.

I couldn't tell if the closure was temporary or permanent. Either way, this was not a town in good shape. If anything, it was worse off than I'd been led to expect. The current state of the economy probably wasn't helping matters, either.

I wondered again how any of the people who still clung to this place survived. And why they stayed.

Maybe they had nowhere else to go. I couldn't imagine they'd be able to sell their properties here for much money.

Joe directed me to an empty gravel parking lot around the back, and I pulled in next to a door that said *Brenton Bugle* in those cheap stick-on letters.

Joe ushered me in, flicking the light switch as he did so.

The place was huge, and mostly empty. Where I'd expected to see some kind of immense printing machine, there were a few long tables and chairs. A fairly old Mac computer occupied a small metal desk, with a cable connecting it to a laser printer, and a stack of boxes of legal paper beside it. Other than a bank of dusty filing cabinets occupying one wall, and a couple of offices with doors closed on the other, that was it.

"I guess you have most of your printing done out of house these days?" I said.

"Nope." He strolled across the room, slapped one hand down on the laser printer. "This is her."

"You put out a newspaper on a laser printer?"

"This is a pretty small town. And a lot of folks like to get their newspaper online these days. This way, I can serve all of them."

I looked around me again. "Why so much space?"

"Room was designed to hold a big old Linotype press. Still used it for a while for specialized jobs, then sold it to a collector a while back when he made me an offer I couldn't refuse."

I looked around again, mentally kicking myself for my preconceptions. The *Brenton Bugle*—and Joe—were not what I'd expected. "What about the archives?"

He gestured to the bank of file cabinets. "They're all in there. Help yourself. I'll go put some coffee on. Want some?"

"Please." No way I was going to make a dent in those cabinets without caffeine.

He nodded, disappeared into the farthest office. I could hear water running. I turned to the file cabinets—which weren't labeled —and I started at the far end, top drawer.

Five minutes and a few sneezes later I'd figured out that the *Bugle* archives did have a filing system, and it was roughly chronological. That helped. I started by going back twenty-two years.

I was engrossed in reading when Joe set a cup of coffee at my elbow.

"Thanks," I muttered, barely taking my eyes from the article I was reading. I reached for the cup, swallowed. That got my attention. Wow.

"You make good coffee."

"Glad you like it," he said with a grin. "I see you found something, so I'll leave you to your reading. Let me know if you need anything."

"Thanks. I appreciate this."

He shrugged. "Sure."

Before his footsteps reached his office I was absorbed in an article about a town council meeting. It was clear that Brenton then had been very different from Brenton today. Tourism had been a reliable and growing source of income, and the town was diversifying beyond it in a real way.

One of the major concerns was about keeping what they called their "unique identity" while maintaining those growth levels.

The town council and the chamber of commerce had worked together, and many of the same people served on both, including James Deeping, Danny's dad. Marie's father had served on both too, and he'd been the Treasurer of the Chamber of Commerce. Made sense for a banker.

So what had happened?

I kept reading and making notes. I found a couple of mentions of Swan when her art started to sell, but otherwise she seemed invisible. I was on my third drawer of papers and my seventh page of notes, with no answer in sight, when I realized I was starving. If I was going to stay coherent, I needed fuel.

"Joe?" I called, standing and heading for his office. No answer.

The door was ajar, so I poked my head around. "Joe?"

The office was surprisingly tidy, and mostly empty. It held a streamlined desk and ergonomic chair, a cell phone, a recent iMac with big screen and a color laser printer. A counter on the back wall held a small sink and a coffee maker, with a mini fridge below and storage cupboards above.

Joe was intent on the computer screen, his fingers tapping quickly.

I rapped on the door. He started, then hit a couple of keys that blanked the screen. "Sorry, I get pretty focused."

"Hot story?"

A grin. "Something like that."

Which suggested he was working on something quite different. I wondered what, but dismissed it as unimportant.

"Can I ask you something?"

"Sure."

"Know anything about Anthea Swan?"

"Huh. Guess you found a couple mentions."

I nodded.

He swallowed some coffee, placed the mug carefully on the desk. "She was an amazing artist."

"And as a person?"

"Not so amazing."

"Did you know her personally?"

"Not sure anyone around here could say that. Knew her to say good morning to, that's about it."

"Did anything change after she was discovered?"

"Not so's you'd notice. She was around a bit less then, that's about it."

I nodded. "Okay, thanks."

If there was something there that would help explain my client, he wasn't going to tell me. I'd have to do the digging on my own. And it didn't look like that would be in the *Bugle* archives.

"Anything else?"

"I need to get some lunch. I can bring something back if you're planning on staying here. Unless you'd like to join me?"

"Thanks, but I need to finish this up," he said. "I'd appreciate it if you could bring something back."

"What would you like?"

"Bet will know. I assume you're going back to the diner?"

"Yes."

"Take your time. It'll be busy, and Bet would be mortally offended if you don't take time to talk. I'll be here when you get back."

Gotta love small towns. There's no such thing as privacy.

And I'd be glad to leave this one.

CHAPTER SEVENTEEN

The parking lot was full and so was the diner, and loud with the sound of men who worked hard and had earned both a break and a good meal. These were regulars—they knew Bet and each other. The daily lasagna seemed to be a favorite, and I was lucky to get the last order.

Bet brought it over with a big smile and a mug of fresh coffee. "Good to see you again," she said. "Can't talk right now, but I'll catch you later."

I could see why the lasagna was popular. Meaty, cheesy, with a thick tomato sauce that had to be homemade, it was the definition of comfort food on a blustery day. I finished every bite, though I passed on the garlic bread. The thick buttery slices smelled wonderful, but not after last night's dinner and skipping my run this morning.

Bet topped up my coffee twice before the place cleared out enough for her to stop by my table. She looked at my plate, nodded and grinned at me. "I do appreciate a girl who eats my food, instead of asking for salad all the time."

She topped up my coffee again, snagged a cup for herself. "The coconut cream pie is today's dessert special, and it's even better than the lasagna. I've got a couple pieces left, if you want to try some?"

I am a total sucker for anything coconut, and especially a good old-fashioned coconut cream pie. "Sure, I'll have a slice."

I'd run tomorrow. Twice, if I had to.

"And more cream for that coffee?"

I nodded. "Please."

"I could get to like you, girl."

I grinned at that, unable to decide if it was too bad her diner was so far from Vancouver, or a good thing.

"So, how'd you make out with your morning? Did you find Old Joe?"

"I did. Which reminds me. I promised to bring something back for him."

"He's at the paper?"

"Yes."

"So no re-heating. Okay. He's not fond of lasagna anyway. I'll throw a sandwich together for him. And some pie—he's a big fan of my coconut cream pie."

The man had taste. I scooped up another creamy mouthful, followed by a swallow of rich coffee. "I have a question for you."

"Shoot." She sat back, sipped her coffee and watched me with narrowed eyes I couldn't read.

"I found the name of the kid I was looking for. Danny Deeping. Remember him?"

Her expression clouded. "I don't recall the boy, but his dad James was the local realtor, and one of the ones hit hardest by that mess. Not only had he invested too much and borrowed to do it, his business vanished along with the town's economy, and with it any possibility of repaying that loan. No-one was buying houses here, not then."

"So what happened to him? Did you keep in touch?"

She shook her head. "No, that was the saddest part. He knew everyone in town, he'd grown up here. And he and the bank manager were best friends. Night after Guy died, James left with his family, just packed up in the middle of the night. We never heard from him again."

"No idea where he went?"

"None. Sorry, hon."

"Funny thing is, I found Joe at the Broken Antler, along with about five other guys. When I mentioned that I couldn't find any trace of the Deeping family since they left Brenton years ago, there was this odd silence. Everyone was carefully not looking at each other. Any idea what that means?"

"You don't miss much, do you?"

I suspected it took one to know one. "I try not to."

"Then yes. There were a few other families lit out in the dead of night and vanished. We didn't hear from them again, either. They'd all lost everything, and they left behind some debts."

"You're saying they built new identities?"

She shrugged.

"Wouldn't it have been easier to declare bankruptcy?"

"Maybe for some, but these folks made other choices. Now, I think I'd best get that sandwich together, before Old Joe gets too hungry."

Was she kidding me? I felt like I'd wandered into a 40's dime novel, complete with menacing strangers and the kind of gangsters that just didn't exist in BC back then.

What wasn't she telling me?

———

BACK AT THE *BUGLE*, I delivered Joe's lunch, waving aside the money he tried to give me, and dived back into the files with relief. I knew where I was in dealing with black and white facts, even much editorialized facts.

Unfortunately the facts weren't a lot of help. I found all the doings of a small town. I noted that James Deeping, Danny's father, advertised in every edition, often with several properties for sale. He seemed to cover quite a stretch of property up and down the highway from Brenton, doing what must have been a profitable business.

If Bet was right and he'd chosen to run in the dead of night—then where had that money gone? Certainly nothing in the *Bugle* stories hinted at anything big enough to destroy a town.

News was related to Church events, Sunday school picnics, bake sales, sports days, farm market days, and other small town events. Names were given of the families who'd moved to town, and new businesses starting up.

The main industries were clearly logging, mining and tourism, or as much tourism as being a stop on the main thoroughfare between Vancouver and the interior could bring. Which was considerable.

In the first drawer, the *Bugle* had been a twenty-four page twice-weekly paper, on standard newsprint. Then came the stories of mine cutbacks, and layoffs in the local lumber mill. The *Bugle* still printed twice a week, but it was down to sixteen pages, then twelve.

Another round of layoffs and the Bugle was down to an eight page weekly. The occasional photos of the Chamber of Commerce showed worried faces and false cheer. Real estate ads showed the same listings, week after week. Events were being cancelled. This was a dying town.

Several months in, the paper was still an eight page weekly, but real estate listings were turning over again. Events were being held, and an air of optimism seemed to underlie the announcements.

"How are you making out?" Joe asked from somewhere behind my shoulder.

I jumped. Immersed in picturing the Brenton of twenty years ago, I hadn't heard him coming. "I'm making some progress, but I'm not sure I really understand what I'm seeing."

"Oh?" Voice and face were both neutral. How did he do that?

"Hmmm. For instance, here—and I showed him the eight page paper—the town is dying. Yet less than a year later, things are expanding again. The town seems to be growing. Am I right?"

He nodded. "You seem to be understanding it pretty well to me."

"Here's the part I don't get. The mine is on its last legs and the mill is still closed. So why the growth?"

"Ah. Well, small towns can be funny, Brenton maybe more than most."

I waited, sure he was going to say something else. He didn't. "And so?"

"So?"

"So did the growth continue?"

"For a while. Then it became clear that the mine wasn't going to be viable again, and everything fell apart. Most folks lost more than they could afford to lose."

"Why did people think the mine might be viable?"

He shrugged, grinned. "Something to do with new technologies for retrieving gold and copper from played out shafts. Never did understand high finance, never mind metallurgy. It's why I'm editor and publisher of a failing newspaper."

I grinned back. I didn't believe him for a second. Which tied in with what Bet had said.

"Right. Did people start investing their life savings in the mine?"

"Some did."

But not most, from the sound of it. "Any chance of another cup of coffee?"

"Sure. I still owe you for lunch."

"Forget it."

"You planning on being here a while yet?"

I glanced at the six drawers I'd gone through and the three I hadn't got to yet. There might not be any answers in there, either, but I wasn't giving up yet.

"Probably. Why, did you need to be somewhere?"

"Eventually. But it's getting late, and I know you weren't planning on staying on."

I glanced over my right shoulder at the window. He was right—the sun was getting low and I hadn't even noticed. It had stopped raining, though.

"I like driving at night. If it doesn't inconvenience you too much, I'd like to stay until I've got through these. Is that a problem?"

He shrugged. "Not for me. I'll get that coffee."

"Thanks," I said and turned back to the files. Good thing I'd had that pie, after all.

Three hours later, I closed the last drawer with a sigh, and looked at my notes, all twelve pages of them. It didn't feel like I'd accomplished much, but I had some information on the Deeping and Deslauriers families.

I'd found nothing on the Kovicks, Hanlon or Stephanos families. I was pretty sure that meant they'd never lived here.

I also had a feel for what had happened in Brenton—at least in economic terms—if not why. And I wasn't sure it mattered, at least not to this case, though my ever-ready curiosity wanted to know. I had enough names of the key players that I might be able to find some answers when I got back.

"You done?"

I jumped. Again. How did he do that? "Oh. Yeah, I am. Thanks."

I checked my watch. After six. "I'm sorry, I hadn't realized it was this late. You should have said something."

"I had stuff to do," he said with a vague wave in the direction of his office. "You heading back now?"

I nodded. "And thank you again."

"Anytime."

———

IT WAS past eight by the time I got back to Vancouver, but I headed for my office anyway. I wanted to review what I had while it was fresh, and catch up on anything I'd missed.

Which included a message from Cathy Yip in Missing Persons, asking me to get in touch. Finally.

Though why hadn't she called my cellphone? She hadn't left me her cell number either, and not surprisingly, she wasn't at her desk. Maybe she just didn't like working with private investigators?

Two cups of coffee later, I got up to get a third cup. And stopped. My eyes were tired from reading small type all day—and I was no closer to finding Celeste. I had too many unanswered questions, starting with where had Danny Deeping and his family gone when they left Brenton. Staring at the same data on my computer screen half the night wouldn't get me anywhere, and more coffee wouldn't help.

The thought of Guido's crossed my mind. Good music, good company, good wine. Lots of good wine.

I shoved the image away. I didn't have time for that, not until I found Celeste. Guido could help me celebrate when this case was done.

Pushing away the thought that there might not be anything I felt like celebrating after this one, I sent off an e-mail to Marie, updating her on the little I'd learned in Brenton. Then I took a last quick look at my notes.

Twenty minutes later I put my notes away, still with no answers for that niggling voice in my head.

I still felt like I was missing something key, and I still didn't know what it was. Cursing under my breath, I headed home.

I couldn't sleep, so I painted. By the time I finished, the sky was lightening to that thin gray that precedes dawn.

I looked at my easel. This might be the best thing I'd ever painted. It might also be the scariest.

As I stared at it, my eyes following the curve of light and shadow, that seemed to obscure the figure of a red-haired woman standing in the lee of a cliff, I tried to figure out if it was hiding her, or obliterating her.

A yawn caught me by surprise. I glanced at the clock. I could catch a few hours of sleep before I had to be up again.

CHAPTER EIGHTEEN

The following morning, I woke groggy from too little sleep and too much driving the day before and went for a longer run than usual. It helped, but it didn't lessen the voices in my head. My trip to Brenton hadn't exactly provided the answers I'd been hoping for.

Back in my office, I dealt with some minor stuff—the downside of not having staff is you do everything yourself. The upside, for a control freak like me, is that stuff gets done up to my standards. Usually, anyway.

Then I was free to focus on the Brenton connection.

I knew that Celeste's mystery date was Danny Deeping, that her aunt had been Anthea Swan—which still blew my mind—and that Kovicks, Hanlon and Stephanos had not come from Brenton. Not under those names, anyway.

I called Jaimie Grandis, and arranged to meet her at Café Buzz after work. I was just starting to dig deeper when my office door banged open. I jumped, looked up as my nephew Cory burst in.

"You have to help me." He dragged one of my vintage guest chair over to the window and dropped into it.

Time was Cory would've called me Auntie Barb and looked at

me like a sad puppy dog when he asked for help, but those days were gone. Now that he's growing up, he doesn't seem to know what to call me, and his expression is usually pretty sullen.

"Okay. Want some coffee?" For a fourteen-nearly-fifteen year old he was awfully fond of coffee. Not that I was one to talk. But for today it was common ground, and that was more important.

"Yeah. Whatcha got?"

"French Roast or Sumatran."

"The good stuff."

Which meant French Roast. The boy had taste. "Coming right up."

What was he doing here on a school day, anyway?

I hadn't heard from Susanna, which meant she didn't know he was skipping school. She might not even know anything was wrong.

This couldn't be good. And it was no time to tell him I was in the middle of a case. No matter how urgent Celeste's case was.

As I ground beans and measured out enough for a full pot, I debated my approach. Decided on honesty. When we were that age, my mother had tried to sugarcoat things for her daughters. I'd noticed Susanna had picked up the habit.

I wasn't a fan.

"You seem pretty upset. What's going on?" I said, walking around the back of his chair and handing him a mug.

"Just stupid shit. I wanted to get away from it. And you usually talk sense."

"Thanks."

He grinned at me, then buried his face in his mug.

"So what can I do for you?"

"Can you talk to Mom? She wants to confiscate my laptop."

Uh oh. I could think of a few reasons for that, none of them good. "Why?"

He wouldn't meet my eyes. "It wasn't anything much."

"Uh huh. So what was it?"

"I've missed a few classes, and I wanted to know what it had done to my grades. And I didn't want to ask our guidance counsellor. He doesn't get it. And he preaches."

"So, instead you…?"

"I just had a look. A quick look." He gulped some coffee. "It's not like I changed anything. And I could have, easy." His voice was nearly whiny now. "I mean, their security sucks."

"You hacked into the school's grading system. This is what you're telling me?"

"Well, yeah. But it wasn't hacking, not really. I just looked. I didn't do any damage."

He had to be pretty good. I'd known computers came easy to him—but if this wasn't handled right, it could be dynamite. "So you want me to talk to your mother. And tell her what exactly?"

"Well, that it was a mistake, but just a little one. And I know I shouldn't have, and I won't do it again."

Not until the next time, anyway. "Your Mom obviously doesn't think it was a little mistake."

He looked mutinous. "She can't take my laptop. She just can't."

It probably wasn't the best solution. But even if I could figure out what to suggest, what were the odds of Susanna listening to me on this one? I was likely to get the "it's not as if you have children of your own" lecture.

No, thanks. "So what do you think is fair?"

It obviously wasn't the response he'd been expecting. Before he could think of an answer, the office door flew open.

———

MARIE STOOD FRAMED in the doorway, looking pale but resolute. Worry lines were etched in her forehead and she clutched a can of Red Bull in one hand. This was the woman who lectured me about coffee being bad for me?

Through the frosted glass panel I could see the outline of her bike. She saw where I was looking and grimaced at me. "I'm not going to risk it being stolen."

"So you dragged it up seven flights of stairs?" No way it would have fit in my building's ancient elevator.

"What of it? And what are you doing about my sister?"

"Calm down," I said. "I'm making progress."

I wasn't, or at least not what I considered progress, but there was no point telling her that. "And this isn't a good time. You'll need to schedule an appointment for later today."

"I don't care if it's a good time for you. Celeste is in danger. And no-one's taking me seriously," Marie said, planting herself in front of my desk. "Not you. Not the police."

She obviously hadn't noticed Cory, half hidden by the chair back. "My sister could be dead before you get off your asses and really look for her."

I noted the assumption that Celeste was still alive. I hoped she was right at the same time I wondered if this was wishful thinking. Or based on some intuitive knowledge.

She'd grown up in Brenton too, after all.

"Has something happened?" I asked her.

"I talked to the police. Again. They're not doing anything. At all. And they won't listen to me. They'll never find her."

I doubted the first statements. Unfortunately the last was possible, even likely. Celeste had been missing for four days. Most disappearances still unsolved by this point do not end well.

"What are they not hearing?"

"They don't seem to care about the guy from Brenton," she said. "And I got your e-mail from last night. Why did you go there, anyway? What a waste of time!"

This wasn't the time to explain that eighty percent of every investigation was a waste of time.

And had Cory not been sitting there, hearing every word, I would have asked Marie about her aunt. And the odd answers I'd been getting about everything related to the woman.

Later. "We have a name for him now," I said. "That's progress."

She snorted. "You don't even know what name he's using now."

"You're pretty quick to assume he's changed his name. Is there something you're not telling me?"

She just glared at me. I was getting tired of all this attitude.

"Most of the records I need to find him are more than twenty years old," I said. "They may not even be online yet."

"I bet I could find him."

"Where?"

She shrugged.

At this point, I'd take whatever I could get. "I haven't found any trace of Danny Deeping or his family once they leave Brenton. Think you can do better?"

"Yeah."

"Then why haven't you found him already?"

"That's why I hired you."

There was something here, something important. "Marie. Why did you hire me?'"

She started to say something cutting from the look on her face, then stopped and really looked at me. "You really want to know?"

"Yes."

"Okay. I saw those articles on that last case you solved."

I shuddered. Where had I heard that before? "Go on."

"I figured you'd know what needed to be done to find Celeste. You're the investigator. But you haven't found her."

"And all you've done is criticize and hold back key information. Your sister deserves better."

She drained her Red Bull, crumpled the can in her fist and slammed it down on the table. "Fine. I'll find Danny for you."

Finally. "When can I expect to hear from you?"

"When I'm done."

Right. "I'll be out of the office most of the day. You can reach me on my cell."

"Fine. I'm outta here."

"Marie. Was there anything else about Celeste the cops aren't hearing?"

She was already halfway to the door, but she turned at this and scowled at me. "They don't believe she's still alive, I can tell."

The helplessness hiding under the scowl took my breath away, and the last of my anger with it. "They've seen too many cases gone wrong, that's all. It doesn't mean this one will."

No way I was mentioning the stats.

"It isn't some case. It's my sister." She stomped the rest of the way to the door, then turned again. "Do you think Celeste is dead?"

I hated this question.

I couldn't lie to her, not on this. But I couldn't think of something reassuring that wouldn't be some variant of a lie, either.

"I don't know," I said. "But we've found nothing to suggest she is. Sometimes that's really important."

"Like she's not a victim of the Stalker," Marie said. She really was quick. "Doesn't mean some other weirdo hasn't taken her and killed her."

"No. But it doesn't mean they have, either. And your seeing her with this Danny means it could be more personal."

"And even deadlier. I know what the stats are on people getting killed by people they know."

Of course she did. And she probably knew the forty-eight hour rule, too.

So I asked her. "Do you really think your sister is dead?"

She stared at me. "No. No, I don't." Her voice broke. "I can't."

"Then hold on to that. We'll find her."

She stared at me for a moment more, then she was gone.

———

AFTER MARIE HAD THUMPED her bike down the first set of stairs, my nephew's head emerged from around the back of the vintage leather chair. "Let me help you."

I jumped. Oh no. In the intensity of the conversation, I'd forgotten he was there.

I quickly ran through what had been said. Not enough to do any damage, thank God.

"Cory, everything you just heard was privileged. You can't repeat any of it." Might as well cover myself. And him.

"As if I would. But I'm serious. I can find more information on this guy for you. Probably faster than she can."

Right. "You can find someone using a name they haven't used in a twenty years or so."

"Easily."

I hadn't expected that. "Legally."

"Oh." His brow creased. "Yeah, that would make it more challenging. Okay, sure, legally."

He seemed pretty confident. "I thought you didn't have your laptop?"

That stopped him for all of ten seconds. "There are computers in the library I can use. We're allowed to study there."

Well, at least it was more likely to be legal that way. And I needed to find Danny Deeping. Why not?

"Okay, I'll make a deal with you. If you can find a last name for this guy or his parents, I'll take you to dinner anywhere you want. Or give you the money to take a couple of friends for burgers and a movie. Deal?"

He thought about it for a moment. "If I do this? I want something else instead."

"What?"

"I want to work for you."

"You're too young."

"I don't mean full time."

Good thing. I was pretty sure what his Mom's opinion of that would have been.

And some months my business barely supported me. I wasn't sure it would stretch to someone else. "I'm not sure I have enough work for you."

He shrugged. "Whenever you do have something, you call me

in. We can agree to an hourly wage. I'm fast, so it won't cost you a lot."

"Why do you want to do this?"

"Are you kidding? What you do is cool. It would be way cool to be part of it."

Maybe it would give him a focus that would keep him out of other, more dangerous pursuits? "I can't promise anything until I talk to your Mom, but I think we can work something out. If you can do this, that is. Legally."

He groaned. "Yeah, yeah. Legally."

I printed off the few facts I had on Danny Deeping, handed them to him. "You're on."

That earned me a huge grin that made him look about three. "I'll get going on this search."

He popped up out of the chair, gave me a hug.

I had to swallow hard. He hadn't hugged me since he was twelve. For a while there things were pretty strained between his folks, and he started acting like he didn't care about anything.

His folks' relationship recovered, but he never seemed to. "After school, you mean?"

"Umm, yeah. Yeah, after school."

"Because if you start missing school, the bet is off. And you know there's no way your mother would let me hire you in any capacity if you were skipping."

Thoughts chased themselves across his face. I wished I could read them. After a moment he nodded. "That's fair."

He must really want to work for me. I wasn't sure whether to be flattered or worried. "You know I'll find out if you don't."

"I know. It's why I want to work for you." He grinned at me again and was gone.

I decided to settle for worried.

I debated calling Susanna, but if she didn't know he'd skipped school today, I wasn't going to be the one to tell her. I'd wait to see if he really did deliver on Danny Deeping's current identity.

CHAPTER NINETEEN

It didn't take long for Marie to get in touch.

Her choice of coffee shop was tiny and crowded, the decor a mix of scarred wood tables with dark leather chairs and white counters with white bucket chairs. High white ceilings, white walls and big windows completed the look. Most of the tables were communal, and the place buzzed with conversation. At least the sound system wasn't blasting.

My client was easy to spot.

She'd staked out a table in the far corner. With her spiky red hair she'd have been hard to miss anyway, but she looked electrified, as if she'd been gripping live wires.

It wasn't a good look for her. Not that I was losing patience or anything.

"What is so urgent?" I asked, pulling out a wire chair opposite hers.

"I found him."

"What? Already?"

"Told you I could."

And I hadn't believed her. But I was more than happy to eat my words. "Where is he?"

She grabbed her energy drink, took a swig. "Don't know yet."

"What did you find?"

I was trying to be patient, but there must have been an edge to my voice, because she glared at me and swigged down some more Red Bull before she answered. "I figured out where his family went, and what name they were using."

"That's impressive." And it was. "What was it?"

"Farrow. And they came to Vancouver."

Of course they did. "Did Celeste ever mention a Farrow to you?"

"Nope. He was here, though, and recently."

"In Vancouver?"

"Yeah."

"Any address?"

"Nothing current."

"So he's either changed his name, died or left the country."

She nodded, her expression pinched. "I knew Celeste shouldn't have been meeting with him. I just knew it."

She drained her drink, then glared at me. "So what are you going to do?"

"Find him." Now that I had a name.

"Good. I'm gone." She shoved her chair back and started to rise.

"Marie."

At the note in my voice, she froze, staring at me. "I have a few questions about your aunt."

"And I don't see what that has to do with finding Celeste."

No, she probably didn't. I wasn't sure I did, either, but I had a gut feel on this one. And I'd learned not to ignore those.

"I'm the investigator, remember?"

I could see the struggle in her face, but in the end she sat back down, shoulders tight. "What do you want to know?"

"How long did you live with your aunt?"

"I told you, until I was thirteen."

Her expression was hostile. I ignored it. "What was she like to live with?"

One hand clenched on the desk. Her jaw tightened. "I don't want to talk about it. And I don't see how this is helping find Celeste."

"If you don't want me to do my job, then fire me."

She scowled, but didn't say anything.

"Okay then. So what was Anthea Swan like to live with?"

"She was a horror." It burst out of her like it had been held back for too long.

"In what way? Did she mistreat you?"

"Oh, not that one. She made sure I was warm and dry, clothed and fed."

"But?"

Marie's tone was bitter. "But that was all. I might as well have been invisible. I wasn't important, not at all."

"What was important to her?"

"Her art. My dad. Her art."

"Not Celeste?"

A bitter laugh. "Why do you think Celeste got away the minute she could?"

I could think of a few reasons.

"I just wish she'd taken me with her," Marie muttered.

I wasn't sure I was meant to hear that part. "You were alone with your aunt for—four years?"

"Nearly five."

"Why did she commit suicide?"

A shrug. "Why did she do anything?"

"Those five years. Your aunt's paintings were a sudden sensation…"

"Ha!"

I waited. She shrugged, bolted down a mouthful of her energy drink.

"Nothing sudden about it," she finally said. "She'd been working for it for years, ever since my Dad died."

"It?"

"Painting. Being a success. It was all she thought about, all she did. She ate, dreamt, thought painting. She remembered us only enough to make sure our food and clothing were taken care of. And to feud with the town."

This was what I'd been waiting for. "Feud?"

Marie smiled. It wasn't a pleasant smile. "They had it in for her and she for them. Watching it was the only amusement I had after Celeste left."

"What happened?"

"Cold War. Like the spy books my dad used to read. All very nice on the surface, but the battle lines were drawn. An insult here. A quick snipe there. Every delivery was late. Bill payments got lost. They hated her, and us. She hated them. I just wanted to leave."

"What happened when your aunt's art was discovered by the art world?"

"Hah. She rubbed everyone's nose in it. And that's when they all found out."

"Found out what?"

"What her real revenge was."

"And what was it?"

"Have you ever seen the paintings?"

I nodded. Of course I had. Studied them, too.

"Seen them since you started looking for Celeste?"

"No."

"Go look. And think about Brenton. And all of us living there."

"What will I see?"

She laughed, a harsh sound, and swigged down the last of her drink. "Just go look. Then call me and I'll meet you."

Now I was the one worried I was wasting my time. "You're sure now is the time for this?"

"You think the answer's there, don't you? That someone in Brenton has it in for us because of my aunt. In addition to Danny, I mean."

She was shrewder than I'd been giving her credit for. "Maybe. They know something. And we need a break."

"Go look at the paintings. You're the investigator."

"I'll look this afternoon. Then we'll talk."

"Okay." The chair scraped across polished concrete floor as she rose. "And Barbara? Thanks."

She was gone before I could react.

————

I'D JUST GOT BACK to my office and was checking for messages when the door burst open. Cory.

I glanced at my watch, surprised but pleased to realize it was just past noon. He wasn't skipping school, then. Not for the next hour, at least.

His grin said he'd found something. In fact, he looked pretty pleased with himself.

"So I'm guessing you think you've won the bet?"

"It's why you're a top P. I., right? You see things."

I'd have been more flattered if I hadn't suspected him of buttering me up. I was tempted to tell him Marie had come through with the name already, but I let him have his moment.

He had been pretty quick. Maybe we could chat about him doing some contract work for me.

I shuddered, just thinking of the conversation that would require with my sister.

"Something wrong?"

He might have the makings of a decent P. I., himself. "Not a thing. So, what did you come up with?"

"His family changed their name to Farrow. His parents died in a house fire about five years ago. His brother was overseas and died in an accident about eight months ago." Cory said. "And..."

"And?"

"And Danny Deeping became David Farrow. Who then changed his name to David Whyte."

I was impressed. He'd found the same information and a bit more than Marie had, and nearly as quickly. "His brother died eight months ago? Let me guess. His latest name change came right after that."

He nodded. "I think maybe he came into some money, because that's when he bought a condo in Yaletown and quit his job."

"After his brother died?"

A nod. Cory pulled a much folded page from his pocket and handed it over. I glanced at it. Address and phone numbers. "So he has no family left?"

"None that I could find."

Was that why he'd gone looking for Celeste? "Was his name change to Whyte legal?"

"Nope. But he's good with his computer—he buried it pretty deep."

"And what about the family name change? Legal?"

"No. They didn't hide it very deep, though. If he didn't buy his new identity, he's learned some serious shit."

My mind connected the dots. "He'd have to be really good with computers."

"Yeah." His tone said 'Well, duh'.

"You found all this out since this morning?"

A shrug. "Sure, wasn't hard."

And he'd done it on the library computer. I was going to have to hire him. "That's impressive."

"So do I get the job?"

"Well, technically Marie found the information first…"

He scowled at me. "She did?"

"But since she only had the Farrow name and not the address or any of the details, I think we can say you won the bet."

"So I get to work for you?"

"You do. Provided your mother agrees. And it will only be on a project basis. You're underage."

"All riiiight." He punched the air and turned to go. Then he hesitated. "So what will you do now?"

"Now? Try to find Danny Deeping. Now David Whyte." And talk to my client.

"Can I help?"

He'd done enough for one day. Any more and I'd have to talk to my sister immediately.

My eyes went to the clock on the wall behind his head. "Don't you have to be somewhere?"

His gaze followed mine and he looked sheepish. "I have time. I rode my bike so I would."

I just nodded. Some of my sister's favorite phrases had leapt to mind, but I bit my tongue. That wasn't my role—I was the aunt. "Just remember our deal."

He looked thrilled. "I will. You're sure you don't need more help?"

"Actually…" I said slowly, thinking it through.

"What? What???"

"It might also help to have a list of this guy's records since he got to Vancouver. Schools, jobs, anything like that. But it has to be done legally."

He grinned. "Sure."

"Okay. Consider that your first assignment. We'll negotiate a rate later. After I talk to your mother."

"Great!"

"Uh huh. Now go."

"Bye, Aunt B." And he was gone.

I glanced at my watch. If I was going to see many of Swan's paintings, I'd better get going.

I dashed off a quick e-mail to Cathy Yip, and headed for the door.

The phone rang. I glanced back at the display. Cathy Yip. And returning my call so promptly? That was new.

"Barbara O'Grady," I said.

"This is Cathy Yip," she said. "You e-mailed that you had new information for us?"

So that's what it took to get her to call me back. I'd have to remember to use the same message in future.

"A couple of them, actually," I said. "Danny Deeping went by the names David Farrow and, more recently, David Whyte, with a 'y', while he was in Vancouver."

"How did you find the names?"

"An informed source." Which was true. Sort of. "And I have a question for you."

"Go ahead."

"Celeste's donors and potential donors at VU—did they tell you if she'd met anyone new in the last month or so?"

"We didn't ask for that kind of data."

"I think it would be worth asking. Something might pop up."

"Do you know something, or is this a guess?"

"Call it an informed guess. They were hiding something."

"Noted. Anything else?"

"No. But you'll share what information you can?"

"You know the drill."

All too well. And it was probably Danny Deeping/David Farrow/David Whyte I was looking for anyway.

"But thank you for the names," she said.

"Anytime."

CHAPTER TWENTY

My stomach was growling so I grabbed a falafel wrap on the way downtown. I checked with the Vancouver Art Gallery first, because I knew they had at least two of Anthea Swan's works in their permanent collection. It turned out that they had five paintings, but none were currently on display.

Was it worth calling Cassie? As a board member, she could probably get me in to see them—and it wasn't a request I wanted to make by e-mail. Too embarrassing for both of us if it leaked in the wrong circumstances.

Favors like this one weren't necessarily wrong, but they could be open to misinterpretation. Especially in the art world.

I decided to do a bit more digging first.

The Omega Gallery was next on my list. One of the best small galleries in town, they'd been Swan's representatives for much of her career. I figured they'd know where most of her stuff had ended up. I just had to convince them to tell me about it.

Since I'd known one of the owners, Ian Wong, for quite a while, it should be possible. And it was, sort of.

"I can't give you the names, I'm afraid, Barbara," Ian told me.

"But I can talk to a few of the bigger collectors, see if they are willing to show you what they have."

I smiled at what he hadn't said. We both knew that most collectors love to show off what is either their passion or their investment. "Thanks."

"We do happen to have an assembly of her selected canvases in the back, though, if you would like to see them now? They aren't all hung yet, but I know you'll see past that."

Finally, something was going my way.

"I'd appreciate it," I told him.

I wanted to ask who they'd been assembling the collection for, but I knew better. "What period are the paintings from?"

"It's something of a retrospective, covering some of the key moments of her painting career. Not just from the time she was discovered, which is what many collections have, but including some of the essential early works."

The description made me pause. It sounded like something Kathleen Marshall would put together.

Kathleen was a former client who had turned a hobby into one of the most exclusive galleries in the country. I hadn't heard she was interested in Swan, but with the right client I suspected the challenge would be irresistible. And if so, it made sense she'd be working through Omega, for the same reason I was here.

Kathleen was an interesting contrast. Emotionally she was a bit of a flake, and that was putting it kindly. She was, however, a very astute businesswoman with an amazing nose for which works of any given artist would be the most collectable over time.

If it was Kathleen's collection, I wondered who her current client might be. If Kathleen was willing to pay Omega's notoriously steep fees, she must be confident that she would make even more on this deal. Interesting.

I wondered if Ian knew who the end client was.

He glanced sideways at me, maybe catching the tail end of my grin at that thought.

He didn't comment, though I'm sure he knew what I was thinking. The art business is a funny one. It's like a gossip machine fueled by client confidentiality.

He led me down a narrow hallway opening into a large, well lit area with canvases stacked against the walls and large rolling display boards holding framed works. These would either be for his next planned show, or, more likely, for commissions like the one for Swan's work.

I glanced from side to side, trying not to look like I was taking it all in. I noted a couple of Jack Shadbolt and Toni Onley paintings I hadn't seen before. I wondered if they were planning a retrospective and made a mental note to find out about upcoming shows.

Then I stopped thinking at all, as Ian led me around a display board and into a twelve by twelve temporary gallery with walls made from display boards. I gasped.

Swan's work surrounded us, framed and unframed, and the combined impact was—there were no words. I had no breath for words.

So much conflicting emotion leapt out at me from those canvases—despair and hope, joy and fear—it felt as if I'd been punched in the chest.

"It's something, isn't it?" he said softly. "Our client has a real eye. I've handled almost all of Swan's works, and yet I'd never felt this impact until we started to assemble this specific collection. I don't know how our client knew which ones to ask for."

I was still trying to figure out how to breathe.

At the same time, my eyes were darting from canvas to canvas, looking for the source of that emotion as much as for any key to the riddle that was Celeste, Marie and their life in Brenton.

Somehow these paintings were tied up in what was going on now. But how?

Ian laughed quietly. "I'll leave you to it. Just come out front when you're done. And I'd be interested to hear your thoughts—when you've recovered your voice, that is."

I barely noted him leaving. I was still staring at the canvases.

It wasn't Swan's choices of color. Most of the tones were dark, but there were slashes of bright, even primary color here and there.

It wasn't the subject matter, either. She'd painted everything from landscapes to buildings, worksites to street scenes. There were even a couple of portraits.

I didn't know Swan had done portraits, which meant she likely hadn't done many of them. Taking last look at the whole collection, I moved closer to consider the first portrait.

It was a man in early middle age, with close-cut sandy-blond hair and intense gray eyes. His face was long, the bones sharp and strong. It wasn't a handsome face, not exactly, but it was compelling. He looked like a man I would have liked.

And his gaze held such despair I could barely stand to look at him.

Who was this?

I moved slightly sideways, and his gaze followed me. Something in the shape of the eyes, the slant of the forehead reminded me of Marie. Was this her father?

If so, I had a pretty good idea when this had been painted.

I checked the date on the canvas. Yes, it was the year he'd died— if this was indeed Guy Deslauriers.

I leaned closer. No date, but the author's signature was there— and a title. Guy.

On either side of the portrait were two landscapes I didn't recognize, but they held the same despair. One was a sweep of hills and sky, painted at dusk. It should have been peaceful. It wasn't.

The other captured an afternoon thunderstorm—and it felt as if even the violent storm wouldn't be enough to wash the landscape clean again.

I turned my back to the portrait and landscapes and let my gaze sweep the room.

My eyes stopped on four smaller paintings, off to one side. I saw—Brenton. The bank, the hills behind the town, the streets, the bar.

It took me a moment to recognize them because somehow the

buildings, the scenes all had a glow of purpose. That sense of purpose was entirely missing from the Brenton I'd visited a few days ago.

Something else was different, too. The emotion in these scenes was not despair, but something much different. Joy?

I scanned the room again, and focused on another portrait. A women this time, late teens or early twenties, a lovely redhead with blue eyes and a half-smile. A Swan portrait was unusual enough, but the sitter's eyes held hope, in sharp contrast to the despair in Guy's portrait.

I was guessing I was looking at Anthea Swan's sister, Celeste's mother. It was clearly a very early work, technically strong, but lacking heart.

It could not have been more different from the later painting of her husband. Interesting.

I turned, scanned the paintings again. This time I noticed a stack of unframed canvases against the far wall. I flipped through them.

These I recognized—the buildings of Brenton. Here was the pub, the post office, the diner. There was the bank, the real estate office, the *Bugle* office—all very different from the previous four of the same scene. What made that difference?

I stepped back again, considering. My eyes traveled slowly from one painting to the next and back again. These buildings looked uncared for, almost derelict. Not too far from how they looked now, in fact. And certainly not the way they must have looked when these were painted.

Then it clicked.

Brenton was the model for Anthea Swan's "Forgotten" show. Those iconic paintings of a dying small town had become a byword for lost hope.

I spun around, looked at the first set of Brenton paintings—the landscapes, a mall, a house, even the bank sparkled. If I believed in fairy dust, I'd say she'd been sprinkling it.

Or perhaps I'd say Swan was happy when she painted them.

If so, it was the only time—and I counted only the four paintings—that she'd been happy. My gaze went back to the small diamond on her sister's hand.

I'd see if I could date those four happy paintings, but I had a gut feel that they'd been done after her sister's death and before Guy Deslauriers committed suicide. Before she declared war on the town of Brenton.

Now where had that thought come from?

I went looking for Ian.

―――――

"SO WHAT DO you think of our little collection?" Ian asked.

That was an easy one. "The more I see of it, the more impressed I am. But I do have a couple of questions. There are four paintings in particular…"

"Ah. I have won. Juan, you owe me twenty dollars. Barbara has indeed spotted our anomaly."

"Nice try. I know your ways. And I will need a little more than that before I pay over a penny!"

Juan da Costa, Ian's long time partner in the Omega Gallery, wandered over with a warm smile. "And how are you, Barbara? It is good indeed to see you. But what is this I hear that you will be exhibiting with our competitor?"

It shouldn't have surprised me that he'd heard about my show, but it did. I could feel my cheeks heat a little.

"Yes, Margaret Courtland saw a couple of my recent works and offered me a show."

"Congratulations," Ian said with a smile and an assessing look.

Juan beamed at me. "Indeed. But why is it Margaret that you are taking these new works to and not us? Should we not get a chance at representing you?"

For a moment I was actually at a loss for words. Was he serious? But no, he couldn't be. Omega represented cutting edge artists— which I was not.

But they were competitive, and they didn't like to lose.

"Next time," I said with a laugh and a meaningless gesture.

"I will hold you to that," he said lightly.

But I saw the look he and Ian exchanged. Now what was all that about? They hadn't even seen my paintings.

"If we could look at these four paintings?" I suggested.

"Yes, yes, of course," and Juan led the way back into the makeshift room. "So, which ones? And what did you want to know?"

I pointed them out. "I'm curious if you know exactly when they were painted?"

Ian smiled at his partner. "You see. I'll have that twenty now, please."

He turned to me. "Most of Swan's paintings aren't dated, and you probably know that she left very little documentation on her painting process. Because she had such a body of work completed before she was discovered, relatively few of her paintings can be dated based on their exhibition dates, either."

I nodded. The sheer number of her completed works was one of the reasons that her discovery caused such a sensation. The breath-taking quality of most of them was the other.

"However, changes in technique and materials have allowed us to group together paintings into broad time periods. Since Swan was not forthcoming with details of her biography…"

"I've read several very detailed biographies that were put together as part of her shows," I said, watching for a reaction.

"Yes, well," Ian began, glancing at Juan.

"She had a little help with those," the latter said smoothly. "She was most reluctant to put together even the barest of facts. We worked with her to create something more detailed."

"How accurate was it?" I asked bluntly.

He shrugged, an elegant movement that caused barely a ripple in the shoulders of his beautifully cut dark suit. Was that silk? Probably.

I knew that the Omega Gallery did very well, and had done so for a long time. Vancouver has more than a few dot-com million-aires, as well as the money that has settled here from overseas in the last couple of decades.

"I suspect she was more creative than most," he said gently. "She was a difficult, troubled woman. And her art was sublime. It was not worth upsetting her over."

"Why? Does it matter?" Ian asked. His eyes were fixed on my face, watching for subtle indication of what I was really thinking.

I shrugged. "Maybe. Probably not. She's tangential to a case I'm working on now."

I suspected tangential was less than accurate, but it would do for now.

I wasn't about to explain myself to these two—discreet as they were when clients were concerned, their love for gossip found other avenues. Frequently.

"What do you know about the timing of these four?"

"We now assume they were painted in the same time frame," Juan said. "Seen like this, the style is quite distinct from any of the other works. She has other similar works, but she released them one by one, mixed in with later works, so even we didn't realize they were earlier works.

In fact, the contrast between this style and her later, darker works was part of what cemented her reputation for great emotional range."

"Do any of the paintings date from before these four?" I was pretty sure about the portrait of her sister, but were there others?

There were. Ian nodded and strolled over to the wall, flipping expertly through the canvases stacked there. "These aren't as good as her later ones, but you'll see they have a similar feel."

"She was a complex woman. And not a happy one," Juan contributed.

I watched Ian pull out about a dozen canvases. These were mostly cityscapes, and I recognized the Vancouver of a few decades ago. All were in dark tones, all grim. If I had these hanging on my wall, I'd be wanting a drink every time I looked at them.

No, Anthea Swan certainly hadn't been a happy woman, except for those four paintings. And from the little I'd seen, Swan was fixated on two things—her painting, and her sister's husband. What had she done when he'd been driven to suicide?

Marie had implied she was cruel, and that she'd got even with the town. How?

And how had her nieces—especially Marie—survived living with her?

CHAPTER TWENTY-ONE

Kathleen Marshall's gallery, simply called 'Journeys', is located in an up-market section of Burrard Street. Small but elegant, it shimmers in shades of silver, gray and white that detract nothing from the spectacular art. When her assistant let her know I was there, Kathleen didn't keep me waiting.

"Barbara! How nice to see you. What can I do for you?" she asked as she led me towards her office in the back.

I was relieved to see she was in full professional mode today. "I'm working on a new case, and I need your assistance."

"Anything I can do for you, Barbara, you just need to ask. You know that. I owe you."

"No, you don't." Her very obvious gratitude embarrassed me. She'd been a client, and I'd done my job.

I don't know why I bothered protesting, though. It never did any good. And it didn't this time.

"We both know that I do. Now, how can I help?"

"I need to know more about Anthea Swan."

"Go on."

What to say without exposing Ian? "You know a lot of the major collectors. Can you tell me who might collect her work? And be willing to let me view it?"

She beamed at me, a wide smile breaking through. "No, I can't. I'm sworn to secrecy."

She laughed. "But I can do better than that. I can show you a collection that I'm having put together, for a client who shall remain nameless. When would you like to see it?"

This was a Kathleen I'd never met before. She was impressive, and a little overwhelming. "How about now?"

She nodded, called out to her assistant. "Brigitte, I'm going out for a few hours."

"Sure thing," came a cheerful voice, and we were gone.

———

STANDING ONCE AGAIN in the back room at the Omega Gallery, Kathleen and I stood gazing at the extraordinary collection she'd begun to assemble. Seeing it for a second time, I could appreciate nuances that had escaped me in a first viewing.

I'd thought I knew a lot about Swan as an artist, but seeing these particular paintings hung together gave me a new insight into her work.

Kathleen's pride in what she'd done was evident, but so was the passion she felt for it.

"When I decide to collect an artist, whether I'm looking for one pivotal painting or a series of the works that define a career, I research that artist, learn everything about them," she said. "No detail is too small. I must understand them, their lives, why they create the art that they do. Then, if I am very lucky, I can recognize the works that matter."

I don't know why this surprised me so much. I'd seen the obsessive side of Kathleen's personality before, when she'd obsessed over a man who didn't care. I just hadn't seen it applied to her business.

No wonder she was so successful as a collector. She would

pursue something she wanted with a focused determination, and she'd keep going past obstacles that would stop most people.

I liked Kathleen—despite getting off to a very rocky start in my first encounters with her—but I'd underestimated her. Badly.

I'd even felt somewhat sorry for her, which was embarrassing now.

"Can you tell me why you focused on these works in particular, and what they tell you about Swan?" I asked her.

Kathleen nodded, strode across the room to one of the framed paintings. In this place she was in her element, confident, in control. I wouldn't have believed it if I hadn't seen it.

The other thing that surprised me was the work she was pointing to.

It wasn't where I would have started, being neither one of her early works nor a portrait. It was a landscape, with nothing I could see that made it more meaningful than the three or four other similar canvases nearby.

"See there," Kathleen was saying, pointing to a couple of black and grayish shapes that I suddenly realized depicted part of Brenton, dwarfed by the surrounding mountains, perched high on a cliff above a turbulent river.

"And here," and she pointed to a tiny glimmer of sunlight reflected in the Fraser far below. "Her landscapes are about emotion, not scenery. How much do you know of Swan's life?"

"Just the basics," I said. How much of what I thought I knew was even correct?

"Okay. She lived in this small town," and she tapped a careful fingernail against the black and gray smudges. "Up the old Canyon highway, during her most productive painting years. She never said much about it, but her paintings say it for her. This one speaks of anger and frustration, with just a bit of hope. But see how small the town is, how insignificant in the landscape. That small glimmer of light is the only sign of hope, and the first one she'd ever showed in all her paintings of the place."

"When was it painted?"

She told me the estimated date. A few years after Guy had died, and right after she'd been discovered as an artist.

"So what happened with the next paintings? Did that glimmer grow?"

"Yes, though not by much. She did a whole series of paintings with glimmers of light, that were part of her 'Darkness and Dawn' show."

I remembered learning about that show. "Didn't that one sell out?"

"Yes. To rave reviews. Critics called her work powerful, riveting, emotionally compelling."

"So what came next?"

She moved on. "This one."

I looked, and for a moment. The glimmer was gone, but otherwise I couldn't see much difference between the two, though I could feel the emotional difference. The second canvas made me shiver, though I couldn't have said why. I looked closer.

"It's the shadings in the sky and the river, isn't it? The whole thing is threatening that town, and there isn't a glimmer of hope anywhere."

Kathleen nodded, then moved on to show me several others. They were like a roller-coaster: better, worse, better, worse, worse…

"These are in chronological order?"

"Yes."

"The mood is trending down. Was she clinically depressed? Is that why she committed suicide?"

Kathleen shook her head, a small frown between untidy brows. "Not exactly. Her suicide came many years later. Let me show you what she painted next."

She moved over to a group of the buildings I'd recognized earlier. "Look at these."

I looked at them, compared them to the landscapes from the 'Darkness and Dawn' series. "These pit beauty against ugliness. And their emotion…" I stood back, stared at them again.

"Hate, I think," Kathleen said. "But she's made it compelling. That was the contradiction of the woman. It's why her paintings are so collectible."

"It's the energy," I said, moving closer to examine the textures she'd used. "Look at the brush strokes. They're alive, practically dancing off the canvas."

Kathleen smiled. "I know. Now have a look at an early painting of the same subject." She pointed.

This was one of the four anomalies I'd spotted earlier. I looked back and forth, thinking about what Kathleen had said.

"The early one is more accessible," I said slowly. "But it's more than that. She's captured a vanishing small town, bathed it in golden light, pitted against a menacing landscape. In many ways it's a typical Canadian painting—survival against the elements. All the virtues of a small town. But she's painted genuine emotion, not nostalgia."

And now I could identify the emotion. Gratitude.

"Yes. She did a few more of these in the same time frame, but I chose these four to represent this phase of her work. Now compare them to this one."

And she pointed to another dark Brenton landscape.

I stepped back, considering it. "There's no energy in this one. Nothing as strong as hate, either. If anything, I'd say it's full of resentment."

Kathleen laughed. "No wonder I like you, Barbara," she said. "You see clearly. That's it exactly. And yet there's something threatening about it."

I considered the painting in front of me. She was right. "When was this one done?"

She pointed at the tiny lettering in the far right corner. This one was dated. I peered closer, held my breath. It was a week after Guy Deslauriers had committed suicide.

What had Swan been saying with this painting? And what had she done about it?

Time to talk to Marie again.

I thanked Kathleen for her help and left.

I had an artist's revenge to track down.

———

JAIMIE GRANDIS WAS ALREADY SEATED at Café Buzz when I got there, sipping on a large cup of what looked like green tea. I shuddered, and headed for the counter to order a large cappuccino.

"I'm sorry I'm late," I said as I joined her, tucking my cell phone away.

"No worries," she said with a strained smile. "I'm a little nervous these days, but it's nothing to do with you. I'm not sleeping well."

I nodded and sipped my drink.

She took it as encouragement, which is what I'd intended. "I can't stop worrying about Celeste. I just have such a bad feeling about this whole thing."

"Any idea where she met this guy?"

"Through Two Hearts."

"I just verified that he's never been one of their clients."

Jaimie pushed dark hair out of her eyes. "You're sure?"

"They seem to be."

She sighed. "So Celeste must have thought I'd disapprove of how they met. She did say it felt like it was meant to be. I suspected he'd somehow engineered their meeting, but she just laughed at me, said I was getting as paranoid as her little sister."

I didn't want to like Jaimie, but she kept sliding out of the categories I tried to put her into. "I think you were probably right. So the real question is, why did he want to meet her, and what is he up to?"

"I'm worried he isn't quite rational about Celeste," she said. "I think he might have created some story in his own mind, centered on her. And however he met her, he had to know quite a bit about her."

"You think he was stalking her?"

She nodded. "It makes sense, doesn't it?"

It was one possibility. Didn't mean she was right, though.

I pulled out the sketch Marie had given me. "Have you ever seen this guy before?"

She looked at it carefully. "No. Is it him?"

"Yes. His name is, or was, Danny Deeping."

"He's changed it?"

"Yes. Several times."

She held it away from her, looking at it from several angles. "He looks just like Celeste described him."

"So if you're right about Danny stalking Celeste and you don't recognize him, he must have been pretty careful. If you and Celeste spend much time together, that is."

"We get together at least two or three times a week. If he's a stalker, he would have been around." She glanced at me, looked back at the sketch. "How accurate is this?"

"Several people have recognized him from it."

"The artist is very good, then. And I'm seeing something I didn't expect."

"What?"

"There's a vulnerability there. Which isn't the energy I'd been picking up from him at all. And it means that there might be hope for Celeste. Where was this drawn?"

"Here, when he had coffee with Celeste. Why?"

"Because it would be good to know what kind of situation can make this guy feel vulnerable. I'm just surprised I never picked up on his energy…" She went white. "Oh my God!"

She looked like she was about to faint. I half reached for her. "Are you okay? What is it?"

"I did pick up on it. That's what it was. I could feel it around her, and I thought it was a stray dog that Celeste was going to end up adopting. She did that kind of thing, much to Marie's dismay."

Really? Jaimie seemed to know Celeste pretty well. But what she was saying didn't seem to match Celeste's immaculate home. "I've been to her place, and I didn't see any sign of animals."

"Marie is allergic, so Celeste could never keep any of her rescues. Most of them ended up with her ex."

Probably not Callum. "Ben?"

She nodded. "He's got a pretty big place, and he's really good at finding homes for the ones he can't keep."

Interesting relationship Celeste had with her exes.

Jaimie wasn't done. "This guy—he's running both kinds of energy—the lost soul and the controller. Somehow he's fixed on Celeste as his answer. And she isn't going to be able to fix him the way he hopes. And I'm afraid his reaction could be—drastic."

And there she went with the weirdness again. But at least she'd confirmed that the sketch was the same guy Celeste had told her about.

Jaimie wrapped both hands around her mug, practically inhaled her tea, then met my eyes. "Barbara, you have to find her. And fast."

Yeah. That's what I was trying to do.

———

I SWUNG by my office and checked the answering machine and the e-mail. Mixed in with the mundane stuff was an e-mail from my nephew.

Cory had been busy. He'd sent a copy of Danny-as-David Farrow's most recent curriculum vitae, updated just before he'd ditched the Farrow name to become David Whyte. How had the kid got hold of that?

I decided I didn't want to know, but we were going to have another talk about legality once this case was done. I didn't need him shutting down my business because he had something to prove.

I sent back my thanks, then printed off the CV and grabbed the rest of my notes on Danny.

I could use an early night.

Once I was home, I poured a glass of Mission Hill Cabernet and carried it and by notes though to the sofa. Half-way there a sound from behind had me freezing. What was that?

Looking over my shoulder, I had to laugh. Cat was lying on his back, paws in the air, making a pathetic little "mrrt" sound.

My nerves really must be shot. He was lying half-under the dining table and I'd walked right by him without noticing.

"You must be feeling mellow," I told him. "You're not usually this subtle."

He just lay there, white underbelly exposed and big eyes staring at me.

"Okay, okay. I've had a hard day, so you probably have too," I told him, and he rubbed around my ankles while I put his tuna out.

I was still smiling when I started to read Danny's CV, but the smile didn't last.

If Danny was responsible for everything Marie accused him of, everything I'd begun to suspect him of, he'd done a great job of hiding it.

His life as David Farrow had been under the radar—way under. He had a decent job doing IT troubleshooting with a big firm, but no promotions and no sign he was capable of the kind of coding magic Cory assures me he'd have to be.

As David Farrow, he hadn't changed jobs often and he didn't list any hobbies or interests. No-one would look at him twice.

I went back through all my notes on Danny several times without finding anything useful. Finishing my wine I called it a night.

Cat curled up at my feet, purring loudly. Maybe Mrs. Pinkton was away. I was glad of his company anyway.

CHAPTER TWENTY-TWO

It wasn't long after sunrise, and I'd only had time to put on the coffee when my office door banged open and a small whirlwind swept in and grabbed hold of my arm. "Marie?"

"He's dead. He's dead. And it's all my fault. You have to do something."

"Take a deep breath, then tell me again. Slowly. Who is dead?"

"Callum. Celeste, Celeste's…."

She gulped in a ragged breath that ended on a sob, and the tears rolled down her face. "C–Callum. Is. Dead."

I freed my arm and guided her to a chair, then grabbed a guest mug and filled it, adding two spoons of sugar and a couple of dollops of cream. Didn't matter that she didn't usually drink coffee. She was in shock.

Putting the cup in front of her, I folded her hands around it. She held it as if grateful for the warmth, then took a sip.

Despite my need to know exactly what had happened, and whether they'd found Celeste, I turned away and refilled my own cup. Marie needed time.

I drank. Maybe I should be putting sugar in my own mug. Not that I'd cared for Callum, but the news was still a shock.

What had happened to him?

And how had Marie found out?

When Marie's sobs had quieted a little, I topped up her cup. "Marie? What happened?"

"I—I don't know. They came. To the door. They were looking for her. Celeste."

"Who came?"

"He still has her listed. And I told them she was gone. They wanted to know when. And they told me."

Listed? Oh. Was Celeste still listed as Callum's next of kin? Which would make "they" either the hospital or the police. Most likely the police, if he was dead.

"Marie? Who is they? And what did they tell you?"

"Police. West Van. And they said he was dead. Shot. In his apartment. Sometime early this morning." She gasped a little, her breathing harsh and broken.

That was a little clearer, but not much. "Focus, Marie. Why did you come to see me? What do you want me to do?"

"It's about Celeste. It has to be. Ben'll be next. You'll see."

"How is this about Celeste?"

"I'm afraid I've killed him. And I'll be next."

"Take a breath, Marie. Killed who?"

"Callum. I think I killed Callum. I asked him to look into a few things for me. Stuff I couldn't find, and he could…" She faltered, drew in a harsh breath. "That he could find faster," she managed to say.

And now Callum was dead. "What did you ask Callum to look into?"

"He's good with a computer. And it's the same bank my father worked for. And they keep records."

Records of what? Exactly what had happened in Brenton all those years ago?

She continued before I could ask. "If Callum wasn't careful, and if he did more than he said he would, then Danny might have been able to track him. And know we were after him. And he'd have gone after Callum first. And then he'll come for me."

She was talking so fast her words ran together.

I was starting to follow her thought patterns, which was probably a very bad sign. "You're thinking that Danny would kill to keep whatever happened in Brenton hidden? And that since Callum was digging into computer records, Danny would spot it and come after him. And then you?"

"Not thinking. He will. He has her, now he wants the rest of his past gone."

It made a twisted kind of sense, but it was a huge leap based on very little. "Marie? Have you learned something more about Danny?"

"No."

"Then how do you know what he's thinking? Or even if he's the one who killed Callum?"

Mascara streaked down her cheeks, her eyes were huge and lined with red, but her jaw was thrust out and her lips set.

"I just know. And I'm right, you'll see. And you have to do something. Save her. Keep anyone else from getting killed."

"I'll need more information. Did you find out anything else about Danny? Anything at all?"

She shook her head. "N-no. No, I didn't. But I know this is him. I know it."

She was close to hysterics. "Calm down. We can solve this."

"How? We can't even find him." She sniffed, buried her face in the mug again.

"That's what you hired me for."

She didn't respond.

"Tell me more about the records Callum was looking into."

"I can't. I can't."

"Marie!"

No response. She was shaking. How much sleep had she had last night?

"More coffee?"

She shook her head. "I hate the stuff. I'm okay."

I doubted that. "Look, you need to answer some questions for me. But maybe you need to get some sleep first."

She swallowed again. "I'm afraid to go home."

Was she over-reacting to Callum's murder? Or was she right about Danny—in which case, she had every right to be terrified.

"Is there someone you could stay with?"

She shook her head. "No-one I could trust. Except maybe Ben, and that would just put him in danger. He's Celeste's past, too."

She gave me a watery attempt at her normal grin. "We'd just be giving him a two-for-one."

"There must be someone you could stay with? A relative? A friend? A colleague?"

She shook her head. "Nope. Celeste is the social one. Most of my friends are on-line, not local. And I can't go. Not until I know Celeste is safe."

"I could stay in touch with you," I said, a tad desperately. I could see where this was going.

Marie just shook her head. I think it was the anxiety in her eyes combined with the stubbornly out-thrust chin that did it.

"You can crash at my place for today, if you like, I have a futon." I'm not sure which of us was more stunned by my words.

"You mean it?"

I nodded. Too late to back out now.

"When you wake up, we'll talk," I said. "And figure out where to go from here."

And it was done—I had a house guest. Have I mentioned I hate sharing my space? At least it gave me extra incentive to solve this case.

Not that I needed it.

Getting Marie set up was more unsettling than I'd expected. I kept seeing a vulnerability in her that she'd kept hidden from me up till now. She felt like a young girl, suddenly abandoned. Was this what all those prickles had been covering?

My apartment felt smaller than ever. A quick glance around

showed no sign of Cat, which was just as well—hadn't Jaimie said Marie was allergic? I showed Marie to my study.

She looked around the crowded room, gaze lingering on the paintings stacked against the far wall. I pulled out the futon and made it up without a single word from her, though she helped by taking the far side of the sheets and blankets.

I kept waiting for a smart remark. Nothing.

She must still be in shock.

I nearly offered her more coffee, but a glance at her white, shell-shocked face dissuaded me. I sat her down and poured two fingers of scotch instead.

After she'd gulped down some of it, I gave her the spare key and drew the curtains.

"Call me when you wake up and we can talk about Callum as well as about your aunt and her paintings. I'll be at the office."

———

WHILE MARIE CAUGHT up on her sleep, I started digging into the facts on Callum McLaughlan's murder. There wasn't much more information than what Marie had told me. He'd been shot and killed in his home, and it seems he had invited his killer in.

There was no sign of a struggle, and the neighbors had heard nothing.

Police were checking his movements in the past day and canvassing the neighbors. I was guessing that ballistics didn't tell them much, and they were looking for a motive or a lead among his circle of acquaintances.

An ex-wife would certainly be a person of interest. A missing ex-wife? Even more interesting. Which left me exactly nowhere.

So what did Callum's death do to my search for Celeste?

If Marie was right and Danny had killed Callum, then I had to wonder if he'd killed before.

How had his parents died? And his brother? I texted Cory,

asking him to find out what he could about those deaths, and whether there had been anything suspicious about them.

Was there anything that would help me find Danny faster?

The resume Cory had found was useless. No leads there—even if I interviewed his former colleagues, I doubted they knew him at all. I'd do better to go back to Brenton, see what they remembered about him before he was forced to change his name and identity.

But I still just had Marie's fears and Jaimie's "vibes" pointing to Danny as the person who'd kidnapped Celeste. Granted he'd been the last person seen with her, and granted no-one could find him, but—what if it wasn't him?

If Marie was wrong—and Danny hadn't killed Callum—then someone else had. Was it possible that both Callum and Celeste were connected to that someone? And Marie was panicking over a bogeyman named Danny?

I picked up the phone. "Ben? It's Barbara O'Grady. I met with you earlier in the week, about Celeste."

"I remember. Is there any news of her?"

"Nothing yet, I'm afraid. But have you heard about Callum McLaughlan's death?"

"Yes, it's running like wildfire through the legal community. How did you find out?"

"Marie told me. And she's convinced that it's related to Celeste's disappearance, and that the killer will come after her next. And possibly you."

"Ah." A pause. "And what has she based this theory on? Or do I need to ask?"

I laughed, as he'd meant me to.

"It's a feeling, I'm afraid. She has no evidence of anything," I said. "But I called you because I can't tell if her fear of this guy from Brenton is based on something real, or if she's paranoid because of some trauma associated with her childhood there. It's definitely a strange place."

"You've been there?"

"Day before yesterday. Have you ever been?"

"No. Celeste wouldn't go back, even though I suggested it a time or two."

"She was as affected by it as Marie seems to be?"

"More so, I'd say."

Hmmm. Since I took on this case, everything seemed to point towards the Deslauriers' history with the town as the root cause of Celeste's disappearance. I distrusted things that were that easy. "Did you know Callum McLaughlan?"

"Sure. Not well, but we went to law school together. In fact, I think it was through me that Celeste and Callum first met. Some reunion thing or other."

"Then Callum and Celeste were involved before the two of you divorced?"

"Before we…? No, she didn't take up with him until a few years after our divorce. Surprised me, that. I can't say I was particularly surprised the marriage didn't last, though."

He wasn't the only one. "And did Callum have enemies?"

"Probably, but since he specialized in corporate law, they weren't the kind of enemies that are likely to shoot you."

"Do you know of anyone who might have shot him?"

"No, I really don't. Including some bogeyman from Brenton."

"Then you don't agree with Marie that you're both in danger?"

"I'm not about to change my daily routine."

That's what I'd expected to hear. "Ben, have you ever seen Marie react like she's doing now?"

"Yeah, I have. It was right after Celeste and Callum got married, and there was discussion about Marie living on her own. She freaked. Just couldn't handle the idea of living alone. Her argument was that she wouldn't be safe, but given her general disregard for her own safety, I never believed that was it."

"Was that what broke up Celeste and Callum?"

"I hadn't heard that before, but it wouldn't surprise me if it was a factor. Celeste really felt responsible for Marie, and Callum was from the "eighteen and you're out" school of child raising."

Ouch. "Marie says it was the reason."

"Marie probably thinks it was. And that it was a victory for her."

"The last time we spoke I asked what you thought might have happened to Celeste. Any further thoughts?"

"I've thought of practically nothing else. Just wish I'd come up with something."

"Anyone else I should be talking to?"

"No. Unless it's some connection through her job."

Her job. Which was also connected to Callum. Maybe that was the link, and not Brenton at all. It might be time for another visit to Alicia at VU.

"Thank you. You'll get in touch if you do think of anything?"

"I have your number. And Barbara? Good luck."

Yeah. "Thanks."

CHAPTER TWENTY-THREE

Alicia Chambers was not pleased to see me. She was one of the people that made me wish I was worth tens of millions, just to see the expression on her face when she found out. In my version of the world, she'd find out right after she'd treated me like a waste of her time.

Come to think of it, the only time I buy lottery tickets is when I've just dealt with one too many Alicias. I grinned at the thought. Pretty childish, Barbara.

It still amused me, though, and I wasn't likely to stop buying the tickets, childish or not.

"Ms. O'Grady? What can I do for you today?" she said.

Judging by her tone, visions of me as a lottery winner were not dancing in her head. Oh, she was polite, and you could tell she'd spent time in an "every contact is a potential lead" school, but her body language spoke volumes. Her time was valuable. Mine, presumably, was not.

Hell, maybe I'd buy two tickets.

"I wanted to offer my condolences," I said.

Alicia went white. You never think the phrase is meaningful, until you meet the kind of people who really do lose all color from their face, leaving them looking paper-like and fragile. Her makeup stood out like the mask it was.

"Celeste? She's—dead? That isn't possible!"

"I'm sorry, I assumed you'd have heard. No, Celeste is still missing. But one of your volunteers has been killed."

"One of mine? Dead?" Her voice rose to a near-screech, yet somehow it was fragile too, and more real than anything I'd heard from her yet.

"Callum McLaughlan was murdered last night."

"Callum was? But that's not possible. He's MC'ing our donor event next week. He's coming in this afternoon for a final run-through. With Celeste away, I'm dealing with far too many details for this event."

Shock. It'd hit her in a minute.

It did. She blinked at me, and licked lips that had narrowed to nothing. "Callum's dead?" she said. "Callum McLaughlan? How?"

"Shot. A neighbor found his body. That's all I know, I'm afraid."

"It's not possible."

"Oh?"

"He was at a dinner last night. I saw him there."

That was interesting. "What time?"

"It started at seven and ran until nearly eleven. It was supposed to end at ten, so we were there until midnight, cleaning up."

"And Callum?"

"I know I saw him just before eleven. I don't recall seeing him after that."

"So he may have left then?"

She nodded. Then swallowed hard, and said, "I suppose so. But how could he have been shot that same night?"

"Someone may have waited for him at his home," I said. "Or perhaps whoever shot him was with him."

"Oh." Another nod.

I waited.

"Just a minute. You're not saying that someone from our event might have gone home with him and killed him?" Her voice rose again.

"I'm not saying anything of the kind. But now that you mention it, is it possible?"

"Of course not."

"So you did see him leave?"

"No, I told you—Oh."

"Who would know if Callum McLaughlan left your event alone?"

She looked about to argue, then gave up. "Karine Jang," she said. "If you'll wait a moment, I'll introduce you."

———

KARINE WAS a decade younger than Alicia and was more obviously shaken up by the news of Callum's death. She blanched, fell back in her chair, then reached for her energy drink on her cluttered desktop with a shaking hand. After gulping down what looked like half of it, she looked at me. "How...?"

"The police seem to think he was shot not long after he arrived home last night," I said. "Alicia said you might know what time he left the event."

Alicia had sunk down in the empty chair of the other desk in the small room.

Karine glanced at her, looked back at me. "Ummm—I'm not really sure," she said. "I was kinda busy."

I looked over at Alicia. "Would you mind?"

She obviously did mind, but what could she say? With another insincere smile and a reminder to stop by her office before I left, she left, closing the door behind her.

Karine and I both watched her go. She turned to me and smiled. "I'm glad you caught that."

"Something you didn't want her to know?"

"Well, something I didn't want her to hear, at least."

"Well?"

"I'm so sorry to hear about Callum. Did he suffer?"

"I don't know, but it sounds as if it was pretty quick."

"Oh."

"What did you want to tell me?"

"I'm the one went home with him. With Callum."

"You were?"

She nodded, swallowed hard.

"I thought you were part of the crew clearing up after the event. Alicia said you were there to midnight."

"How would she know?" She caught my expression, started to laugh, remembered Callum and choked back a sob. "She didn't stay, once the big donors were gone. She just assumes I was there."

"And were you?"

"No. Callum left just after Alicia did. And I went with him."

Somehow I didn't think this was a confession of murder. "And how long were you there?"

She gave me a weak smile. "A couple of hours. I had to be in early this morning, to cover for the ones who covered for me last night."

"You were at Callum's place?"

"Yes."

"And he was alone last time you saw him?"

She nodded.

"This would have been what time?"

"One? One-thirty?"

That fit with what I'd heard. "Did you notice anything unusual on your way out?"

She paled even further. Obviously she'd figured out why I was asking. "No. Nothing."

"And was Callum expecting anyone?"

"He was asleep."

I'd take that as a no.

"I left a note and let myself out," she added.

How to ask this diplomatically? "Did the door lock behind you?"

"That's why I'm glad you got rid of Alicia," Karine said. "I have a key. And the buzzer code."

"Were you two together?"

"We weren't exclusive, if that's what you mean. But we'd worked so many events together, we'd become friends."

Her eyes filled with tears and her voice tailed off as she reached for a tissue. I felt bad about asking her anything else, but I couldn't let it go. "Do you work with Celeste Deslauriers?"

She nodded, and reached for a second tissue. I felt worse, but waited for an answer. It was my job.

"Celeste? Oh my God, Celeste. She's not dead too?"

"Not as far as I know. But she is still missing."

"And you think this is connected. Callum's—death?" Her voice squeaked again and she dabbed at her eyes.

"I hope it isn't. But I've been hired to find her, and I can't ignore the fact that it might be connected. Is there anything you can think of that might help me find Celeste?"

"I wish there was."

"Nothing out of the ordinary that you noticed about her over the last few weeks? No fights with anyone? No accusations from colleagues or donors?"

"Celeste? As if!" Then her eyes tightened. "There was something…"

"Yes?"

"It's probably nothing. And it's nothing to do with work. It was something Callum said."

"Go on."

She swallowed hard. "I probably shouldn't say anything. He told me in confidence."

"And now he's dead and she's missing. If what he told you has any bearing on Celeste's disappearance, I think you can afford to break that confidence. In fact, I think you have to."

"You're right. He would tell me the same thing." She reached for another tissue, dropping the crumpled, soggy mess that was all that was left of the previous one on the desk in front of her. "In fact, he would have insisted on it."

She paused, swiped at her eyes. "He said something about Celeste being too soft-hearted for her own good. And then he said he'd told her more than once that this job was wrong for her. Then I think he remembered I work with her, and asked me to forget he'd said anything. So I did."

The job? "Do you know what Callum was referring to? And why he thought she should quit?"

"This is off the record, right?"

"I don't work for this organization. My only interest in what you tell me is how it will help me find Celeste. Nothing else."

"And Callum's killer?"

"That too. But I'd suggest you tell the police all of this yourself."

Her shoulders squared under the fitted suit jacket she was wearing. "Okay, then I'll tell you. I know Celeste and Alicia don't get along. But there's nothing new there. None of us like Alicia much. Senior management loves her."

Another reason I'm so glad I've managed to steer clear of the corporate world, even the university version of it. "Any idea why the two of them didn't get along?"

"Specifically? No."

Uh huh. "Or why Callum thought she should quit?"

"No."

"How about the soft-hearted comment?"

"I just assumed he meant she put up with too many of Alicia's stupidities."

I wondered if that was all it meant, or if Callum had been as concerned as Marie was about Celeste's attitude towards the citizens and former citizens of Brenton.

I certainly couldn't ask him now.

Karine had lost the fight with her composure, and was sobbing quietly. "Is there anything I can do for you?"

She shook her head. I stood up and handed her another tissue.

"Thank you for your help, and your honesty," I said. "I'll see myself out."

I put my card on her desk. "If you think of anything that might help, please give me a call."

———

AS I LEFT the VU offices by the back door, I glanced at the shrubbery half-concealing the old cement-block building, wondering why the fundraising unit wasn't in one of the newer buildings. This place didn't exactly inspire confidence about the success of the university. On the other hand, if you're asking for money, maybe it doesn't help to look like you're throwing it around.

But Jayson always used to say that when you ask for money, never look like you need it. And Jayson understood about playing the angles.

Good thing I'm in the business I'm in. I get paid to ask questions, not to know the answers.

I climbed the slight incline to where I'd left my battered Civic, and wondered if I should be upgrading my image. I could probably lease something for less than car payments on a new car would cost me. Yeah, right.

No matter how big a bargain a lease was, it was still more than my paid-off monster. And I liked the Beast, it suited me. Any client who couldn't deal with the image wasn't a client I wanted in the first place. Too much trouble.

What about the world Celeste and Callum operated in? It wasn't a world I understood. Was that part of the problem?

It wasn't a world Marie understood either, was my guess.

Maybe that was why she was focused on Brenton and Danny Deeping? And until Callum's death, her view seemed to make sense. Especially given all the innuendos I'd found in Brenton.

Now I wondered.

Was I missing something critical because I didn't understand the dynamics?

I stopped for a red light, stared at the Mercedes bumper in front of me. Who could give me the insight I needed?

Ben? He'd chosen to leave this world. Was he connected enough to tell if I was missing something?

What about Jaimie? I definitely wanted to talk to her again, but was she the person for this?

No, there was only one person I was sure had the level of access to that rarefied level of society that major gift fundraisers and corporate lawyers served. I stopped for another light and I made the call.

CHAPTER TWENTY-FOUR

Half an hour later I was ushered into a sparely furnished study, all glass and black metal with lovely clean lines. If it hadn't been for the huge Lawren Harris painting on the wall, and Cassie Stewart sitting behind the desk, I'd have thought the maid had showed me to the wrong room. The housekeeper brought in a tray of coffee and small scones and departed.

"Thank you for seeing me on such short notice," I said.

"I'm happy to help if I can." Cassie raised the silver pot. "Coffee? You take it black, I believe?"

As I nodded she poured out a thick dark stream that smelled as rich as my surroundings and handed me the cup. "Scone?"

"No, thanks." I sat back, waited while she added a hint of cream and lightly buttered a scone.

"How can I help you?"

"You've heard about Callum McLaughlan?"

"Yes. I'm utterly shocked by it. He was a lovely man."

I nodded, though lovely was perhaps not the word I'd have chosen. "Celeste Deslauriers is still missing."

"There's been no word at all?"

"No, nothing. I was looking into her background, but with

Callum's murder, I'm wondering if there is some connection. Something that ties back to their world, or something they have in common. And since I don't know their world..." I paused, sipped my coffee.

"You thought perhaps I could help?" she asked, with absolutely no expression in her voice.

"Yes, I did." Had I just put my foot into it?

Apparently not. Cassie smiled, and her eyes danced. "I have never seen myself as an investigator," she said, "but I've always loved detective fiction. And I do notice things."

Cassie Stewart read detective fiction? That was the last thing I'd expected. "Can you think of any connection between the two of them and some recent event which could have provoked his murder and her disappearance?"

"Hmmm." Cassie sipped her coffee. "Recently? They were both involved in the big gala event that is coming up at VU, but I can't think that would trigger a murder."

She took a tiny bite of her scone, her face thoughtful. "In fact, I can't think of anything that would provoke violence towards either of them."

"Were there connections between her donors and his clients?"

"Yes, of course. You see the same people at all of these functions. But are you thinking of a donor he might have introduced to her?"

"I suppose." I wasn't satisfied with the explanation Alicia had given me. "A donor, or perhaps one of Celeste's prospects?"

"Someone who is capable of murder? I can't imagine it. But I could ask a few questions of my circle, if you like. Discreetly, of course."

Of course. "That might help. Are you aware of anything other than their marriage and their links to VU that Celeste and Callum had in common?"

"I'm afraid not. You would need to speak with her friends or colleagues for that." She sipped her coffee, leaned forward a little. "Although, I did hear that they might be thinking of getting back together."

"Celeste and Callum?" I couldn't keep the surprise out of my voice.

She nodded, smiling a little. "They made a nice couple."

How did Karine's recent revelations tie in?

And how many people would have been upset to see Callum and Celeste back together. Karine herself? Marie?

"How solid was this rumor?"

She set the cup back in its saucer. "My source is usually fairly reliable. You think it might be of interest?"

"Could be. Can you check out the rumor further? See if there's anything more to it?"

She nodded. "I can do that. Anything else?"

"There are probably questions I don't know to ask. It's why I came to you."

"I'm flattered. I will see what I can uncover."

"Thank you. I do appreciate this."

She smiled. "I still owe you for what you did for Brian and me. And I will let you know if I hear anything worth following up."

I couldn't have asked for more. She saw me out herself, using the opportunity to ask me the question that had me stewing all the way back to my office.

"How is the painting coming, Barbara?" she asked with a warm smile. "I am looking forward to seeing your new works."

———

AS I GOT behind the wheel, my phone beeped at me—incoming text. Cory?

It was.

He'd found the information I'd asked for and was sending links. I cracked the driver's window for air and settled in to read.

James Farrow and his wife Lily had been killed in a house fire. Danny-David and his brother had both moved out the previous year, and the senior Farrows were alone in their bungalow. Arson was suspected, but results were inconclusive. No motive was ever uncovered.

So it was possible Marie was right and Danny was a killer.

Or not.

I wondered if they'd even looked at Danny for the murder of his parents. Given the resume I'd reviewed last night, I was guessing not. Why would they?

There was no obvious motive, unless there had been money?

Cory had also unearthed the details on Aaron Farrow's death on a worksite in Indonesia. This one was not suspicious—a temporary retaining wall had collapsed in a freak rainfall. Danny's brother, an engineer, was one of four men unfortunate enough to be in the way of half a ton of mud and water.

Must have been tough on Danny. I wondered what losing his brother so soon after his parent's death had done to his state of mind.

I glanced at the time—school had been out for just over an hour.

How could Cory learn anything if he was constantly responding to texts and e-mails? I've heard a theory that his generation is using texting and instant messaging so much that it's re-wiring their brains to multi-task more efficiently.

I found the whole idea unsettling. I couldn't decide if I wanted it to be true because it made their constant connection okay—or if I wanted it not to be true because it meant my world could change beyond recognition in my lifetime.

I felt a sudden stab of real sympathy for my mother, who had gone to school before even calculators existed, let alone personal computers. When she joined the work force, a computer filled an entire room. Spreadsheets were kept in large paper ledgers. It made my brain hurt trying to envision how I'd have done my job then.

Shaking my head, I skimmed through my e-mails.

Mostly junk, but Isabella had confirmed that neither David Farrow nor David Whyte had ever been Two Hearts' clients. Fair enough.

I texted Cory back my thanks, and asking him to find out who had benefited from James and Lily Farrows' deaths.

After a moment's consideration, I sent Jerry a quick e-mail, asking him if they had anything more on the Farrows' deaths—and whether there was any chance Danny could have been the perpetrator—then I started the car.

———

I SAT across from Jaime at a tiny, battered table in a shadowy corner at Café Buzz. Which fit my mood. This case seemed more impossible now that when I'd taken it on, and with everything I learned it seemed to get worse. I lifted the heavy earthenware mug with the bee logo, drank.

At least the coffee was good.

The place was busier than last time I was here, and we'd been lucky to get a table at all. It was also noisy enough that no-one could hear a word we said. Even Jaimie had trouble hearing me until I leaned closer. Which I did.

"I've heard that Celeste and Callum may have been thinking about getting back together," I said.

She nearly dropped her soup spoon. "Celeste? And Callum?" Her voice rose, causing a few heads to turn our way, even in the lunch hour racket.

I hid my grin behind my coffee mug and took another fortifying sip of the best dark-roast Sumatran I'd tasted in quite some time. I do like to catch people off-guard—I get some of my best information that way. And Cassie's tip about Celeste and Callum had definitely caught Jaimie off-guard. "Is it possible?"

"No!" She thumped her cup down. "Where ever did you hear that?"

"Sorry, that's confidential. But my source is usually pretty accurate." Well, Cassie was, though I wasn't sure about her source. "Are you sure?"

"Well,…" Jaimie sat back, rested both hands on the table and closed her eyes. What was she doing? Surely she wasn't doing the psychic thing? Here? Now?

Her eyes flew open. Her face was white and her eyes looked like she was in pain. "Something's happened to Callum. Is he—? He feels…" She stared at me, and swallowed hard.

"I'm sorry." And I was. I put my hand on her arm. " I thought you would have heard. Callum was killed last night. Shot."

She shook her head, swallowed again. "No. I only knew him through Celeste. And I never watch the news."

"So how did you know?"

"I felt it."

"Felt it?"

"When I reached out, just now. I felt a void where his energy used to be, and a dark ugly energy surrounding it."

I must have looked as blank as I felt, because she took another mouthful of herbal tea then gave me a shaky half-smile. "This must all be very strange to you," she said.

She had that right. This case just kept getting weirder. "Why did you—reach out?"

"If Celeste and Callum had reconnected, it should show in his energy field. Maybe even be a link I could follow back to Celeste."

"And?"

"No links, just the void. I knew he was dead. And that the death had been violent. There is an energy around the void where Callum used to be and I'd have to call it an angry energy. It's buzzing, and feels to me rather like a swarm of hornets."

I took a breath. I needed to focus, because I wanted to challenge nearly everything she'd said, and that would end the conversation. If it would help solve this case, I'd even take advice from a psychic. "Is the killer the guy from Brenton?"

"I'm not getting anything that would identify the killer. I can't even tell you for certain that it's a man. It might help if I could go to the spot where Callum died."

I could just imagine trying to explain that one to the West Van police. "Is there anything you can tell me about the killer?"

She closed her eyes for a moment, then they flew open. "He or she was interrupted. It's why they were so angry when they left the murder scene. They nearly got caught."

Uh huh. "Any sense of who might have interrupted them?"

Jaimie put a hand to her throat, then reached for her teacup. She swallowed several mouthfuls. "No. Whoever interrupted them didn't leave any energy at the scene, or at least nothing strong enough for me to pick up. Maybe they never saw the body."

"If you can read these energies so clearly from a distance, can you read anything from Celeste?"

"No. And that's what I don't understand. We're close enough, I should be able to read her pretty clearly, especially if she's experiencing strong emotions."

"Which she would be if she's been kidnapped."

Jaimie nodded. "But I'm getting nothing."

"And you don't think she's dead."

"No. I don't sense the void that tells me she's died. I just—don't get anything at all."

Which was hardly confirmation that Celeste was alive. And likely Jaimie knew that—probably why she looked so drawn. "What about Celeste's date? The guy from Brenton. Can you pick up anything from him?"

"No. He's gone too. Which is less surprising, because I never met him in person and I never did have a very strong read on him."

"Is there anything that might help me find her?"

"I wish there was."

Right. Back to square one. So much for psychics.

CHAPTER TWENTY-FIVE

I drove back to my office on auto-pilot, my mind spinning. I couldn't to completely discount everything Jaimie had said. I might have trouble with the idea of psychics, I couldn't ignore the insights of a trained psychologist who was Celeste's best friend, even if she was a little weird. Okay, a lot weird.

And Celeste had been missing too long. The odds of finding her alive were getting shorter every day.

Unless she wasn't really missing and had just gone AWOL for some reason of her own?

No. That didn't make sense—not given everything I'd learned about Celeste and her life so far. Just vanishing was too far out of character for her.

But there had still been no ransom note, which ruled out a normal kidnapping, and The Stalker's latest victim had already been found. What did that leave?

As I pulled into my underground parking spot and automatically checked every shadow before getting out of my car. Celeste's life formed a very tight pattern. One that would make me feel like the walls were closing in, but it seemed to suit her. Or so all her friends and acquaintances said.

What if it didn't? What if she'd grown fed-up with the narrow little life she'd created for herself, with its obligations to others and its rules, and just thrown it all over. Skipped town. Done a bunk.

Pressing the "lock" button and heading for the stairs, I shook my head at my own fantasy. It was too far-fetched to be true.

But it was the first time I'd really tried imagining myself inside Celeste's head, inside her life. Why had it taken me so long on this case?

Celeste was very different from me, sure, but that had never stopped me before. Maybe it was the similarities I didn't want to face. Was that what my subconscious was trying to tell me with this cut-and-run scenario?

Celeste and I were both oldest children, with a strong sense of obligation to our families, even if I like to pretend I'm running away from mine most of the time. We shared a strong work ethic, and a tendency to over-work.

Neither of us was very good at relationships, but neither of us gave up on the possibility of having a good one, despite my somewhat vociferous protests to the contrary.

I opened my office door and headed straight for the coffeemaker. Uncomfortable truths called for caffeine. I checked my voice mail and e-mail, but there was nothing of interest, and my brain refused to be distracted.

This was important. Even if I wasn't quite sure what "this" was.

If I looked at Celeste's actions from the perspective of the traits we shared, what did that tell me?

She wouldn't have left voluntarily. She might have felt like it, and wished she was the kind of person who would just leave, but she'd never do it. An overdeveloped sense of responsibility—I knew it well.

Celeste would have known Marie would worry if she disappeared, and she'd have got in touch. It might have taken her a day or two, but no more than that.

That felt right. So Celeste hadn't intended to be gone this long, or she had no way to get in touch. Or both.

What else? Given the traits Celeste and I didn't share, even if she had intended to leave for a time, it would have been meticulously planned.

Well, that was one explanation for why we'd found no trace of her. But the more I considered it, the more I had the feeling that this was a false direction and I was still missing something.

I poured a cup of coffee, pulled up my notes on the screen. I scrolled through, trying to look at it with fresh eyes, looking for anything I might have missed, forgotten or misinterpreted. If I assumed that all of my informants had their facts right but their interpretation wrong, what did that tell me?

Nothing. Not one blasted thing.

I felt out of control. It was a good thing Marie hadn't called to bug me—if she had, I'd have been tempted to quit. Except that I hate to give up. On anything. And Celeste was too intriguing a person to give up on.

Wait a minute. Why hadn't I heard from Marie? It was nearly 2:00 p.m.

I called her cell phone and then my home number without response. Had she woken and gone out?

Concerned, I drove back to my place. The apartment was suspiciously quiet.

The sliding doors in the living room were open about half an inch. Surely she hadn't gone out and left them open? Someone determined enough could easily climb the tree outside the window and drop down onto the balcony that ran halfway along that side.

Could she still be asleep?

There was no movement from my spare-room. The door was ajar, though.

I paused outside it, listening. Nothing. Nudging the door open, I peered cautiously around it.

The sofa-bed rowas closed up, the bedding piled neatly on one edge. There was no sign of Marie, though my paintings were stacked differently. She'd gone through my work.

I felt a flare of anger.

I stared at the empty room for a moment, not sure if I was more stunned that she was gone or that she'd neatly made up the bed. The latter didn't fit my image of my difficult client.

The former, unfortunately, did.

———

BY THE TIME I got back to my office, I was increasingly concerned about Marie. There was still no sign of her. No calls or messages, and she still wasn't answering her cell.

Maybe she'd gone out to get something to eat?

Marie's earlier panic was apparently contagious. Reminding myself that she'd been looking after herself quite well for quite some time, I called Ben's number again.

While I waited for him to answer, I wondered where Marie might have gone, and what time she'd left my place. By the fifth ring, I was about to give up when he answered.

"Ben? It's Barbara again. Have you heard from Marie today?"

"How is she?" Quick concern in his voice.

"Distraught. And missing."

"Missing? Like Celeste is missing?"

I hoped not. "No. She was afraid to go home this morning, so she crashed at my place for a few hours. Now she seems to have decamped without a word."

He gave a relieved laugh. "That's typical Marie behavior, I'm afraid. She doesn't like to be obligated, and she really hates saying goodbye."

"So where would she have gone?"

"She's probably at work."

Right. I had that number. I'd call her there.

But there was no answer from Marie's company, and still no answer on her cell phone. And I couldn't help worrying about her, even though I knew I probably didn't need to.

I got up to get a glass of water, then stood at window, staring at the clouds drifting by. The sky was pearly gray, the clouds mixed shades of darker gray and white.

Good, no rain, decided one part of my brain, while the other part debated how I'd paint something so monochrome. The flatness of the light against the buildings across the way made for a challenge that had my fingers itching for a paintbrush.

Marie was missing.

The police were working on Callum's murder, and I wasn't likely to hear anything soon.

I couldn't afford to assume that Celeste's disappearance was because of something that happened in Brenton, but nor could I assume it wasn't. I was going to have to pursue both possibilities.

And I was going to need some help.

I dialed Marie's cell again. This time I got an "out of service area" message. Oh, that wasn't good.

Had she panicked and left town without saying anything? I could track down the phone company she dealt with, but I wasn't likely to get far until she'd been missing longer.

I called Marie's company again—they hadn't heard from her. It didn't seem to worry them, though. They'd simply reassigned her route.

"Does this happen often?" I asked.

"Oh, sure. It's always something with our bike guys. They think of themselves as independents who choose to work from us when it suits them. Mostly it suits them."

"With Marie, I mean."

"Same, same."

"Can you ask her to call me if you hear from her?"

"Sure thing."

Right. I finished my water, locked up and headed for the car. Maybe Marie had gone home.

I cruised by their house, rang the bell. Nothing. So not only did I have a missing persons case, I now had a missing client on the same case.

I tried Ben again. He still hadn't heard from Marie, nor had he heard any further rumors about Callum's death. I checked my notes.

Kyle Hanlon. He was the Two Hearts guy who said he'd met once with Celeste, and I'd seen him talking with Callum at Mandino's. It was time to pay him a visit.

Maybe it would shake loose some bit of information that would make this case come together for me.

CHAPTER TWENTY-SIX

Kyle Hanlon's office was on a high floor, very sleek, with far too many reflective surfaces for my taste. I name-dropped shamelessly to the receptionist and was shown into a spacious meeting room with a spectacular view of the harbor, despite my lack of a prior appointment.

Kyle himself joined me in less than five minutes, all smiles and charm, which was replaced by a flash of confusion as soon as I introduced myself. Then the smiles were back.

"Ms. O'Grady. It's a pleasure to meet you. And did I not see you at Mandino's the other night, with a very charming friend?"

"Thank you for seeing me," was all I said. "I appreciate it."

"And what can I do for a private investigator?"

"I'm looking into the disappearance of Celeste Deslauriers. She's been missing nearly a week now, and one of her friends mentioned that she had coffee with you a week before she vanished."

"I'll do anything I can to help, but I barely know her." His tone was deep and sincere, and his gaze direct.

It set off my bullshit detector. He probably practiced that look in front of the mirror. You can't tell me anyone does that naturally.

"When did you meet?"

"We had coffee at Starbucks one evening, a couple of weeks ago. Let me check." He pulled out his phone. "Yes, on the fifth. We met at eight, and we went our separate ways around nine-thirty."

"You haven't heard anything from her since?"

"Nothing at all, I'm afraid."

"Did she say anything that might give me some clue as to where to start looking for her?"

"No, nothing."

"Nothing about upcoming travel plans?"

"Nothing at all, I'm afraid. It was a first meeting, and we mostly talked about generalities."

"Like what?"

"Oh, like where we grew up, our jobs, our hobbies, things like that."

"And what are Celeste's hobbies, do you recall?"

"Golf, mostly," he said. "Though I recall she said she'd like to travel if she ever had both time and money to do so. We compared notes on places we'd like to travel."

"Do you remember hers?"

"Buenos Aires, which surprised me, and Paris, which didn't," was the reply.

"Oh?"

"What woman doesn't dream of Paris?" he said. Yup, there was something condescending there. "But Buenos Aires?"

"Did she explain?"

"Tango lessons. Apparently she loves to dance and has always wanted to learn to tango authentically."

Interesting. I was betting this was another fact that Marie didn't know about her older sister.

I wondered whether checking flights to either city for the day Celeste disappeared would be a total waste of time. By now I was clutching at straws. I wasn't happy about that.

I still took time to irritate Kyle, though. "And where would you go?"

"Africa on safari. And the Amazon jungles."

Had a little cliché of our own at work, did we? I had to bite my tongue hard to keep the words back. It's always a challenge when I find suspects annoying.

I keep wanting to slap them down verbally, but that just makes them less likely to let fall those incriminating details. "What about her job? Is there anything she mentioned that stuck with you?"

"Nothing connected to her disappearance, I'm sure."

"At this point I think we need to consider anything. Please share what you do remember."

He looked a little uncomfortable. "Some of her donors are clients of ours."

"Surely you didn't compare?" It wasn't the idea that he might do so that shocked me—I didn't have much of an opinion of him anyway. I had trouble believing Celeste was capable of such pettiness.

"No, no. I already knew they had buildings named after them, so they were major donors. And none of them are my clients directly."

So much for his professionalism. "Did Celeste mention any difficulties at work, or with any of her donors?"

"We'd just met. It was too soon for confidences," he reminded me.

"No good natured complaining, or little jokes?"

"Celeste?" Now he sounded shocked. "She's much too elegant for that kind of behavior."

Hmmm. Yet another facet of the woman. "What about your backgrounds? You talk about them?"

"Sure, she came from some little whistle-stop a few hours out of town. She said she was very happy to leave there."

"She say why?"

"No, I'm afraid not."

"And where are you from?"

"I fail to see how that is relevant."

I grinned at him. "It isn't. But I like to do an informal survey, to see exactly how many people are really from somewhere else. So far it's running 90% non-Vancouverites."

He smiled back. "I'm sorry I can't reduce that statistic for you. I'm from Toronto. And you?"

He was lying. Why? "Vancouver girl, born and raised."

"One of the few, then."

I nodded, then hit him with it. "And how do you know Callum McLaughlan?"

"Callum? Oh, that's right. You would have seen us at Mandino's." He sobered. "I was shocked to hear the news of his death."

"Yes. Can you tell me how you know him?"

"We share several clients. And I'm afraid I can't tell you any more. But why are you so interested in how I know him? Is there some connection to Celeste's disappearance?"

"Celeste didn't tell you?"

"Tell me what?"

"Callum was her ex-husband." I wasn't mentioning Ben if she hadn't.

He went white. "And you think Celeste may be…?"

"I hope not. But I need to find her, and soon. So I have a few more questions."

He nodded, face still pale.

"Now that you know about the connection between the two of them, did Callum ever mention anything that might have a bearing on her disappearance?"

"No. Nothing."

"And do you know of any enemies Callum may have had?"

"Callum? No!" He still looked shell-shocked, and it felt genuine.

I handed him my card. "If you think of anything, anything at all that might have some bearing on our finding her, please give me a call."

I still didn't like him, but I didn't think he'd been involved in Celeste's disappearance or Callum's death. Leaving me back at square one.

Jerry was my next best option, and he still hadn't called me back. And there was still nothing from Marie.

So what did I do now?

———

I WAS HALFWAY BACK to my car when the phone rang. I glanced at the number. Jerry. Maybe he had news?

No such luck. What Jerry had was more questions. It seemed that this case had far more questions than answers.

"Any chance you've heard from Marie Deslauriers recently?" he said.

"This about Callum McLaughlan's death?"

"Yeah. We need to talk to her. Don't suppose you'd know where to find her?"

I briefly debated telling him only the basics, but we needed to find Marie, and fast. Confidentiality needed to take second place. "I've been trying to get in touch with her since this afternoon."

"You know where she was this morning?"

That's my Jerry—doesn't miss anything. "Yeah. She showed up at my office, distraught. Crashed at my place for a couple hours, then vanished."

"No note?"

"Nothing. You have any leads?" I asked as I reached my car, and unlocked it.

"No. We've been trying to locate her," he said absently. "So she came straight from talking to us to your office?"

I slid into the seat, locking the car doors with thunk. "I don't know," I said. "She got to the office not much after seven."

"That's about when we finished talking to her."

"Then yes, she came straight to my office," I said, and wondered exactly what that meant. Probably nothing good, the way this case had been going.

"Huh. I wonder why."

"She said something about asking Callum to look into records from the bank branch her father managed twenty years ago. I gather she was afraid that he'd done a search that had somehow caught Danny Deeping/David Farrow-Whyte's attention."

"Yeah, she tried to tell us something like that. She was pretty incoherent, and it didn't make much sense."

"I think it's worth looking into, Jerry."

"Some twenty-year-old unproven bank fraud? Do you know how stretched we are?"

"Yes, but it could be the root of this whole thing."

"We'll get to it."

I could just imagine when. "What about the deaths of Danny Deeping/David Farrow-Whyte's parents? Did you get my e-mail?"

From the silence I knew he hadn't read it. "What about them?"

"Apparently the deaths were suspicious. I wondered if any of that suspicion fell on Danny? And how strong his alibi was?"

"How long ago?"

"Six years."

Jerry groaned. "I'll get back to you."

"It's important, Jerry. And it could be a stronger link to Callum's death than the files Marie thinks Callum was digging into."

"Okay, okay. I'll get to it as soon as I can."

"And let me know if you find Marie?"

"Yeah, yeah."

I wasn't going to be able to sleep easily, so I started the car, drove home and started a new painting.

Spreading strong color onto a blank canvas was strangely satisfying, even though I was mainly doing the underpainting, blocking in the main shapes. I could have used Cat's company, but he didn't show up.

Which was probably just as well. He's far too interested in the movement of wet brushes on canvas. And I was too distracted by my thoughts to keep him from participating.

CHAPTER TWENTY-SEVEN

I called Marie's cell far too early the following morning. Still nothing.

I was getting really concerned about her.

Was it possible that whoever had kidnapped Celeste had grabbed her too? I needed to bounce ideas off of someone. Jaimie came to mind. Even if it was too early to call anyone.

But Jaimie immediately agreed to meet me before she saw her first patient, suggesting a Blenz near her office. Apparently she liked the tea there. Luckily they had good coffee too. I was going to need it.

The coffee shop was warm and brightly lit, a nice contrast to the chill drizzle outside. The place was mostly empty, except for Jaimie at a table by the window and a young couple near the back. Jaimie already had a pot of tea steaming in front of her.

I shook the rain off my jacket, took an appreciative sniff of fresh roasted coffee, and went to grab a cup.

"If I hadn't told her about it in the first place, I don't think Celeste would even have told me about joining Two Hearts," Jaimie said, raising her teacup. "I think she was a little embarrassed."

I downed half a cup of their strongest coffee. "Did she tell Marie before she told you?"

"I doubt it. As far as I know, she didn't tell Marie at all."

But Marie had known. They lived together—it probably hadn't been hard to find out. Unless Marie was the link to Danny finding out about Two Hearts?

"Can I ask you something else?"

She tilted her head a little, her eyes assessing. "It's about the case, but it makes you uncomfortable." It was a statement.

"Wait a minute. Is this the psychologist or the psychic talking?"

She grinned, but it didn't undermine the calm certainty she seemed to wear like a blanket. "A little of both. What is it, Barbara?"

So this was her professional persona. I was impressed, but oddly pleased to see the airy spirit I'd first met peeking through. I began to see why she and Celeste were friends. "What's your take on Marie?"

"Marie?"

Just the question, nothing more. Definitely the professional persona.

I nodded. "I'd rather not tell you why just yet, but I'd appreciate your impressions of the relationship between the sisters. Especially Marie's relationship with Celeste."

She was watching me closely, nodding a little. "So you've already figured out that Celeste is very protective of Marie."

Again it was a statement. Knowing that she claimed to be psychic made her certainty a little eerie.

"Yes. It's been pretty clear from everyone I talked to. What I'm curious about is why she's so protective. Marie's an adult now."

"And this will help you find Celeste?"

"Let's just say I think I need the information now or I wouldn't be asking."

She considered that for a moment, taking a sip of her tea. As I waited for her decision, I wondered how many people successfully lied to this woman. Not many, I was guessing.

Finally she nodded. "Celeste has only told me parts of this, the rest I've put together. Their childhood was—not easy, particularly after their father died."

"Yes, Marie told me about the bank failure, his death and something about their aunt."

"She did? She must be more worried about Celeste than I'd realized. Normally she won't talk about any of it."

Jaimie didn't wait for a response. "I don't know how much she told you, but the aunt was a—difficult personality. Very artistic, and very bitter. Celeste escaped from her as soon as she could."

"By going to university," I said. "And leaving Marie behind."

"Yes. Celeste has always felt guilty about that."

Given my own reactions to Swan's paintings, to the bitterness and the gloom in them? The idea of a young Marie being trapped in that house—I could see why Celeste might feel guilt. "There wasn't much she could do."

"That doesn't matter to how she feels about it, though."

No, it wouldn't. "Any idea how Marie feels about it all?"

"She didn't tell you?"

"She might have been going to. She asked me to look at her aunt's paintings, and then talk to her."

"And?"

"I didn't get the chance. Marie's disappeared."

"What?"

"She came to me right after she found out about Callum's death, said she was afraid to go home. She had a nap at my place, then left the key and vanished. I can't reach her."

"Oh no." Jaimie closed her eyes and her face took on that listening expression.

I waited. Skeptical I might be, but if she could find Marie, I didn't care how she did it.

But when her eyes opened, she shook her head.

"Nothing?" I said.

"No."

"What does that mean?"

"Might not mean anything. Finding people is not one of my strong gifts."

Okay then. "So what is your impression of Marie's relationship with Celeste?"

Jaimie sighed. "I've never even told this to Celeste. But I think she loves her, is overawed by her and resents her, all at the same time."

"Over-awed?"

Another shrug. "Celeste succeeds at everything she does. Or so it appears from the outside."

"Except relationships?" It takes one to know one.

"Well, yes. On the other hand, there's Marie, who never went to university, has no career, seems to have few friends and has no obvious relationships."

"You're hedging."

A broad smile. "And you're good. Yes. She hides much of her life from Celeste, and I suspect she has both friendships and relationships that her sister never learns about."

"But the resentment is real?"

"Yes. Very real. All the stronger for being largely repressed."

"What if something triggered it? How would Marie react?"

"Badly. And it could be an excessive reaction." She sipped her tea, but her expression was strained. "You're wondering if Marie had a more active role in Celeste's disappearance than we'd assumed."

"Hypothetically, can you think of any incident that might have triggered such a thing for Marie?"

"Is this Danny guy real?"

I nodded. "Very real."

"Then it's possible Marie either helped him meet Celeste or hired him," Jaimie said thoughtfully.

Hired him? That hadn't occurred to me.

Why had it occurred to her?

"So it had to be something that ran deep, something tied to childhood," Jaimie was saying. "Celeste didn't mention—wait a minute. She said something about Marie being unrealistic again, thinking she could be like their mother. What Celeste called Marie's refusal to live in the real world was a recurring theme."

"Any idea what she meant by that?"

"She wouldn't tell me."

"What about the reference to her mother?"

"She'd never mentioned her before."

Neither had Marie. And I was going to find out why.

———

THERE WAS no sign of Marie when I got to the office. It was still pretty early, though. I opened my laptop, started searching into Marie's background. It beat worrying about her.

Tracking down Marie's mother proved no easy task, though. All I could find were the basics—name, dates of birth, marriage and death. Her name was Eleanor, and she'd been born in Vancouver, as had her sister Anthea. She had died in Brenton, too—the same as her husband and her sister had. Though Eleanor had died in childbirth, not by suicide.

Brenton hadn't been a lucky town for that family.

Eleanor had graduated high school and married young. Celeste didn't come along for a couple of years, but I couldn't find any record of a job. Didn't mean there hadn't been one, just that I couldn't find it.

A little more digging told me Celeste had been born in Vancouver, Marie in Brenton. I wondered why they'd moved. Guy's job? Something else? That was as far as I got.

Much as I hated to admit it, I needed Cory on this one, too. I checked my watch. He should be up now, right?

I sent a text, just in case. "You free this morning?"

"Yup. Why?" he sent back.

"Breakfast is on me. Check with your Mom it's okay."

"Pancakes?"

I wasn't in a cooking mood and my apartment was a disaster,

which tends to happen when I get caught up in a case. Or a painting.

But Guido's is open for breakfast on weekends. I could count on a quiet booth, and I can't resist his pancakes. "Sure. I'll collect you in twenty."

———

ONCE WE EACH had a stack of fluffy goodness in front of us, dripping with butter and Guido's homemade blackberry syrup, I told Cory that I had another project for him. "Are you up for it?"

His eyes lit up. "Same case?"

"Yes."

"Cool. What d'you want me to do?"

"You're on the clock now. Twenty dollars an hour to start?"

I hadn't seen a grin that wide since Jerry was his age. I'd never seen it from my sometimes too reserved nephew.

"Yes!" He punched the air.

I hid my laugh, grinned back. "Okay, then. Keep track of your hours. And don't forget to count the time you've already spent on this case."

He poured syrup with a lavish hand. "I'll invoice you. How much detail do you need?"

Huh. I hadn't expected this degree of sophistication. At his age I'd probably have jotted time spent on a sheet of paper torn out of a notebook.

"Well, I'll need to know which case you're working on—I'll give you a case number—then the project I've asked you to work on and the hours against that project. Can you do that?"

"No problem. How often do you want to be billed?"

Whoa. I had a budding entrepreneur here. I hoped Susanna was ready for the kind of kid she was raising. "Make it weekly for now, so I can get a feel for how long various things take you. Later we'll switch to monthly if that suits you?"

He didn't look up from cutting his pancakes. "Sure. But I don't do credit. You need to pay me right away."

I wondered if Godfrey talked business at the dinner table. Maybe there were positives to my workaholic brother-in-law that I'd overlooked.

"Fair enough," I said. "For this project, I need to know everything you can dig up on my client's late mother. I did some basic digging and didn't find much. But I need it fast. Any chance you could come back to the office for an hour or so now, see what you can find?"

"Mom's not expecting me home 'till dinner. I've got as much time as you need."

"Then eat up. You'll need the energy."

———

WHEN WE GOT BACK to my office, Cory made a beeline for the computer. He sat down and reached for the keyboard, then looked at me. "This okay?"

"Sure. I wanted to think some stuff through anyway." I grabbed my notebook and pen. "Want some coffee?"

"Yeah."

While I fixed our coffees, I watched him, fingers flying. He had that air of confidence you can't mistake. Computers were his thing.

Putting the coffee down beside him, I retreated to the guest chair with my own cup. "Cory?"

"Yeah?"

I waited until he pried his eyes from the screen to look at me. "If you're going to do this kind of work for me, you'll need a good computer."

He shrugged, but looked a little worried. "Mine will do what I need it to."

He'd misunderstood. "No, I meant that if you need to upgrade to a new computer, I'll advance you the money against future earnings."

He looked like I'd just given him the best gift ever. Who knew it was so easy to be Super Aunt?

"Really, you mean it? Any computer?"

I'd had a couple of lucrative cases lately so I was pretty flush—for now—but I know better than to offer a techie a blank check. "Within reason. Work out what you need for the work you'll be doing here, then we can talk about it."

"Wow. I can design exactly what I need, get it built…" Then the grin faded. "My mom won't let me."

"Let me talk to her. As long as the computer's not too expensive, I think she'll agree."

"Wow. Thanks!"

He reached for the mug I'd put beside him, gulped down a mouthful, and looked back at the screen. "I guess I'd better…" and I'd lost him.

I was deep in a review of Celeste's file, and had just started wondering where I'd put my notes on Danny when Cory's head popped up again. "I'm done."

Already? "What did you find?"

"Not a lot after she got married, but before that, she and her sister were both artists. Did you know the sister was some big-name artist, years later?"

"Yeah, I knew that," I said absently. Both sisters had been artists? "How did you find out?"

"They both studied art, here in Vancouver. Just for a year, though. Then the younger one left, and the older one did another year but then she quit too. Didn't finish, either."

"Where?"

"At Vancouver School of Art. Some pretty big names taught there."

"Yes, I know." It was now part of the Emily Carr University of Art and Design. "Anything else on them?"

"Well, I found a kind of assessment of the first year class. The guy teaching it put it in his journal, and now it's online at their archives."

That would be gold for a Swan scholar. "And?"

"Well, the younger sister was the better artist."

Wait a minute. The younger sister? "And Anthea was the older sister?"

Something in my voice had him staring at me. "Yeah, why?"

Because it helped explain part of her bitterness. "But the younger sister, Eleanor, she didn't paint again after she married?"

He shrugged. "No record of it. And she didn't exhibit anywhere."

"Is there any work still around from those years?"

"Nuh-uh. But in those same journals? I found the prof's reaction to some exhibit the first year students did. And then, the next year on how the second year students did."

"So both sisters would have exhibited the first year, but only Anthea in the second year, right?"

"Right."

"Let's see."

He nodded, hit a few keys and the printer warmed up. He handed me three sheets of paper. "These are all of the comments I found."

I skimmed through them. Whoa. This guy really hadn't liked Anthea Swan's work. Called it too dark, hated the edge of bitterness. He loved what he called the warmth and humanity of Eleanor's work.

But it was the description of the first year exhibits that stopped me cold. He described two paintings, very similar in look, completely opposite in tone.

"Any chance this professor is still alive?" I asked Cory.

"Nope. None of the teachers from back then are still around. And this was the only guy whose papers I could find online."

Still, I was lucky to have the journal entries. "Okay, thanks."

"Yeah."

I was getting a bad feeling about this. And I really wanted to see those paintings in Kathleen's collection again.

CHAPTER TWENTY-EIGHT

Afternoon sun glinted off the lettering on the Omega Gallery's windows. As I pushed through the glass doors, Ian Wong came forward, hand outstretched. "Barbara. It's a pleasure to see you again so soon."

I smiled, shook his hand and answered the unspoken question. "And you, Ian. I was hoping to take another look at your Swan collection."

He beamed, there was no other word for it. "I thought perhaps that was it. Your timing is superb—the collection will be moving on within a day or so. And I have new works to show you."

"It's nearly completed? Congratulations!"

I knew enough of his world to appreciate the hours and the connections it took to track down and purchase this many works by one artist. It meant that the collector, whoever he or she was, had very deep pockets. I wondered again who Kathleen was assembling this for.

"You must have been burning the midnight oil to pull it together so quickly."

He dipped his head in a funny little half bow. "It was a challenge I enjoyed. Now come with me so I can show it off."

I was more than willing to do so. "Before we do, I'd like to ask your opinion of a sketch, if it isn't too much of an imposition?"

"Not at all. Your work?" he asked, looking intrigued as I pulled the folded sheet that Marie had given me out of my bag.

"No. And I can't share the identity of the artist without permission. I wanted to verify my own opinion first."

"Ah." Eyebrows slightly raised, he reached for Marie's sketch of Danny. He considered it in silence for several moments, holding it closer to him then further away, angling it to catch the light. "Interesting. Very interesting."

He sounded intrigued, or was I imagining it? Ian's poker face is very good—perfected by years as an art dealer. "Oh?"

"Hmm. Does the artist have more work?"

I had no idea if Marie had done other things, but I suspected she must have. The lines and shading of the drawing were too assured to be an early work. "Yes."

"There is talent here. It needs training, but I certainly see possibilities."

From him, it was a rave review. That's what I'd thought.

Yet Marie didn't seem to be following that spark. Why not? Was it a result of being raised by Anthea Swan?

Ian handed back the sketch and preceded me down the hall. When we reached the back room where the Swan's were displayed, I stopped, stunned.

The temporary room holding the paintings had been expanded with more of the ubiquitous dividers on wheels, and all of Swan's paintings were framed and hanging. The impact was overwhelming.

"Wow." I stood there, letting my eyes sweep from work to work, taking it all in. "Just wow."

Another little smile. "I knew you would appreciate it."

I wondered if Kathleen had seen it, and if it met her expectations. How could it not? In one room, she'd captured the evolution of an artist.

I looked again. No, that wasn't quite right. What was it I was seeing?

I turned to Ian. "Which works have you added since I last saw it?"

"You can't tell?"

I looked again, pointed to a particularly strong evocation of a decaying Brenton. "That one."

"Correct. It was one of her last paintings."

"Which one is her final painting?"

He frowned. "We weren't asked to collect that one."

Interesting. I'd have to ask Kathleen why not.

I looked around the room again, then focused on the early paintings. "That one—the portrait of the artist. That wasn't here before."

He nodded again. "You have a good eye. Yes, that one was very difficult to acquire. It's a pair to the one of her sister, yet the emotional texture is quite different.

It's closer in spirit to some of her other early works, whereas the one of her sister ties better to her later works. Obviously the relationship with her sister was a source of deep conflict for Swan."

He strolled over to the paintings in question. I followed, my eyes glued to the new acquisition.

"Which is the better painting?" I asked him.

"Technically the one of the sister. However, this one," and he indicated Swan's harsh features and tightly controlled hands. "This has more depth. Her self-knowledge, even at that age, was extraordinary. It allowed her to paint a stronger, more mature portrait."

If she'd painted it.

I looked from one portrait to the other. Two young women, clearly related. The sister was pretty, and Swan might have been called handsome were it not for the bitterness in her eyes. But what was a good bone structure in one was too strong in the other.

I glanced at their hands. On the sister's left hand was a small engagement ring. Even in paint it seemed to sparkle. I glanced from the ring to Anthea's bitter eyes. Had Eleanor just become engaged to Guy when these portraits were done?

I glanced around the room, wondering if the student works described in the journal might be here, but didn't see them.

I offered a copy of the journal fragment describing Eleanor's painting to Ian. "Does this sound like a painting you've ever come across?"

He read it rapidly, then gave me a considering look. "Where did you get this?"

"I'd rather not say at the moment. But when my investigation is complete, I'll come back and tell you."

"Fine. On that condition then." He looked at the page he held. "Clearly this describes one of Swan's early works—it sounds very like this one," and he nodded towards a sunny landscape of Brenton. "If it still exists, it could be very valuable indeed."

Hmmm. I handed him the page where I'd printed out the description of Swan's student painting. "And this one?"

He scanned it, and I could feel his excitement. "Another early work, but this one presages the passion and the vision of the later works she'd do. Side by side, they capture a soul in conflict. I must ask again. Where did you get this?"

My mind was spinning.

Without answering him, I walked over to examine each of the early paintings more closely. Tags had been added with the painting's title and estimated date when it was painted. In a few cases, the painting itself bore the date, but most did not.

"How accurate are these dates?" I asked.

Ian came to stand at my shoulder. We both looked at a bright landscape.

"It depends. Some we have been able to date very accurately. Others are guesses."

"What about the later paintings?"

"The ones painted after Swan's discovery are accurate."

I nodded, continuing my slow circuit of the gallery, noting

painting styles and dates, correlating them with what I knew of Anthea Swan's life. And her sister's.

I was now pretty sure that at least a dozen of the works on display were done by Eleanor, and not Anthea. I was itching to ask Ian questions that would confirm it, but to do so would probably let him know exactly what I was thinking.

And I wasn't sure I could trust him not to use that knowledge before I'd sorted out the implications for my case. And my client.

"I need to know more about Anthea Swan, as a person, not an artist. Did she have friends that might talk to me? Fellow artists she was close to?"

He was already shaking his head no. "Swan was a loner. She kept herself to herself. We were her dealer for years, and our relationship never progressed past the professional. Despite our best efforts. I suspect that the only ones left alive who knew her the way you're talking about are her nieces."

And maybe her former neighbors in Brenton? "There's no-one else?"

"I can't think of anyone. Sorry."

"Who handles Swan's estate?"

He named a prominent legal firm. "Ask for Jonathan Saddler."

I could see he wanted to ask more questions, which he probably knew I wouldn't answer. Not yet.

"Thanks," I said, and meant it. "I'll be in touch."

That little smile appeared again. This time it made me uncomfortable. "I'll be expecting your call."

Something about his tone reminded me that I now had a foot firmly back in the art world, and this man had power in that world.

But I refused to be intimidated. Not now, nor ever again.

"I'll keep it in mind."

———

JONATHAN SADDLER WAS EXACTLY the executor I would have expected Swan to appoint—high-powered and connected, though he had to be pushing seventy now. I had wondered if she'd managed to make real money from her belated fame. One look at Saddler's understated office told me she'd done very nicely, thank you.

"I understand you're a private investigator. How can I help you, Ms. O'Grady?"

"I represent one of Anthea Swan's nieces, who is currently missing. The case is complicated, and I can't give you details, but I need to know if your client left anything to her nieces?"

He stared back at me across an expanse of polished wood, then leaned back in a tall, webbed chair. I'd expected smooth Italian leather, to go with the wood, but I guessed he had a bad back. It made him more human, and I liked him for it, even if he was spending too long deciding whether to tell me anything.

"Since Brian Stewart speaks highly of you and since neither of the two young women benefited, I suppose I can share at least that information," he said, just as I was about to prompt him.

I'd assumed that there had been some amount, though the frugal way they lived suggested it wasn't lavish. "Nothing?"

"No."

"So where did the money go? I assume there was quite a lot of it."

"Charities, mostly. And yes, she left a tidy sum."

And nothing to her nieces. There was a story there. "Do you know who handled her brother-in-law's estate?"

"One of my former colleagues did so. It was left to my client, in trust for the daughters."

"I understood that the estate was primarily a life insurance settlement?" It was a guess, but I was pretty sure I was right.

"Correct. And I believe almost all of it went to raise the children."

I wondered how much of that had been spent on paint and canvas. "So there was no ongoing income for them, once their aunt passed on?"

"I can't speak to specifics, but that was my understanding at the time."

That explained quite a bit.

I wondered if the estate had stretched to cover Celeste's university costs, or if she was still paying those off?

And no wonder Marie hadn't gone to university. Or art school, despite the professional quality of the drawing she'd done.

No wonder she didn't want to talk about her work. And had an aunt-sized chip on her shoulder.

"Will that be all?"

I started to say yes, then realized that something was niggling at me. "I'd like to speak with your colleague, Guy Deslauriers' lawyer. Does he still practice?"

He gave me an odd look, but nodded and picked up the phone. "He doesn't see many new people these days, but I'll put in a word."

I walked out with an address and a time for my appointment, thanking him profusely. And he got up from behind his desk, took my elbow, and escorted me to the door.

You don't see the old-fashioned courtesies much any more. Probably just as well. They make me feel like an awkward teenager again.

———

GUY DESLAURIERS' former lawyer could not have been more different from the one his sister-in-law had chosen. Partly retired or not, I suspected the craggy face and rumpled suit hadn't changed much over the years. Nor would the kindness I saw in his eyes.

When I explained what I wanted to know, and why, Edward Chalmers hesitated for only a moment before explaining in some detail. I took notes carefully.

"So the insurance paid out?" I said as he finished. "I thought Guy committed suicide?"

"It was my understanding that, officially, suicide wasn't proven."

Ah. You gotta love small towns. "So, when he committed suicide —he knew it was the only way there would be money to feed his kids?"

"That would be it."

I wondered if Marie knew that. I was guessing Celeste did, though I don't know what I based that on. Maybe just the fact that Celeste seemed to have got on with her life, while Marie just seemed—stuck.

Almost as stuck as Danny Deeping seemed to be.

Now where had that thought come from?

I thanked him and left, wishing he still had an active practice. I needed a good lawyer.

CHAPTER TWENTY-NINE

I was beginning to get a sense of what was going on, but I needed to talk to an expert. And Jaimie the psychic-psychologist was the only one I could trust to understand the whole picture.

How odd was that?

I unlocked my car and called her. We arranged to meet at Café Buzz again after she saw her last client. She didn't even ask why. I guess there was something in my voice.

I got there early, so I grabbed an Americano and sat down to think about what I'd just learned. From what I'd seen, Anthea Swan had always resented her younger sister. Eleanor had not only been the better artist, she'd probably quit art school to marry the man Anthea had wanted.

And then Eleanor had kept painting instead of devoting herself to her husband and family.

I suspected most of those early paintings were Eleanor's. I was guessing Anthea Swan hadn't started painting again until after her sister's death. Maybe she couldn't afford to, and it was only when she came to keep house for Guy Deslauriers and his motherless daughters that she took it up again.

Or maybe she felt she couldn't compete with Eleanor. Whatever. Then when Guy died, she channeled all of her grief into painting, almost completely ignoring the girls.

I considered everything I'd learned about Benton. And Bet's reaction to Anthea. Did Anthea just blame Brenton for Guy's death?

Or had Bet tried to talk to Anthea Swan about how she was raising the two girls?

Anthea hated the town so much she made it a byword for small town gone bad. And she resented her sister's daughters so much she didn't leave them a penny of her new-found wealth, even though some of it came from their mother's paintings.

Maybe I was totally wrong. But if I wasn't?

What would Eleanor's paintings be worth now, if they weren't seen as Anthea Swan's early work?

Maybe nothing. But then again… Who could I trust enough to ask? Ian? Kathleen?

Given her specialty in the defining works of certain artists, Kathleen might know how to position such a discovery so that both artists' work grew in value. Or she might want to ignore it, depending on how much she was making from her current client. Either way, it wasn't likely to benefit the girls.

All of Swan's paintings had been sold long ago. Marie and Celeste would have a claim against their aunt's estate, though—if it could be proved that some of that estate had, in fact, come from paintings their mother had painted and Swan had taken.

But sorting out the details of such a claim and the paintings involved could take months, if not years. Which wasn't going to help Marie.

It struck me that I still didn't know why Anthea Swan had committed suicide. I gave a half-laugh. Maybe Marie found out about her mother's paintings and threatened to expose her.

Now where had that thought come from?

Marie hadn't even known her mother. Though she clearly had artistic abilities of her own.

Anthea Swan had to have stored her sister's paintings somewhere. When had she produced them for her dealer? And had she always intended to pass them off as her own?

Had Marie even seen them?

And what about Celeste? Did she remember her mother painting? Her comment about Marie suggested that Celeste had at least known her mother was also an artist.

All this art history was fascinating, but it wasn't getting me any closer to finding Celeste. Or Marie. And if there was any possibility that Danny had killed before…

Before I could get myself any further tangled in my own thoughts, Jaimie arrived. I waved her over.

"Thanks for coming," I said. "I'll get us some wine. Red?"

"Please."

When I returned with our glasses, she'd taken her suit jacket off and was looking more relaxed. I peeked under the table. Yup, her shoes were off too.

"Long day?" I asked, putting the glass in front of her.

"Complicated day," she said. "Cheers."

"Cheers."

"You look like you've had a pretty long day too."

"You could say that."

"Any closer to finding them?"

I shrugged. "I wish I knew."

She glanced at the notes I'd been making. The page was covered with cross-outs, arrows, and comments jammed in any which way. "Need a sounding board?"

What the hell. "Please."

"Why don't you lay it out for me."

I glanced around. No-one near enough to hear, and the few occupied tables on the other side of the room were mostly wearing headphones and focused on their laptops. "Can I ask you to keep this confidential?"

She grinned. "Give me a dollar."

"That works for psychologists, too?"

"Sort of. It's as good as anything. For the next hour you're a client, and I'll treat everything you say in confidence."

"Thanks." And I proceeded to lay it out for her, the whole mess, speculations and all. She listened without speaking the whole time, her attention focused on each word.

"That explains some things," she said slowly once I'd finished. "And did you say Marie is an artist too?"

"I think so. She drew that sketch of Danny."

"I hadn't realized that was hers." Jaimie paused, sipped her wine. "And their mother was an artist? So that could be what Celeste was referring to when she said Marie was being unrealistic. Apparently her latest plan was to take tattoo lessons, and Celeste refused to help her pay for it. Which of course put an end to that."

She nodded, seemingly to herself. "If the tattooing plan was the latest in a series of artistic interests for Marie, it would explain the underlying resentment I've seen in her. She hasn't been able to follow her passion, maybe can't even admit it to herself. And after her aunt's stellar example, Celeste could be ruling out anything artistic as a career option for her much younger sister."

It fit with what I'd seen. "Which Marie would just resent more."

"Especially since she's basically always been dependent on her sister."

"I'm guessing as a psychologist you'd see that as a warning sign?"

She nodded. "I've even tried to talk to Celeste about it, because it isn't healthy for either of them, but she just gets defensive."

"How not healthy? Would Marie helping Danny get closer to Celeste fit that kind of not healthy?"

"Yes, especially if she didn't know he came from Brenton."

I still didn't know how seriously to take Marie's latest fears about Danny. Not until I had more than an uneasy feeling about his role in his parent's death. "So how do you see Danny's motivation?"

"My guess is he's fixated on Celeste, and that's why he's kidnapped her. She could have become symbolic for him of a lost, idyllic childhood. Could be revenge. Probably a combination of both."

"How would you describe Danny?"

"In psychology terms? Given what you've told me, he's a loner, very good with computers, not so good around people, a planner. Possibly delusional."

"A sociopath?"

"Probably, or at least somewhere on that scale. This is all about him. Everything that's happened to him will be about how it impacted him. Celeste may be a bonus, a reparation…"

"Or a sacrifice."

"Yes."

"But if he's kept her alive this long?"

"We don't know he has," she said bluntly. "And you're saying that now he may have Marie."

"That's what I'm afraid of."

"Then you need to find him, and fast. But you already know that."

"I know his new name, his address. He isn't there. How do I find him?"

She shook her head. "I don't know. You need to begin to understand his patterns. As it is, you have no way to reach him and no way to predict what he might do next. You need more."

"Brenton, here I come?"

She nodded. "That's what I'd suggest. You need to get at the root of his patterns. It might be worth talking to people from his university days, his last few jobs. But since his relationship with Celeste dates back to childhood—I think that's where you're most likely to find the connections and the patterns that might help you."

I nodded. "You're confirming what I was thinking myself."

"Can you go to the police?"

"I've given them what I have, but there's not enough to tie Danny to Celeste's disappearance. Not without Marie."

"And there's still no sign of her?"

"Nothing."

———

I WAS JUST STARTING the engine when my cell rang. Jerry. I turned the car off, grabbed for the phone.

"Jerry? Have you got something for me on the Farrow deaths?"

"Yeah. I've just got the highlights—that's all they've digitized. Doesn't look like the sons were in the frame anyway, but your Danny has an alibi. He was working that night. Seems he's some kind of computer guy and he was online at the pertinent time."

Cory had said Danny had to be an awesome hacker to have changed his identity so thoroughly. "According to my source, Danny can make computers sing."

A pause. "And manufacture alibis?"

"That would be my guess. Was there anyone else they suspected but couldn't link the arson to? Any firebugs with similar patterns?"

"Apparently not. But even if your Danny was involved in his folks' death, that was arson, and this one's a shooter. There's nothing to suggest he's the guy we're looking for now."

"Except Marie."

"Who's missing. And who wasn't making a whole lot of sense before she went missing."

I could imagine. "Just let me know if you hear from Marie. Oh, and it might be worth letting Cathy Yip know, too what you've found out." Just in case.

"Already did," he said, and rang off.

Well, that was helpful. But his information could put Danny in the frame for the murder of his parents. Which led me to wonder whether he'd had anything to do with the rash of suicides that seemed to surround this case.

Or was I reaching?

I wasn't getting any closer to finding Celeste—let alone Marie— and it felt like I had a clock counting down in my head.

Jerry was right. I couldn't afford to focus solely on Danny Deeping—what if he wasn't the guy who'd taken Celeste?

CHAPTER THIRTY

The following morning I was on the road for Brenton by five, despite the pouring rain. I couldn't help noticing how few truckers were on the Canyon Highway. Would towns like Brenton eventually just wither away?

The diner was open, but mostly empty at this hour. I pushed open the doors, to be welcomed by a cheery jingle of bells and the rich scent of fresh-brewed coffee. I could have done without the bells.

Bet came out of the back room at the sound and raised an eyebrow at the sight of me. "You must have been up early?"

She knew there was a story. "Coffee first."

With a grin she poured a stream of fresh black goodness into a thick mug and handed it to me. "Just brewed."

I might just survive today.

"And the muffins are still warm. Oatmeal-rhubarb-raspberry and chocolate-pineapple-coconut."

For food like that I'd double my run. "I'll have one of each. And more coffee?"

She plated the muffins and topped up my cup, then poured

herself a cup and lit a cigarette. Seeing my eyes on the smoke, she waved a hand at me. "Too early for the tobacco Nazis to be out. You don't mind?"

I love the scent of fresh tobacco burning, but I loathe the smell once it's gone stale. I'm not big on what it does to the lungs either, but hey, it was her place. And if smoking would get her in the mood to talk, I'd put up with it. "I don't mind."

"Then shoot."

I grinned. "No pleasantries for you, huh?"

She snorted out a laugh, waved the cigarette at me in a "go on" gesture.

It was time to put everything on the table. "I'm still looking for Danny Deeping. He's been going by Whyte lately, though the family used Farrow after they left here. I need to know anything you can tell me about what might have caused him to kidnap Celeste Deslauriers a week ago."

I sat back, took a bite of chocolate, coconut and banana and nearly stopped breathing, it was that good. Then I glanced over at Bet and lost my breath again.

She'd gone white, and her face was tight and pinched-looking.

"Danny Deeping kidnapped Celeste Deslauriers?" The voice was wispy, almost too soft to hear.

"Yes."

"Oh, God."

"What? What do you know?"

"I'd hoped never to have to think about this again," Bet said.

"Celeste's life is in danger."

Possibly. Probably. Danny might not be a killer, though, and if he was, he might not kill Celeste.

I didn't care. I needed to find her. And Marie.

She let out a long stream of smoke. "First you need to know the facts, I'll also tell you what I suspect. Then you need to go talk to Old Joe."

I got out my notebook. "Go on."

"When the mine failed and all the loans got called, some folks left town right away. James Deeping was one who hung on, tried to make a go of it. Or so it seemed. Guy Deslauriers tried to help him and others like him, even though he'd been demoted back to assistant manager. Wasn't a lot he could do, but he tried."

She took a long drag on her cigarette. "Poor Guy. He lasted a couple of years, getting more gaunt by the day, until finally he couldn't take any more."

"How did he die?"

"Suicide."

"No, I meant how did he kill himself?"

"Oh. Gunshot. To the forehead."

I wrote it down, frowning. It's one of the less reliable ways to kill yourself. "Who did the investigation?"

"Sheriff. He's dead now. Wasn't much of an investigation anyway. They had the gun, the body and everyone knew how guilty Guy felt. Nobody questioned it."

"What about the coroner?"

"Local doctor. He didn't question it either."

"He around?"

"Died years ago. Fourteen?" She paused. "No, it'd be seventeen years now." She sucked smoke into her lungs, held it as though trying to hold onto a memory.

"What happened to the Deepings?"

She watched smoke blow up to the ceiling. "They left town a couple months later, followed by a bunch of bad checks he'd been writing. Some pretty ugly customers came looking for him. Never heard if they found him."

"Ugly customers?"

She shrugged. "Fighters. Scars, cauliflower ears, guns."

"Guns? You mean hunting rifles?"

"Nope. Vegas-style ugly customers."

Maybe Danny wasn't responsible for his father's death, after all. Maybe James Deeping's past caught up with him. "Was he a gambler?"

She grinned. "We all thought he was our most upstanding citizen, the one destined to go far. Turns out he'd been speculating in the real estate he was supposed to be selling, and he'd tried to make up the deficit at the tables. Guess it backfired on him."

Wait a minute. "You're telling me one small town had a stock scam and a real estate fraud within a few years of each other, and they weren't connected?"

"I'm not telling you anything of the kind. You might try talking to Old Joe about stuff like that."

"I'm asking you."

She got up, poured us both more coffee. "Another muffin?"

She wasn't going to answer. Fine. For now. "I'll take another one of each, but to go. Those were amazing."

"Thanks. I'm pretty proud of those recipes."

"You should be." I added some cream to my coffee. "What can you tell me about Anthea Swan?"

"I think she was the only one not surprised when the Deepings left town so fast."

"Oh?"

"I always thought she blamed James Deeping for Guy's death. And she went out of her way to make sure he knew it. She was like a rattlesnake with prey. Waiting for the slightest move to attack."

Ugh. "Why did she blame him?"

"Neither of them ever said. But it got the town wondering. And the more we wondered, the more nervous he got, y'know?"

"You think Deeping senior killed him? Guy?"

"Question is, did Anthea think he killed Guy? I don't know. I always suspected she thought James said or did something that finally made Guy give up."

Something was niggling at me. "What was Danny doing during all of this? He'd be what, eleven or so?"

"Twelve." She didn't even have to think about it. "And he was in school, and mooning over the oldest Deslauriers girl."

"Celeste."

"She the one that's kidnapped?"

"Yeah."

We both thought about that for a minute

"It was kinda funny at the time. You'd never see her without him trailing behind. He'd hang around waiting for her to appear."

"What was her reaction?" I asked.

Pre-teen girls can be pretty cruel, and remembering those years always made me cringe. It hadn't taken much to embarrass me back then, and I'd tended to make smart remarks about whoever had caused the embarrassment.

Bet cackled. "She didn't return the sentiment, that was for sure. But she was good about it. Let him hang around her, but more as if he were an injured puppy that she was being kind to. He was a funny looking kid, quiet, and had that air as if he expected to get beaten."

"Did he? Get beaten, I mean."

She stubbed out her cigarette. "Like I said, his dad seemed like a fine, upstanding citizen. Why would he beat his kid? Or gamble and run stock frauds?"

More motive for Danny to kill his father? I needed to pass this on to Jerry. "What did Anthea Swan make of all this?"

A crack of laughter. "Are you kidding? She hated that kid almost more than his father. Yanked the girl away and sent him home every time she caught sight of him. Wasn't polite about it, either."

I could imagine. I could also imagine the humiliation Danny had felt.

How had it shaped him? "Was Anthea Swan friendly with anyone when she was here? Anyone she talked to?"

"No-one. Why?"

"What about her sister, Eleanor Deslauriers? Did she make friends here?"

"Yes. Everyone loved Nell."

"Anyone in particular?"

She reached for her cigarettes, lit up. "Yeah. Me."

"You?"

"She was my best friend."

———

I HADN'T SEEN that one coming.

Bet had been Eleanor's best friend? Bet?

It seemed an unlikely friendship, given the little I'd learned of Eleanor. I wondered who Bet had been, all those years ago.

"What was she like? Eleanor?" I asked Bet.

"Happy, in love, gentle, loved living here."

Smoke drifted between us, hiding her expression. "Everything her sister wasn't."

"How did Eleanor feel about her sister? About the fact that her sister wanted her husband?"

"Figured that out, did you?"

"Yup. I've seen a couple of the portraits."

"Huh. Nell knew, and it made her sad, but she never blamed her sister. Just didn't see much of her. But when she knew she was dying, she asked Guy to get her sister to help care for the girls."

A pause, a harsh drag on her cigarette. "She couldn't know that Anthea would blame them, too."

Oh, how awful. "Did Eleanor, Nell, paint too?"

"She painted until her second child was born. But she'd been ill leading up to it, and—she didn't survive the birth."

"I'm sorry."

"Yeah. What can you do?"

"Did she paint often?"

A nod. "She loved it. I'd walk out—and there she'd be, surrounded by her paints, at her easel, baby sleeping beside her."

Sounds like I'd been right in guessing who had painted the sunny paintings. "Did she have favorite spots?"

A shrug. "She never said. But she painted some places pretty often."

"Did other people see the paintings?"

"No. She was pretty private about them. Her husband and me, that's about it."

"You ever see any of Anthea's shows?"

"No, never got the chance and I wouldn't have if I could. I saw enough of that filth when she'd hang them here at the diner."

"Why did you dislike them so much?"

"You've seen them?"

"Yes."

"Well, then you know. Dark, ugly things. But for me, mighta been because she painted the same places her sister did. And I couldn't bear the fact that Anthea was alive and painting while Nell was gone."

There must have been more of Eleanor's paintings than the ones I'd seen. Did they still exist? "Bet, when the two girls moved to Vancouver…"

"You mean when the little one went to join her sister?"

I nodded. "What happened to their stuff?"

"All the furniture was sold or thrown away. Paintings went to that smarmy dealer Anthea had, from Vancouver."

"All the paintings?"

If I hadn't been looking hard, I would have missed her look of guilt. "There were more, weren't there? Of Eleanor—Nell's paintings, I mean?"

"Whatever do you…" Then she caught my expression and tailed off. She knew I'd figured it out. "Yes. There were."

"Where are they?"

She indicated upwards with a movement of her chin. "Attic. I wasn't keeping them. Not exactly. But when I saw what Anthea was doing with them, I cleared the rest of them out of there."

"What was she doing?"

"Painting over them. All those beautiful paintings with Nell's personality just shining out of them—and Anthea just slopped her dank ugly soul right over top. Always left just a hint of the earlier works peeking through. Those paintings were a desecration."

That gleam of joy in some of Swan's best known works. "How many?"

"Four I saw for sure. And I know she had others."

She must not have painted over all of them, because I'd seen a few of Eleanor's originals in Kathleen's collection. "How did you get them away?"

"Nell was my best friend. I knew she kept most of her paintings out in the old barn. She'd leave them there so the oil paint didn't harm her baby's lungs. That's the kind of person she was."

Years of pain and rage were spilling out. She couldn't seem to stop. "Not like that harpy who called herself her sister, then did her best to destroy those girls."

"And her girls need your help now," I told her. "Celeste has survived it all, if I can find her before Deeping kills her. It's Marie who's still suffering from what Anthea did to her."

Now I had her attention. "The little one too? What can I do?"

"Marie is an artist, but she's had no training. I suspect she could use some. She wants to learn, and there's been no money. If somebody doesn't help her become the artist she was meant to be, I think she'll drown in Anthea's bitterness."

"The poor kid. I tried to help her a few times, but I couldn't even reach her."

"How many of Nell's paintings rightfully belong to her daughters?"

She didn't hesitate. "All of them."

That's what I'd thought. "I think they might be worth some money. I have a couple of friends who are art dealers. Let me talk to them, see what I can do. If I bring one of them out, can you show us the paintings?"

She nodded.

"How many of them are of scenes that Anthea also painted?"

"Most of them. Even when Anthea didn't know Nell had painted a particular scene, she seemed drawn to it too."

Bet took a harsh drag on her cigarette. "There's a couple of portraits that bitch never saw."

"Portraits?"

"Sure. One of her baby, and one of her husband."

So Anthea had painted the one I'd seen. And it looked like we had a collection of paintings by two artists, sisters, with very different takes on life and their world. But were they valuable?

It had been Anthea's ability to shift from despair to hope that had first caught people's attention, and the apparent dichotomy had brought her fame.

Branding. It could make or break an artist—and the art world can be a fickle one.

What would happen to that fame when Anthea Swan was exposed as a thief? Would her sister's work be equally valuable? Or would Anthea's simply lose all value?

It was worth finding out.

"Tell me about Anthea's death."

She gave me a hard look. I waited, not giving anything away. "I'll tell you the facts, then I'll tell you what I suspect. But it's up to you to prove any of it. And you probably want to go talk to Old Joe."

"Okay."

She lit a new cigarette, refilled our cups before she answered. "You know she committed suicide?"

I nodded. "She took pills."

Bet snorted. "She died in the fire when their barn burned down. They said she took pills first. The barn was demolished, and she was deemed a suicide and given a very public funeral."

Another fire? Why didn't I know that? "Deemed? Wasn't there a note?"

"Caught that, did you? Yeah. There was a note, and I always wondered about it. Anthea was too mean to kill herself, plain and simple."

"So you think it was an accident? How do you explain the note?"

"The note?" She snorted. "Typical complaining. She sounded like that all the time. Life was too hard. She wasn't valued. It wasn't worth living as she had to."

I'd read excerpts from Anthea Swan's journals, which were hailed at the time as glimpses into the tragic soul of a tortured artist. Bet's take on it was almost amusing. Almost. "So why was this one seen as a suicide note?"

"You'd have to ask the cops. Besides, she was dead."

I wondered how the note would have been read in a different context, made a note to take another look at the biography of Anthea Swan I had on a shelf somewhere. It seemed to me that suicide note had been duplicated in it.

"So you do think it was an accident. The barn burning and her death, I mean?"

Bet blew out a cloud of smoke, didn't answer.

Danny's parents had been killed in a fire. "Or are you telling me she was murdered?"

"I'm not telling you anything. But you might want to find out who was in town that weekend."

"One of the facts, right?"

She nodded.

"So can we move on to what you suspect?"

That earned me a grin. "I'll never admit I said any of this. You'll have to confirm it, if you can. Right?"

"Sure. Go on."

"I suspect Deeping senior owed too much money to the wrong people and tried to make it back by cozying up to a stock promoter, running up worthless stock and convincing other people to buy it. Ended up ruining the town and blaming it on Guy Deslauriers. After Guy's death, my guess is Anthea found out something, and hounded Deeping out of town."

Marie must have heard something of this from her aunt. No wonder she said her father was an idiot, not a fraud. "How did Anthea find out if everyone else thought the man a saint?"

"Who knows? The woman was incurably nosy. And it killed her."

"It? Or he?"

She nodded at me. "Yup, you got it. I'm thinking he."

"Deeping again? But wasn't this years after he left town?"

Bet waved a cigarette at me, but ignored the question. "So

Anthea was gone, and no-one here mourned her. Least of all that poor, miserable little girl who cleared town the next day."

"And was Deeping senior in town when Anthea Swan died?"

"Go talk to Old Joe. I've told you everything I can."

"I will. And thanks."

"Don't thank me yet," she said, sucking in a lungful of smoke.

CHAPTER THIRTY-ONE

I called the newspaper office and Joe was already there, so I grabbed a couple of extra muffins and headed on over. The food was readily accepted, my questions less so.

But when I told him what I was looking for, and why, his whole demeanor changed. "So you're not looking for the scoop on Anthea Swan and her death?"

I'd finally worked it out—he was a journalist, it was second nature to protect his sources. And if Swan really had been murdered, he might have a bestseller on his hands.

"No," I assured him. "The only thing I want is anything that would lead me to why Danny Deeping might have kidnapped Celeste Deslauriers, and where he might have taken her."

I paused. "In fact, if you were writing a new biography of Anthea Swan…" I let my voice trail off, watching him closely.

He was an old newspaperman. His face gave nothing away. "Yeah?"

He hadn't denied it. That was all I needed to know. "I have quite a bit of information on her art that might play very well into the kind of story you're telling. And it would cause a sensation in the art world."

"Huh. You looking for writing credit?"

"No. I just want my client and her sister found. Unharmed." And maybe for them to get their rightful share of their mother's work. "After that, anything I've uncovered is yours."

He tapped long forefingers together. "Care to tell me any of it now?"

"My clients are my first priority. And based on what Bet told me just now, I think Anthea Swan's death ties into it. Bet suggested I look into who was in town that day, said you'd know where to look."

I was stretching the truth a little, but I had a feeling…

"Okay. Come into my office."

Seated in the ratty guest chair that was far more comfortable than it looked, I waited while he searched out something on his computer. I could hear the keys clicking softly and a muted hum. Beneath both sounds was the remote roar of the highway.

"Looks like the whole family was here that day," he said eventually.

"The whole—the Deepings?" I hadn't expected that. "Danny too?"

"Yup."

"And you think Deeping senior killed her?"

"That's been my premise. There was what amounted to a blood feud between the two of them. And he might have killed Deslauriers, too."

"I thought they'd been best friends."

"They were. Until the mine failed. They had a big fight just before Deslauriers committed suicide."

Interesting. My mind was clicking through facts and dates. "How old would Danny have been when Swan died?"

"Nearly twenty."

"And do you know what he was up to that day?"

"No clue. You're thinking he might be the killer?"

I was hoping not. I was still hoping Marie was exaggerating her fears about Callum's death, that Celeste hadn't been held all this time by a killer.

But I didn't believe it, not after talking to Bet. "How closely can you document Deeping senior's actions?"

"Not closely enough. It's mostly circumstantial, but it makes more sense than suicide, if you knew Anthea."

I took the leap I'd been thinking about all morning. "What if you looked at Danny rather than his father?"

His eyes gleamed. "I never considered that. You said he used more than one name?"

I told him about Danny's metamorphosis from Deeping to Farrow and then Whyte, sipped my coffee. Waited while he communed with his database. This was taking too long—I needed to get back to Vancouver. Finally he looked up.

"It could work," Joe said, downing half his coffee. "Could work indeed. In fact, based on the facts I have, your Danny's as likely to have killed both of 'em as his Dad was."

"Wait—both of them? You mean Guy Deslauriers too?"

"Uh huh."

"Danny would have been—twelve?"

He nodded. "Killers that young exist."

I was still absorbing that, when he added, "But if he is involved with the two girls, I'd need to write about your case, too."

Hold on a minute. "After this case is over, if you respect that I have to maintain client confidentiality, I might be willing to talk to you."

He nodded, turning his attention back to the computer.

"I can't see how Danny would have worked it. Unless..." His eyes narrowed and he leaned forward to scribble a couple of points on a legal pad. "James Deeping's long dead, but I could interview the son."

"Once we find him. And assuming he's willing to talk."

He waved it off. "Even if he isn't. Just getting the interview..." His voice tailed off.

I called him back. "So if Danny killed Swan, what does that tell us about him?"

I wasn't ready to think about a twelve-year-old killer.

He started, focused on me again. "That he blamed her for something? Maybe his father's disgrace?"

It wasn't ringing true for me. "What else do you know about the weekend Swan died, and about the Deeping family? Where did they stay, what did they do? Everything. And why in the world did they come back here?"

Joe just nodded, pulled out a sheaf of files. The extent of detail he'd collected was impressive.

I left with a briefcase full of copies, and a mind tumbling over itself with disconnected facts.

———

IT WAS STILL RAINING when I merged onto the highway back to Vancouver. As I drove, I took all the scattered facts, and turned them this way and that until it all fit together. Joe had been working from the assumption that James Deeping was a murderer as well as a con artist. But if Danny was the murderer…?

Was it possible Danny had already killed four, maybe five people—Swan, his parents, Callum and now possibly Guy Deslauriers?

My phone chirped, distracting me.

Cory?

Hell's Gate was coming up, so I pulled off at the lookout. Sure enough, I had a text from my nephew.

"He's got another name. William Prince," it said.

"Is this new?" I texted back.

"No, set up a long time ago. For gaming."

"Thanks." Another name, an old one. "Check if he's used it recently."

I listened to the thunder of the rapids far below, watched the wind feather in the tree branches. Yet another name. Why? After a moment, I called Isabella at Two Hearts.

"Barbara. How is it going? Any luck in finding Celeste?"

"I'm still following up leads. If I give you a name, can you confirm if they are a Two Hearts client?"

"Barbara, you know I can't do that."

"He was seen with Celeste the morning she disappeared."

"Oh." A short silence. I let it stretch. "What name?"

"William Prince."

I heard keyboards clicking. I waited, anticipating the no. Instead I could hear a slight gasp, and the clicking stopped.

She'd found him?

While Isabella was still debating what to tell me, I made it easier for her. "Hypothetically, if you did have such a person on your membership list, he'd probably have joined no more than six months ago."

"Five weeks. Hypothetically."

So he must have spent some time researching Celeste and her life. Just the thought gave me the creeps. "But Celeste was never matched with him?"

"No."

"Do you ever have membership mixers, or anything like that where they might have met?"

"No, confidentiality is a primary concern of most of our members. They only want to meet the ones who are selected as their best matches."

Uber-geek rides again. "Your members have an on-line sign?"

"Sure, they each have their own member page with a secured login. That's where they can see and review their matches."

Maybe that was how Danny had connected with Celeste.

"Are you thinking this guy could have hacked our system? Set up a meeting as though it was from us?"

She was good. "Yes."

"Our security is supposed to be fool-proof."

"Is there any way you can tell if it's been done?"

More clicking. You don't hear that much any more. I wondered what kind of keyboard she was using.

"I can't see anything, but let me look into it. If he managed it, that's a security hole we want to plug, asap."

I could just imagine.

"You'll be at this number?"

"Yes, but I'm on the road for the next couple of hours. If you text me, I'll call you back."

She promised to get back to me as soon as she could. Meanwhile, I was going to proceed on the assumption that Danny had joined Two Hearts specifically to give him easy access to their system. And Celeste.

So how had he known she was a member?

I asked Cory. Seconds later, I had my answer.

"If Danny could setup the Whyte and Prince names, he could hack 2 Hearts," he sent back.

That's what I'd thought.

———

IT WAS NEARLY an hour later that Isabella got back to me. I pulled off at the nearest rest stop and called her back. Hopefully she had some answers for me.

She did, though she didn't sound very happy about them. "You were right, Barbara. Our system has been compromised."

Compromised? She sounded like one of those Victorian novels they made us read in first year English. "What did he do?"

"He set up a hidden page, which allowed him to set up any dates he wanted to at Two Hearts. And yes, he'd used it to set up two meetings with Celeste."

"So how did he get in?"

"We're still not sure. But he's really good. Our security guy is still shaking his head and swearing. But he's almost as impressed as he is pissed off. You know what I mean?"

"One pro to another?"

"Something like that."

"So he's not just good. He's very good."

And Cory had to be almost that level of good to track him down, and that scared me. Great. "Was William Prince doing anything else with that identity?"

"Nothing we've found so far. But this guy is way more sophisticated than anything our system guy had seen here, so they're still digging."

"Could you share that information with Missing Persons as soon as possible?"

"Yes. Yes, I'll let them know."

"You'll let me know if you find anything else?"

She promised she would.

I sent Cory a quick text letting him know that William Prince had indeed hacked the Two Hearts database, and asking him to look for any recent transactions under this second identity.

"Will do. Danny and brother split parent's estate. Not much left —father sold house he got from his own parents 10 years before," he sent back.

So money hadn't been a motive for Danny.

"Thanks," I texted him. Then I called Jaimie, who agreed to meet me for lunch.

———

TRAFFIC SNARLED as I exited the freeway, so Jaimie was waiting for me by the time I got to Café Buzz.

"What did you find out?" she asked as I reached the table.

"It looks like you were right about Danny Deeping," I said. "And it's possible he's responsible for the deaths of his parents and Celeste's aunt. He might even be responsible for Celeste's father's death. Which means Marie is probably right about Callum, too."

I filled her in on what I'd learned, including the second identity at Two Hearts.

Jaimie's face paled as she listened, and her hands clenched

around her mug. "I need a minute," she said softly when I'd finished. "If you don't mind?"

I understood. I'd had the drive back to run through everything I'd uncovered, and I was still feeling overwhelmed by the implications. I needed a coffee and something to eat anyway. "I'll be back in a minute. Do you want anything else?"

She shook her head.

When I returned, coffee and grilled chicken panini in hand, Jaimie was looking more herself.

"What can I do?" she asked. "That is why you wanted to meet with me?"

I nodded. "I need your help. I'm going ahead on the assumption that Celeste and Marie are both alive. If they are, it means whatever reason Danny had for snatching Celeste, he doesn't intend to kill her."

"And you need my help in figuring out that reason."

"And where he might be keeping her. Yes."

She swallowed hard. "If he hasn't killed her by now, we can probably eliminate revenge."

That's what I'd thought. "If Danny was responsible for his parents' deaths, something must have changed. I suspect he'd blamed Celeste's father and aunt for everything up to that point."

She considered me thoughtfully. "You have the makings of a pretty good psychologist yourself."

It was supposed to be a compliment. I think. "As a painter, I spend a lot of time watching people."

"This is the first time I've heard you identify yourself as an artist."

Because I hadn't done so for years. I hadn't even realized I'd said it now. "Joe had some pretty compelling facts about Farrow senior's role in the collapse of the town. If Danny finally found out his father had been behind the loss of everything he knew…"

Jaimie obligingly followed my lead, though a narrowing of her eyes noted my evasion. "If you're right, Danny had already killed at least once for exactly that reason."

"Yes. The aunt, Anthea Swan." I paused, drank some coffee.

"So he kills his father, buys a penthouse and a hot car and joins a dating service?" she said.

"Not quite. His father dies, and then his brother. Then he buys a penthouse and a hot car and goes looking for Celeste. I think he joined Two Hearts to get close to her. But why was he looking for her?"

"To replace his lost family," she said softly. "If your theory is right, he'd just lost everything he thought he knew about his childhood. And about his father."

"So Celeste was the one good thing left from his childhood?"

She sipped her chai. "The lost puppy feeling I was getting—this isn't a guy that fits in easily, especially with women. Your informant said Celeste was nice to him as a child?"

I ignored the psychic bit. "She said Celeste was one of the few who was."

"So he might want to get that back. Or to punish her for it."

Wait a minute. "Punish her?"

"I'm going on probabilities here, but if we're anything like close on our profile of him, he could go one of two ways. He could idolize her. Or he could blame her. And in order to find him, we probably need to work out which kind he is."

Great. "So how do we do that?"

"We need more information on him, on how he sees himself. It would help if we knew how he spends his leisure time. He seems like a loner, but is he a reader? A gamer? What about movies?"

"This is why you're the psychologist. I know he was a gamer, but not much more. Hold on a moment."

I texted Cory asking what kind of entertainment Danny as William Prince had sought out online. "This is a long shot, but it might get us something. It could take a while, though. Can I get you another chai?"

"Please."

I was just coming back with our drinks when my phone chirped. I passed Jaimie her mug, then opened the text.

"Interesting. Looks like the younger Danny was a fan of high fantasy."

"Games?"

"Some, but mostly movies. Lord of the Rings. Star Wars. Avatar. Even The Princess Bride. Lots of heroes rescuing civilizations. And princesses."

"I'm not going to ask how you found that out."

I glanced at the text Cory had sent. "Movie-sharing sites. Not exactly legal, but apparently it's all pretty open about who's down-loading what, if you know their sign-ons."

"And you know Danny's?"

I grinned. "He created it years ago, then used it at Two Hearts. Seems nobody knew about it."

She was nodding. "Makes sense."

"Why?"

"Our guy is seeing himself as some kind of romantic hero, in the old tradition. Prince Charming."

"Or Prince William."

Her eyes widened. "William Prince. Yes. Not the most creative soul, then."

"And a pretty violent version of Prince Charming," I said. "So that makes Celeste the princess he needs to rescue?"

"Something like that."

"Means he'll keep her alive, and in pretty good health. Or try to?"

She nodded, took a sip of her chai. "He'll probably try to make her fit into his notion of a perfect princess. If she's smart, she'll go along with it. Otherwise—it could get bad."

"You know Celeste pretty well. Is she smart?"

"Yes, but she's also got a very strong will that most people don't see. And in this situation? He's likely pretty volatile, and I don't know if she's that kind of smart under that kind of pressure."

"And what about if he's got Marie too?"

Her eyes met mine, and she shook her head. "I can't see any

good ending there. Not if he sees Marie as an impediment between him and what he wants."

"Or if he decides she's betrayed his princess?"

"Yes. If he has Marie and she's still alive, I don't think she will be for long," Jaimie said.

She picked up her mug, holding it cupped in her hands as if she needed the warmth. "Not unless Celeste is a way better negotiator than I think she is."

"She's a fundraiser. Wouldn't she have to be able to read people and negotiate pretty well to do that job?"

"Yes. And she's good at it. But she works in a pretty defined environment. Here, she's out on her own, in danger, maybe in pain, certainly confined…" Her face had gone pale.

This had to be hard on Jaimie. I hated to put her through it, but I needed her. Celeste needed her. "Where would a hero keep a princess?"

"In a castle, or a tower. Even a remote fortress. Somewhere he can keep her safe."

"He would have shopped for her, bought her clothes."

"I think so. He'll have money?"

I nodded. "But where? He couldn't get her out of the country, but there's a lot of back country where no-one would ever look."

"Not too many towers in the back-country, though. Princesses either."

I was getting desperate." You still don't get any sense of her?"

"Nothing."

Time to start digging.

CHAPTER THIRTY-TWO

My office looked exactly the way I'd left it, but it felt distant. Like I'd been on a long journey. Or away a long time. There were no messages.

A call to Jerry got me no closer to Danny, though they'd finally found a witness. She saw a man matching Danny's description getting off on Callum's floor just before he'd been murdered.

So Marie was probably right about Callum's death.

I had to find Danny, and fast.

Nearly two hours and a half-pot of Italian Roast later, I stretched out my back and rubbed aching eyes. I'd seen nothing in Old Joe's files that contradicted my theories about Danny and his murderous tendencies. Nothing that confirmed them, either.

Either James or Danny Deeping could have killed Guy Deslauriers and Anthea Swan. Or someone else entirely could be responsible.

No way either death was suicide, though. What had the sheriff of the day been thinking?

I flipped back through the file. Was there anything I could send Jerry and Cathy Yip, that might help them find Danny?

I doubted it. This was a very cold trail. There was no proof and not much in the way of evidence.

There was still no proof that Danny had Celeste, either.

And too many of my conclusions were drawn from my conversations with Bet and with Old Joe. Hearsay. Inadmissible.

I e-mailed Jerry and Cathy with the information that Danny Deeping/David Farrow/David Whyte/William Prince had likely been abused by his father, and that either Danny or his father seemed possible suspects in the twenty-year-old supposed suicides of Guy Deslauriers and Anthea Swan. Couldn't hurt.

It would probably be good if I wasn't within yelling distance when Jerry got the e-mail, though.

Danny's various identities each had a reason behind them. But who was this guy really? And what would he have done after he had Celeste?

I grabbed a legal pad and started a mind map, filling in what I'd learned. Suddenly I could see the missing piece. And I needed some help.

I texted Cory; was he free for a couple of hours?

"Sure. Your office?"

"Yes."

"See you there."

Perfect. I went back to my mapping. When the door swung open, I jumped.

"Hi, Aunt B. You wanted to see me?"

How had Cory got here so fast?

"Aunt B? Hello?"

Oops. I gave him a grin, had to stifle my urge to give him a hug. "Sorry, just following a train of thought."

I told Cory what I needed him to do.

"You think we've got enough to track him down? Cool. What do you need me to do first?"

"Tell me about the second identity at Two Hearts. Prince Charming. Did you find any recent use?"

He chortled. "Prince Charming? Where did that come from?"

I explained Jaimie's theory. "So did he use it for other things?"

Cory was still laughing. "Mostly for online stuff. Downloads," he managed to say.

"So no physical purchases? Nothing sent to an address? No property rentals?"

"No."

I nodded. I'd expected that. This guy was too cagey to be caught that easily.

"Except…"

"Except what?"

"He did place one order."

"What did he order? And when?"

Cory headed for my laptop, then glanced at me for permission.

I nodded.

A few quick clicks later, he had it for me. "He ordered a couple dozen romance novels. And he took delivery at the local UPS on Marine Drive. The one in West Van."

Romance novels. Two days before his 'date' with Celeste. And in West Vancouver?

I'd been right.

And I was going to get this guy, deluded romantic murderer or no deluded romantic murderer.

"Does that help?" Cory asked, watching me with a quizzical look on his face.

"We've got him."

"Really?"

Well okay, maybe it was an exaggeration. But not by much. "Yup."

"So now what?"

"We have a couple of errands to run, then we're coming back here. You want some pizza?"

His grin told me he did.

Stupid question, anyway. He was a teenage boy. And I was a little hungry myself.

———

WHEN WE GOT BACK to the office, we pinned the two huge maps we'd just bought—one of Metro Vancouver, the other showing the southern third of BC—to the cork-board that now covered most of one wall. I laid out our collection of colored push-pins on the edge of the desk.

"Danny has to have a bolt-hole to take Celeste to, and it has to be isolated enough that the neighbors haven't noticed," I said. "How's your geography?"

"Hopeless," he said with a wide grin. "But the computer's really good at it. What do you need?"

"The red pins are for criminal activity." I put in pins showing where Swan's body was found, where Danny's parents died, where Celeste was last seen, where Callum died.

"Why are there only two pins on the map of BC when you've got two on the Vancouver map?"

"I'm only using the large map for anything that doesn't show on the Vancouver map. We can change it later if we need to."

"Huh." I could see he didn't agree with me, but he didn't argue about it. "So what's next?"

"The yellow pins are for every address you've found for him, including any properties he's rented or bought."

A frown between his brows told me how hard Cory was focusing. I watched as he searched for the addresses, then placed the pins on the appropriate large map.

"Now add in a green pin for where he picked up that package he ordered," I said.

He did so.

"Can you think of anything else to add?"

"How about where he worked? And the dating place."

"Good idea. Add them." I glanced from the Vancouver map to the BC map, where a few pins clustered around the canyon highway. Wait a minute.

"Can you add the yellow pins from the Vancouver map to the BC map?" I said.

Cory nodded, and placed them. Then we both stood back and looked at the brightly colored pins.

"They're following a pattern," he said.

"They are indeed."

The yellow pins ran along Highway 1 until it reached Vancouver, then they followed 1A. It hadn't been obvious until it was laid out like this. Just going by the addresses we'd never have seen it, because Danny Deeping hadn't stuck to any particular municipality.

"Can you bring up a map of Brenton that's the same scale as this one of Vancouver?" I asked.

"Sure." A couple of clicks. "Here."

I moved so I could see over his shoulder. "Does this program have any way of adding multiple points?"

"Yeah. But I bet I could figure out how to do that." And he waved a hand at my bulletin boards.

"Later. For now, just add the two pins we have." The barn where Swan died and the house Danny had lived in as a child.

He did so, and we both stared at them.

Cory was the first to speak. "They're the same distance from the highway as the yellow ones in Vancouver. That can't be accidental."

I didn't think so either. I stood back, looked at our creation. "I'm assuming he's created a bolt hole for himself that has some meaning for him. How do we narrow it down?"

"He hasn't lived outside Vancouver in twenty years."

"True."

"What about eliminating everything else?"

I squinted at the map. It made sense, but…

"Good thinking," I said. "But let's try something else first. Can you take the stickies, write a number for the order in which he lived in each place, first, second and so on, and add them to the map?"

"Sure." He did so.

By the time he'd finished, it was clear to both of us what was wrong with his first conclusion. "He's been expanding outwards," Cory said.

I nodded. When you looked at them in order, his pins were spreading further out on the map.

"What…" I started to say, when Cory held up his hand.

"Wait a minute," he said. "Do you have a ruler?"

Wordlessly, I dug it out and handed it to him. I knew better than to interrupt inspiration when I saw it.

Cory was busy measuring the distance between pins and scribbling on the sticky notes. Then he went back to his laptop and began clicking frantically, muttering to himself as he did so.

I couldn't make any sense of what was on his screen, so I grabbed a cola for Cory and a bottled water for myself, then went back through Joe's file.

I could see I was going to have to keep the fridge stocked with pop.

ONCE I FINISHED with the file, I glanced up to see how Cory was doing. He was still muttering to the computer, and the maps didn't look much different. Except he'd added all the Vancouver pins to the BC map.

I stared at it.

Wait a minute. The pins clustered along Highway 1 and 1A. And Highway 99—the Sea to Sky Highway—connects with them both. What if…

I called Ben, and my luck was in—he was home. I told him what I wanted and sent him a scan of Marie's drawing of Danny.

His response was immediate. "I've seen this guy."

So I'd been right. "Where? And how long ago?"

"Here in Squamish. And sometime this spring. Can't be more accurate than that."

"Did you see him more than once?"

"Must have. He doesn't have a memorable face."

No, he didn't—unlike his father. If Danny saw himself as Prince William, his father had been King James. Handsome, charming, memorable—impossible to live up to. And an utter fraud.

I wondered again how Danny had felt learning the truth about his father's past. "Can you remember where in Squamish you might have seen him? This is important."

"I recognize one of Marie's sketches," Ben said. "Is this the guy?"

"I think so."

"Okay." A silence. "I didn't see him at any of the usual places—not the grocery store, or playing tennis, or eagle watching."

"Go on."

"I think I've seen him around town, maybe in a coffee shop. And at the courthouse."

"The courthouse? Where?"

"Land Registry, maybe?"

I covered the receiver. "Cory, can you find any properties he's bought in Squamish?"

I took my hand away. "But you haven't seen him recently?" I asked Ben.

"Nope."

So he'd likely not bought property in Squamish itself. Or he'd holed up somewhere and not ventured out. I explained my theory to Ben. "What do you think?"

"Not here," his voice was definite. "The place is too small. People would notice."

Made sense. "Let me know if you see or hear anything. Or if you think of anything else."

"Sure."

"And do me a favor and be careful, okay?"

I'd been expecting an argument, but I didn't get one. "Sure," he said, and clicked off.

I turned to Cory, filled him in. "Can you check if Danny bought property in Squamish?"

His face lit up. "You think this is it?"

"I think it could be."

He nodded, and turned to his keyboard, fingers flying. This kid was good. Scary good. Suddenly I felt sorry for Susanna.

The phone rang, and I grabbed it, my attention still on Cory. "O'Grady Investigations."

"You have to help me!"

"Marie?" All my attention snapped to the phone. "Where are you? Are you all right?"

"I'm in Horseshoe Bay. At the coffee shop. And I'm afraid he's seen me..."

Her voice trailed off. Had I lost her? Then she whispered, "Just come. Please!"

And I heard the dial tone.

There was more than one coffee shop in Horseshoe Bay, and there was no guarantee Marie would still be there, but I'd take that chance. I turned to my nephew.

"Marie?" he asked.

I nodded. "She's in Horseshoe Bay. I have to go."

"I'll come too."

"No." I pulled a couple of twenties out of my wallet. "Take a cab home."

"But I want to help."

"You have."

"At least let me finish this search."

I didn't have time for this. "Fine. Then go straight home. And lock the door behind you."

"I will."

Uh huh. "I need your promise."

"You got it." When I gave him the eye, he grinned, shrugged. "Okay, okay. I promise."

"Call my cell if you find something. And Cory? Thanks. You've been a huge help."

He gave me a quick half-grin, and turned back to his computer screen.

CHAPTER THIRTY-THREE

Traffic was building up, but I still had two lanes going north as I headed over the Lion's Gate. It took me twenty-seven minutes to get to Horseshoe Bay. Not bad.

But not good enough. There was no sign of Marie in any of the coffee shops along Bay Street. Now what?

I let my eyes scan the clumps of people strolling along the small harbor front. No sign of her.

No sign of Danny, either. Not that I'd really expected it to be that easy.

A footfall behind me had me starting to turn even before I felt the tap on my shoulder. "Marie!"

She looked awful. Pale, tired and haggard. She was still wearing the clothes I'd last seen her in two days ago, and it looked like she'd slept in them. But at least she was alive.

"Shhh. This way, quick." And she grabbed my arm and half dragged me down Royal Avenue and into a deserted sandwich place.

"Marie, what's going on?"

"I'll tell you. But first, I'm starving. Can you buy me something to eat?"

By the look of her face, "starving" was not just a phrase. And I wasn't sure when my next meal would be either. I ordered soup and sandwiches, water and coffee for both of us, then sat impatiently across from her while she wolfed hers down.

I gave her half of mine. "Talk. Where have you been? What's going on? And why did you call me now?"

A wan smile crossed her features. "I've been hiding out. I was afraid he'd find me, too. And I've been looking for him."

"Why didn't you tell me what was going on?"

"I—I..."

"I know you helped Danny connect with your sister through Two Hearts."

She looked stunned. "How...?"

"Never mind how. Why didn't you level with me?"

"I—didn't think it would help. I found out pretty quickly that I didn't even have his current name."

"How did you meet him?"

"He hung around my favorite tattoo parlor for a while. Seemed to know people who knew people."

"And how did he talk you into it?"

"He said he had an in with this tattoo artist who'd take me on as an assistant, give me the training I need," Marie said. "Just to tell him how he could 'accidentally' meet Celeste."

She gulped down some coffee. "But he never told me he was from Brenton. I'd never have told him anything if I'd known he was from there. And once they'd met and Celeste told me he was from Brenton, it was too late. I couldn't talk her out of meeting him again."

"So you decided to look for him yourself? That was pretty stupid," I said.

"Maybe. But she's my sister. And I got her into this—I owe it to her. I'll do anything to get her back safe. Anything."

She rubbed at her eyes, looked up at me. "I know you're doing your best, but no-one else cares about her the way I do. I knew I'd do whatever it took to get her back safe. I didn't know that about you."

"Try me."

She gave me a long look, then her face went even whiter and her bottom lip started to tremble.

"Finish your sandwich," I said, and got up to get her another sandwich and both of us more coffee. When I sat down again, she had herself under control. "So why did you suddenly decide you could find her?"

"Because I read your notes about Danny, that day I stayed at your place. You'd left them in the kitchen. It was the first time I realized Danny's father was the town realtor. My aunt used to talk about Danny's dad all the time. She really hated him."

"So why did that send you running?"

"Because she'd rail about how he came from money, how his folks lived in West Van, not far from the ferry. I was hoping Danny still had the place, and that he'd take Celeste there. I was watching for him."

Danny's folks had sold that house years ago, but I hadn't realized it had been here. "You saw him today?"

She nodded. "Right before I called."

"Hang on a moment." I sent a text to Cory, then turned back to Marie. "Where did you see him?"

"The bakery. He was buying chocolate chip cookies. Celeste's favorite."

So I'd been right. Celeste was still alive. "You're sure it was him?"

"Yeah. He's grown a beard, but yeah, it was him all right."

I could feel my breathing speed up. "Where did he go?"

"He walked along the wharf for a bit, casual like, but I think he was watching for anyone to notice him, y'know?"

"Did he see you?"

"No. I stayed way back."

"Then how do you know what he bought?"

"I asked. After I called you."

Right. "So where did he go?"

"Back to his car. He'd parked on a side street."

"What was he driving?"

"Gray Camry. 2009 or so. I couldn't get close enough to get the license plate, though. Not without being spotted."

"Which way did he go?"

"Onto Nelson and back up the hill."

"He could have been going anywhere."

"Yeah. But those cookies were fresh out of the oven, and Celeste likes them best when the chocolate's still all melty. So maybe he wasn't going far."

Maybe. And maybe this was yet another one of Danny's false trails. Before I could answer, my phone rang.

I glanced at the number. My office. "Cory? What is it? And why haven't you gone home yet?"

"I think I found it."

"Good work. Where?"

"David Whyte a.k.a Danny Deeping bought a small warehouse in Squamish, through something called Regal Land Services."

"A warehouse? He wouldn't take her there." It came out with a certainty I hadn't known I felt.

"No, but Regal Land also bought another property just beyond Horseshoe Bay. It's still in West Van, but pretty isolated. Want to see?"

"Yes."

"Check your e-mail, then call me back."

He'd sent a photo, which showed a large property with a decent sized house in the middle of it. The house overlooked the water. And it had a turret.

I called him back. "A turret?"

I could hear the grin in his voice. "You were looking for a castle."

"I was indeed." This was the place, I could feel it. "How far is it from Callum's place?"

"Address?"

I gave it to him. Moments later he had the answer. "Maybe twelve minutes on the freeway. Closer to twenty if you take the lower route."

It all fit. "You got an address?"

He gave it to me, and I entered it onto my iPhone and asked for directions. Seven minutes from here. Marie had been right. Those cookies would still be warm.

I checked out the satellite view. Isolated enough, lots of trees, hidden from prying neighbors.

"Thanks, Cory. I'll check it out. Now go home." I disconnected, called Jerry.

Voice mail. Not much help.

I sent him a text instead, hesitated, then sent an e-mail to Ms. Yip too. I looked up to see Marie staring at me.

"You've got something?"

I filled her in.

"So why are we sitting here?"

"We can't just confront him. That's for the police—they're trained for this."

"But Celeste may not have time to wait for them."

"Warm cookies, remember?"

"It could be a last meal. You don't know this guy. He isn't sane."

Now she figures it out. But she was right—he was probably the sociopath that Jaimie had named him. Or worse.

And there was no predicting what he might do next.

Which did not make charging in there a good idea. "No, Marie."

"Fine, then. If you won't help me, I'll rescue her myself."

"And have two of you kidnapped?"

We sat there exchanging stares over the dregs of our coffee. She looked away first, but I knew better than to think she'd given up. The minute she got out of my sight, she'd be heading straight for the address I'd foolishly let her catch sight of.

This case was wearing me down. I'd never have made that mistake a week ago.

So how did I get Marie under control? If I could get her in my car, she'd have a harder time getting away from me.

"Okay, we'll drive by," I said. "Once. We can at least see what the place looks like while we wait for backup."

I'd been looking for this guy for over a week. I wanted to see the place too.

CHAPTER THIRTY-FOUR

It was already getting dark as we cruised by the sprawling house, barely visible through the trees.

"Just stop here for a moment, Barbara," Marie said. "We're out of view, and I want to see if…"

"We are not getting out of the car," I said as I pulled off onto the gravel, engaging the child-proof locks as I did so. Not trust my client? Me?

"Fine."

I nearly didn't stop, but my phone bleeped, signaling a new message. Jerry? Cathy Yip? I pulled over, making sure all the doors were locked as I did so.

"Is that the cops?" Marie asked.

"Hope so," I said, signing in.

I never saw it coming.

———

I OPENED MY EYES, blinked a few times. Where was I?

I felt dizzy and my head hurt.

I was only half-aware of someone leaning over me, the locks

disengaging, the other car door opening. By the time I'd shaken off the blow—what had she hit me with, anyway?—Marie was gone.

"Marie!" But it came out as a choked whisper.

I couldn't let her go blundering in there.

She'd either get herself killed, or Celeste killed, or both. Shaking off the dizziness, I raced after her. Or tried to.

Once I got the door open, I had to grab the edge of it to stay upright as my knees buckled under me. I called her name again.

My voice came out cracked and way too soft.

I rested my head against the door frame for a moment, ignoring the hammers that set off.

Focused on breathing slow and deep.

After a moment, I stood up and went after her.

A few broken branches made it easy to see where she'd forced her way through. I'm no tracker, but I'd learned a few things from a Salish friend many years ago, and I still remembered a little of it. Besides, a drunk badger could have tracked Marie, given the trail she'd left.

She wasn't going for subtle.

I just hoped she was at least trying for silent.

As I crept closer to where I knew the house had to be, the trees thinned, making way for a thicket of blackberry canes, half leafed out, their wicked thorns in full evidence. Marie had forced her way through, as evidenced by a few shreds that had torn from her sweater and scarf. I could only hope it had slowed her a bit.

Instead of following her and risking getting slowed down, I took the gamble that I knew where she'd come out and went around.

I was right.

Her trail emerged about fifteen feet closer to the house. She'd left even more white bits on this side.

There was no other sign of Marie.

It was dark enough now that I could barely see the bushes—if she hadn't worn a white scarf, I'd never have tracked her this far. She'd make a great target if Danny was looking outside.

She couldn't be that far ahead of me, surely?

I was trying to track her through yet another clump of shrubs—this one luckily without the thorns—when some instinct stopped me. I fell prone, inching my way forward on the damp leaf-mould.

Four feet from where I'd stopped, the clump of bushes suddenly opened into what looked like untrimmed lawn. The house was right there in front of me, not more than twenty feet away.

All the windows looked shuttered, and I saw very little light coming from inside. Where was Marie?

I could see no sign of her. Was she hiding somewhere? Or had she gone rushing in?

If she had, she'd managed to do it without me hearing her.

A shadow crossed in front of one of the windows. A suspiciously Marie-shaped shadow. And it was on the inside.

Damn it! What was she thinking? Except I was pretty sure she wasn't thinking.

Which meant it was up to me.

I glanced at the house. No sign of movement. Okay.

I crossed the ground at a flat-out run—or as close to one as I could get while staying silent.

Hugging close to the walls, I ghosted around the house, looking for an entrance. How had Marie got in so quickly?

The French doors in the kitchen? No, locked tight. And I hadn't seen an open window.

So how had she done it?

Then my eye caught a slight movement in one of the curtains. A draft. And a window cracked open for a bit for air.

Four minutes later I was standing in what appeared to be a laundry room.

The house was silent around me.

This was so stupid. There were no words for how stupid it was. But I couldn't leave Marie to blunder her way into danger. No, I had to blunder my way in too.

Why was I doing this?

Because I had to. It made no logical sense, but something inside me wouldn't let me do anything else. I heard a soft scuffing sound, and a muffled thunk.

Marie?

Or Danny?

I crept out of the laundry room and down a long darkened hallway, feeling my way. Following the nearly silent shuffling of careful feet.

I was guessing we were looking for a basement.

There was a bit of light coming from somewhere, because I was seeing shades of gray rather than deep black.

I passed an office on the right and the kitchen on the left, glowing eerily blue from the clocks on stove and microwave. It was 8:28.

Had Jerry or Cathy even seen my text yet?

I'd turned off notifications, so I didn't know if I had a message. And I daren't risk a lit phone screen now.

Where were the police?

On my left was a dining room leading into what had to be a living room that seemed to run across the front of the house. I could make out the larger forms of furniture ahead of me.

Where were the stairs?

I'd expected them to be in the kitchen, but Marie—if that's who I was following—had gone straight past.

Ah. That's why.

There was a stairway on the right, leading down into darkness. I wished for a street lamp as I felt my way down the narrow stairwell.

Somewhere ahead of me I heard a whispered curse.

Marie.

At least I was following the right person. Even if she was an idiot.

Well, she wasn't the only one. I felt my way down stair by stair.

Ahead of me, Marie seemed to have stopped. I crept closer.

"It's Barbara," I said in an undertone, just a hint of a whisper, hoping she wouldn't scream.

She didn't.

She froze.

Then she made a movement in the darkness.

Guessing what she'd done, I took her extended hand, squeezed gently.

She let go, moved slowly forward. As I reached the small landing where she'd stopped, I could see what she'd seen.

The stairs below us curved back, then widened into a hallway running towards the back of the house. It was too dark to see what lay on either side of that hall, but at the end was a faint line of light, coming from under a door.

Running one hand along the wall for guidance, Marie quickened her pace.

So did I.

Surely she wasn't planning just to walk into that lit room?

Apparently she was. She reached for the door handle. I grabbed her shoulder, held her back despite her resistance.

"Let me go!" It was the softest hiss I'd ever heard.

I didn't. Charging from darkness into a bright room, when we didn't know what was in there, was beyond foolhardy. We'd be helpless, our vision gone. And Danny wasn't stupid.

He struck me as the kind to have contingency plans backed up by even more contingency plans.

"We need to find another way in," I said very softly.

Her muscles tensed, then relaxed. I felt her nod quickly, once.

Somewhere upstairs, there was a click, and then the sound of locks disengaging.

We both froze.

Where was it coming from?

CHAPTER THIRTY-FIVE

I could hear heavy footsteps coming down the stairs from the second floor.

He—if it was Danny—was making no attempt at subtlety. Maybe he didn't know we were here. Yet.

I grabbed Marie's elbow and half-dragged her away from the door she was still staring at.

"Stop!" she ordered in a fierce whisper.

I ignored her.

We had to get out of there.

Given everything I'd learned about Danny, I was betting he was armed. And even if we both jumped him, the element of surprise wasn't enough against a gun. Not with someone like him wielding it.

I dragged us six feet back down the main hall to where I'd spotted a narrow hallway running off to the left. It had a door at the end of it.

A door leading outside.

Marie resisted me the whole way.

"Windows," I breathed, directly into Marie's ear. She quit trying to fight me. Finally.

I let go of her arm, got to the door and waited, a hand held up to keep her still. No way I was risking a draft of night air when I could hear Danny on the basement stairs.

He'd be coming down that hallway any moment now.

I stood there, listening, feeling way too exposed. I hate that feeling.

It was hard not to just yank the door open and race for the nearest hiding spot.

I fought the urge with everything I had, clamped a hand on Marie's arm again when I sensed the same instincts flaring in her. We listened to the footsteps get closer, barely breathing.

Would he go straight for the lit room?

Or would he glance to the left and see us?

He went straight past us, footsteps pausing outside that lit room.

A key grated, then came the sound of a doorknob turning overlaid by a cheery masculine voice.

"Time for a little nightcap, my dear."

A hoarse grunt that barely sounded human.

Celeste was alive! I'd been nearly sure we'd be too late.

Now we just had to get her out of here.

"Celeste?" Marie whispered, her voice just a breath at my ear. "Was that my sister? What has he done to her?"

"Is that any way to talk when I've brought you this nice cup of tea? And your favorite cookies?" the voice was asking as I eased the outer door open and yanked Marie out with me. "I thought you'd have learned better manners by now…"

I crept outside and along the wall, Marie right behind me. The small windows that had to belong to the room where he was holding Celeste were heavily curtained. He'd used blackout drapes, by the look of it.

No light showed, and I couldn't hear a thing.

I glanced around me. It looked like we were at the back of the house, on the opposite side to where we'd come in. I held a finger to my lips and motioned Marie to a spot concealed by shrubbery and at least fifteen feet from the house before I'd let her speak.

"Why did you stop me? We could have taken him. There are two of us."

"He'll have a gun. If we tried and failed, we'd be far worse off. At least we know he has her, and that she's alive."

"Right. Like I'm supposed to be happy, when she sounds like that? What has he been doing to her?"

"The police will be on their way…"

"How long will it take them to get here? If they're even coming. And how do we know he'll keep Celeste alive? He might have poisoned her tea."

I doubted it, but Marie was right. We didn't know.

And I didn't like the idea of leaving Celeste in his hands a moment longer than we had to. "Trying to take him by surprise would have been stupid," I said. "We can do better than that."

"Yeah? How?"

At least she was listening. "Wait 'til he goes back upstairs."

"Yeah—And?"

"And we grab her." It wasn't much of a plan, but we didn't have much to work with.

At least Celeste was alive.

"So we let him get away?"

"With any luck, the police will get here and arrest him before he figures out anything is wrong. Our job is to get Celeste out of here."

"If that is Celeste."

I bit my tongue against the urge to ask her who else she thought it could be. "You think it isn't?"

"No. Sorry. Can you get that door open?"

I hoped so. "Yes."

"How do we get her away?"

"Out this way. Then through those bushes and back to the car."

"What if he hears us?"

"You get Celeste out. I'll distract him." Somehow.

"But…"

"Here." I handed her the car keys "You'll need these."

She closed her hand around them, gripping hard, but didn't say a word.

"We'll have to get back inside so we can hear when he leaves," I said. "You ready?"

She nodded, and we retraced our steps back into that claustrophobic little hallway.

———

DANNY probably only stayed for half an hour or so, but I was a quivering bundle of nerves by the time he emerged. I was pretty sure Marie was worse off.

Finally I heard the door open and close, then a nasty little half-chuckle. My heart stopped.

What had amused him? I was sure it couldn't be good.

As I heard his footsteps disappear down the hall, I squeezed Marie's shoulder, then moved forward.

The line of light was gone. He'd left Celeste in the dark.

Stopping outside the door, I inserted the pick I'd held ready into the keyhole, trying not to make any sound as I fumbled to find the right fit.

Behind me, Marie's breathing sounded broken and far too loud. I could hear Danny's footsteps in the kitchen, then going into the office. I'd hoped he'd go back up to the top floor, but no such luck.

Still the lock resisted me.

I was sweating under my sweater, and beginning to think we'd need Plan B after all, then finally I had it.

As the lock gave, I heard footsteps again, and froze, listening hard.

He passed the basement stairway, then I could hear him heading up to the second floor. Whew.

My luck was in tonight.

I eased the handle down and slid the door open a crack.

Pitch blackness. No sound. No movement.

Now what?

I opened the door wider, slid my body forward.

"Celeste?" It was the softest whisper I could manage, and it sounded to me as though I'd shouted it.

I paused, trying to orient myself.

Still no movement.

Had he drugged her? Killed her? Was that what the chuckle had been?

Were we too late, after all?

A sudden rush of movement, felt more than seen, had me swinging to my right.

Too late.

A heavy weight hit me full on and I fell to the floor. And not quietly.

The grunt I couldn't keep in echoed in the silence.

"What?" It wasn't a voice I knew.

She sounded hoarse, and shocky. Celeste? "You're not him!"

No kidding.

Before I'd gathered my wits, there was a small cry and I could feel Marie beside me, flinging her arms around her sister.

"Celeste. My God, you're alive. We found you."

"And we have to get her out of here," I said, forcing myself to my feet.

Too late.

He'd heard us—of course—if the feet I heard thundering down from the second floor were any indication.

"Outside. Now!" I staggered to my feet. "Marie, get her out of here."

Somehow they managed not to trip over me and made it to the outer door before he reached the basement stairs.

I hunched in a doorway a few feet further down the hall.

Waiting for him.

I could just see his shadow, lurching down the hall. He looked far larger than the five eleven I knew him to be.

There was no room for any fancy kicks or throws. I didn't have a weapon of any kind. And I didn't know if he was armed.

I was hoping I could either attack him, distract him, or lead him in the other direction from the one Celeste and Marie would be taking. I wasn't sure if I could manage any of them, but I had to try.

First I'd see if I could distract him.

He hadn't turned on the light. Probably figured he knew the basement better than we did. It might give me an advantage, if I was fast and really, really lucky.

I ducked back into the doorway when the first shot went off, cringing instinctively at the sudden flash and muffled whine.

Silenced.

So he had a gun. But where was he aiming?

He had to be shooting blind.

Was he going to keep it up?

Apparently he was smarter than that. I couldn't see, but I could just hear his careful footsteps as he made his way down the hall.

A glance behind me showed Marie and Celeste had made it outside, but were still visible as they raced away from the house.

And Danny was getting close enough—if he was looking, he'd see them.

He was now within two feet of where I was hiding.

Taking a deep breath, I leapt at him, yelling at the top of my lungs.

He went over, but swung his gun hand towards me.

I grabbed for it.

And got a grip, but not a good one. I couldn't get the gun away from him. His reflexes were too good, and even off-balance he was too strong for me.

I ducked, and raced for the stairwell behind him before he could recover his balance.

There was a shot behind me that must have gone wide. I kept running.

Now he had a choice between following me or going to find out what had happened to Celeste.

I was counting on him thinking Celeste was alone, and seeing me as the bigger problem.

I was right. Unfortunately.

He was after me what felt like seconds later, cursing under his breath, feet thumping down the hallway.

I was already around the curve and out of his sight.

I had to get out of there before he could see me again and get off another shot.

I double-timed it up those stairs, my feet moving faster than I think I'd ever moved in my life.

I almost made it.

CHAPTER THIRTY-SIX

The first shot went wide.

The second hit the stair my foot had just left.

Then I was at the top and through the door.

Now what?

There was no time to decide, but no decision to be made, either.

Running through a house I didn't know in the dark was too dangerous. He knew it far better than I did, and all he had to do was turn on a light and I was a perfect target.

I'd have to go out the way I'd come in.

Gasping for breath, I increased my speed, while trying to keep my body mass compact.

No point in making a bigger target than I needed to.

Hugging the wall, I flew down the hall and through the kitchen.

I could hear him behind me—breathing hard, but moving fast.

He wasn't as fast as I was, but he knew the house better. And there was enough light coming from the kitchen that I was headed for that I'd be visible.

I just hoped he couldn't shoot and run.

He couldn't.

The third shot went wide.

But then I guess he figured it out, because the footsteps stopped and the next shot tore through my sleeve, missing my arm by a hair.

Using every ounce of energy I had left, I accelerated towards the French doors. Ripping them open, I dived for safety.

I could just hear a shot over my breathing. For a moment I thought he'd missed again.

Then it seemed as if my right arm didn't belong to me any more. A huge pain spread out from it.

I rolled, hit the ground too hard and came up out of it half-crouched. An almost whimper escaped my lips.

I hurt.

But I had to get away.

And I had to keep him focused on me. The other two had to escape.

It didn't seem like the former was going to be a problem.

Hugging my right arm against my body to provide what support I could, I ran in my half-crouch across the few yards between me and the hedge that had hidden me before.

Another shot whined by.

And missed.

I almost thought I might be safe. Then he turned the porch lights on.

"You might as well give up," he said, in a deceptively rational voice. "I know you're injured. I can see the blood trail. And you haven't got a hope of getting away from me."

Blood trail?

I nearly glanced at the injury, then forced myself not to look.

I squeezed my arm tighter to my side. I'd try to bind it later, but I needed to get further away first.

And I wasn't even going to think about the damage. It felt like someone had stabbed ice through my arm, then set it on fire. But it was probably just a graze.

I wasn't answering him, either.

He just wanted to get a fix on where I was.

The porch light just reached to the hedge, but the bushes were too thick for him to see much.

If I moved, though, he'd see the branches move.

I was trapped.

He walked further into the yard. "Look, it's getting cold out. You need something hot to drink before you go into shock. I'll make a hot toddy, run a bath."

He sounded so reasonable.

The guy was seriously out of touch with reality if he thought I'd believe him.

He was right, though—it was getting colder. Which at this time of year usually meant there was some kind of wind due any minute.

I took a slow breath. I could almost taste it.

I waited.

Around me, the leaves began to rustle, then the branches swayed a little.

Another shot. Then he seemed to realize what was happening. Silence.

The breeze kept picking up, until I judged it safe to ease my way deeper into the bushes.

After thirty seconds I stopped, listening.

No gunfire, and I couldn't hear him.

Had he turned back, gone after Celeste and Marie?

It didn't matter.

I had to get out of there before the ache in my shoulder and the blood I was steadily losing made escape impossible.

With any luck, he'd keep searching for me long enough for Marie and Celeste to get away.

If the wind held for another ten minutes, I'd be back in the trees.

Then a powerful flashlight played over my head and I froze.

Was this it?

No.

After a moment, the flashlight moved on, playing over the bushes from one side of the yard to the other.

Good. He hadn't seen which way I went.

And he must have been lying about the blood trail.

While the light was on the other side of the yard, I half ran, half wiggled my way through and behind a couple more thickets, until I broke into the trees.

Then I ran, still in my half crouch, for what felt like forever. Until finally it felt safe to stand up.

Well, actually it didn't really feel safe, but I couldn't move in that bent posture any longer.

I straightened up and felt my arm, which seemed to have stopped bleeding. The bullet couldn't have gone deep, even if it felt like I was dying.

Probably hadn't left much blood trail, either.

Keeping my arm squeezed tight to my side, I started to run again.

Staggered.

Then found my pace.

It wasn't fast, but it was steady, and hopefully quiet. All that morning running paid off.

And with more than my share of luck, it would get me out of here before Danny and his damn flashlight figured out where I'd gone.

———

I REACHED my car and slumped against it, breathing hard. There was no sign of Marie and Celeste.

I'd given Marie my key, but I kept a spare hidden under the rear bumper—even though I know exactly how stupid that can be if you're worried about your car being stolen.

I've always been more worried about finding myself in a situation like this one.

I fumbled around feeling for the key, trying not to pass out. Trying to hurry while making as little noise as possible was hard.

Focusing on finding it without glancing over my shoulder for any sign of Danny was harder.

Finally my fingers touched the key.

I had my car. And my cell phone. I called Jerry, left a fast message.

Now I had to find Marie and Celeste before Danny found us.

Celeste had been imprisoned for nearly a week. Her stamina was probably pretty bad. How far would she be able to run, even with Marie's help?

Could they have found safety with a neighbor?

Wishing the engine was a little quieter, I eased my way back onto Marine, drove a couple of blocks south before I turned around.

Driving past Danny's property, I was torn between crawling along checking every bush for the two sisters, and flooring it to get away from Danny and his gun.

The taste of terror lingered in my mouth. I glanced at my arm, half expecting to see fresh blood, but it seemed to have stopped.

It felt surreal—everything looked so peaceful.

This was a lush, beautiful part of the city, an unlikely spot for the violence Danny had brought into it.

Or so it seemed. I knew well enough how easily violence spreads into even the loveliest spots.

I held myself to a steady speed well under the limit, my eyes checking every bush, every shadow, every movement.

If Celeste and Marie had made it this far, I wouldn't fail them.

I had no desire to put myself back in Danny's line of fire, either.

I drove just over a mile past Danny's place, then turned around. Tempted as I was to just go get help, I couldn't take the chance Marie and her sister would make it out to the road, and find the car gone.

It would be too devastating, after everything the two of them had been through.

And I had a feeling that the sooner we could get Celeste to a hospital, the better.

I hadn't seen any obvious injuries, but there hadn't been much light. And the little I'd heard suggested Danny had been trying to break her. Which meant he'd have rationed her food, probably half-starved her. Some Prince Charming.

I thought I saw something and hit the brakes.

It must have been a raccoon, because when I stopped the car and cracked a window, nothing happened. No motion. No sound. Even the wind had died down.

I was starting to panic.

Even in this light, Marie would have recognized the car. Where were they?

Had Celeste collapsed?

Or had Danny somehow tracked them down?

I couldn't keep driving back and forth. I'd have to go and get help. We needed people to arrest Danny, people to search the woods.

I started the car, eased off the brake, then stopped again. Some instinct had me turning the motor off, then sitting very still, listening intently.

I couldn't tell you, then or now, what caught my attention. I'm not sure I even knew what I was listening for. But something compelled me to wait.

After a moment, I half-heard, half-saw a motion in the darkness, a rustle in the bushes.

Then I heard it, pitched just loud enough to carry. "Barbara?"

I was out of the car and over to the roadside before I thought about the dangers of a possible ambush.

It wouldn't have stopped me anyway. Though I might have been a little more cautious.

"Marie?"

A rustle, and I could see Marie's face, gleaming slightly in the light of the rising moon.

"Oh, thank God."

It was a voice I didn't know. Celeste.

"You're both here?" I asked as I reached down to help Marie to her feet.

"Yeah. I'm fine, help Celeste," she whispered.

"Get to the car," I told her as I parted the low-growing salal and reached down to help Celeste to her feet.

She staggered slightly. Her grip on my arm was tight, but she didn't hesitate.

"I'm okay." It was a harsh whisper that sounded like it came from a very dry throat, but there was determination in it.

"Come on. Let's get you out of here."

I had her almost to the car, when Danny's voice said, "Not so fast."

We both froze.

Then I gave Celeste a little shove towards the car.

Little rustles told me she'd kept going, though I didn't take my eyes away from the area Danny's voice had come from long enough to look. "What do you want?"

A dry laugh. "Oh, I think you know. I have a gun pointed at you. And if your friends there don't do exactly as I tell them, I'll shoot you. And this time I won't miss."

I'd left the key in the ignition. I hoped they had enough sense to get out of here. "I don't believe you."

Seconds later he stepped out of the bushes, and leveled the gun at me. Light from the solitary street lamp gleamed along the barrel.

I'm no expert, but it looked like he was aiming at my heart. Not a good feeling.

A clicking sound warned me, and as the engine fired on my Honda, I dropped to my knees.

Danny fired. I think he missed, or maybe he was out of bullets. I dropped to my knees, and scrambled for cover. Then realized the car wasn't pulling out onto the road.

It was heading straight for Danny.

He'd been trying to do something with the gun. By the time he looked up, it was too late.

With a yell I could see but not hear over the engine, he flung himself to one side.

Too little. Too late.

The fender of the Honda caught him and he flew a good five feet. He landed hard, and didn't move.

With a great screeching and a thump or two, my car came to a halt inches from a sturdy yellow pine. The air was full of scorched rubber and the chocking sound of the engine cooling down.

In the distance I could hear a siren, coming closer.

CHAPTER THIRTY-SEVEN

Celeste was still under sedation but Marie was already out of bed and popping into my hospital room almost before the doctor finished stitching up my arm. Apparently that bullet graze had been a little more serious than I'd thought.

"I don't know how to thank you," she said, plopping down into the visitor's chair that was empty only because they weren't allowing me visitors yet.

Knowing who was likely waiting in the visitor's lounge, that was probably self-defense on the nurses' part, rather than any medical concern about my condition. "How did you get in here?"

"They weren't looking."

It figured.

"But I really don't know how to thank you," Marie said.

Now she was appreciative?

"I'll send you an invoice." I was more than glad we'd found Celeste, but equally happy to be seeing the end of this particular client. "How is your sister?"

Her eyes filled. I stared.

She blinked hard. When every trace of moisture was gone, she grinned at me. "She's doing great. Underfed and dehydrated, but she's fighting back in a way I've never seen her fight before. I didn't know she had it in her."

Huh.

"And she says I can go to Paris."

Come again? Was the little chat I had all lined up going to be unnecessary after all? "Paris?"

"Yeah. I'm going to art school, the real thing."

Marie's voice broke and she swallowed hard. "When she didn't think she was going to make it, Celeste said it was the one thing she regretted, that I didn't get my chance. She said she'd decided if she ever got out, she'd find a way to send me, no matter where the money had to come from."

Uh oh. I had a pretty good idea where the money was likely to come from, but this particular plan didn't sound like it would help Marie grow up any. And given what I'd learned about Marie over the last few weeks, that wasn't good.

Then she surprised me. Again. "But I can't let her do it. It's my dream—I'm the one who needs to make it happen. Celeste has looked after me long enough."

Uh, what? "She has?"

"Uh huh. She's the one who's paid for everything. I just got dead end jobs, barely contributed to the food. But—she nearly died. And she comes out determined to make my dreams come true. Even if she can't understand them."

She looked down, picking at her ragged fingernails, then noticed what she was doing and stopped. "You know I wanted to be a tattoo artist, right?"

"I figured."

"Yeah. And I'm going to. I'm going to make really good money at it, too. Good enough to pay for Paris, and the training I really want."

She took a deep breath, met my eyes. "Because I think I can be more. And I'm going to try."

She leaned forward, put her hand on the blanket where my

hand lay. "That's what you're doing, right? All those canvases in the spare room. They're pretty decent."

"Thanks." I think. Given her apparent taste in clothes, what did it say if she liked my work?

"You're investigating to pay the bills, but you haven't given up on what really matters," she was saying. "You haven't given up on doing real art."

Wow. When this kid committed, she really gave it everything she had. "Something like that."

"Yeah. So I figured I could do that. Find work that lets me pay my own bills, and get the training I need to do the kind of art I was scared to even dream of doing."

They must have given me really good drugs, because this had to be a hallucination.

And then it got better. Or maybe worse. Scarier, anyway.

Marie looked at me, no grin in sight.

"You need more time to paint," she said. "I figure you could use an assistant. And I owe you. Besides, I think it could be cool."

What? I mean, what? "You want to be my assistant? I thought you planned to make money as a tattoo artist."

"I need more training before I'm ready to do that. I can help you out while I get it."

Okay, then. I pushed the call button. I was so not ready for this conversation.

"Are you in pain?"

Yeah, but it wasn't my arm that was the problem.

"My head's pounding," I said. Which was true. "I'm hoping they can give me something for it."

And remove her.

Maybe I just wasn't up for visitors yet.

———

I MUST HAVE DOZED OFF, because when I woke up, Nick was standing there staring down at me. There was an odd look on his face, like he wasn't really sure what to think.

Or maybe he just didn't know what to do when someone's in hospital.

Nope. He leaned over and kissed me. Wow.

He knew what to do, all right. Even managed it without jostling my various wounds. What can I say?

The man has finesse.

"You doing okay?" he asked.

"I am now."

"Good painkillers?" he said, straight-faced.

I laughed. "Yeah, that."

"I thought you were supposed to leave the rough stuff to us cops."

"It really wasn't me this time. My client…"

He rolled his eyes. "Marie? Yeah, I met her in the waiting area. She's a little—energetic."

"That's one way of putting it."

"Please tell me you're not going to hire her?"

Wait, was she telling everyone that? "No worries. I don't think I can afford an assistant."

"According to Marie, once you sell out that show of yours, you won't be able to afford not to have one."

Marie said that? No way she'd really liked my stuff. "She's just grateful I helped her find her sister."

"Yeah, I spotted that. But I think she really likes your work." A beat. "So when do I get to see these paintings?"

Umm. "They aren't exactly ready to show. Marie was snooping."

He just looked at me. I narrowed my eyes at him. "Says the man who barely has time for dinner these days."

"That should be changing any day now."

My brain was still feeling kinda hazy, so it took me a second. "You've nailed him? The Stalker?"

"Let's just say we're close."

"Nick, that's great." No wonder he looked like he hadn't slept. "Wait a minute. If you're that close, why are you here? Shouldn't you be chasing down loose ends or something?"

"Barbara, you've just been shot."

"So? It's not like it's life-threatening or anything. Isn't even my painting arm."

He gave me that look again. "I'll go back later. Right now, this is where I need to be."

Nope, I really wasn't up to visitors.

Something in my expression must have given me away. My poker face was supposed to be better than that. Nick smiled at me, the worry lines easing in his forehead.

I was happy to see it, in a funny, disconnected kind of way.

"It's a good thing I did come by. Your sister and your nephew are in the waiting room, too. Your nephew Cory, right? He seemed pretty relieved you were going to be okay."

They were? "That's nice."

"Hmmm. Cory also seemed somewhat upset to hear Marie was going to be your assistant. Something about it being his job?"

He slanted a look at me, and his smile widened into a grin. "And I'm pretty sure I saw steam coming out of your sister's ears when he said that. Though I'm sure being injured will save you from whatever the problem is."

Oh no. I'd forgotten about leaving Cory in my office. And I'd only left that one message for Susanna. I never did get the chance to have that chat with her. "I think I need more painkillers."

His grin spread. "Appreciating me yet?"

"Oh, definitely."

"Yeah, I kinda thought you might be."

"I don't suppose there's any way you could get my room quarantined? That I'd really appreciate."

"Last thing I checked, bullet wounds weren't contagious. And neither is stinging nettle."

"Stinging..." Oh. That explained the itching. Damn it.

"But you're looking a bit pale. Like you need a good night's sleep. And no more visitors."

"Now you're talking."

Then I processed the rest of what he'd said. "Wait a minute. They going to keep me in here? I wasn't hurt that badly."

"You lost a fair bit of blood."

Oh. That's probably why I'd felt like I was going to pass out.

"So they want to keep me under observation." I sighed. It figured.

And maybe they had a shot or something for the itching.

"Yup, that's the plan. If you're good, I'll spring you tomorrow. And if you're really good, I'll make it early, before your sister gets here."

"Can you get away?"

"Not for long, but yes."

"You don't need to, you know."

"I want to." And there was a look on his face that stopped me arguing.

I grinned instead, though I suspect it wasn't quite as light-hearted as I'd hoped. "That'll get you bonus points."

"Thought it might," he said. And kissed me again.

CHAPTER THIRTY-EIGHT

It was four days before the itching stopped. And that was with the really good anti-itching cream. Oh well.

Guess that's what I get for going after Marie. And for taking her on as a client in the first place.

Still, aside from the itching—and the bullet wound—it all turned out pretty well.

Celeste was going to be fine, Marie was going to be an artist, Danny—well, Danny was going to be locked away for a long time.

And I was pretty sure it was going to be in a mental facility, not a prison. Maybe they could help him.

Celeste wasn't even mad at him. She'd come to see me the previous morning—still pale—but with that inner strength showing on the outside now.

It felt almost surreal to meet her, when I'd learned so much about her during the course of the investigation. I'd come to feel I knew her, and it was odd to meet her in person and realize what a false assumption that had been.

I knew a lot about what other people thought of Celeste, and a fair bit about what had shaped her, but the three dimensional person with emotions chasing across her translucent skin? Her I'd have to get to know slowly.

I hoped I had the opportunity.

She walked into my office shaking out her umbrella, her steps light, and beamed at me. "Barbara O'Grady," she said. "Is this a good time?"

I nodded, mute for once. I hadn't expected to see her—had, in fact, expected to have the office to myself all day.

"Marie wanted to come, but I told her no, that I was fine now. And I wanted to talk to you alone. She looked a little worried," Celeste said with a laugh.

I could see why Marie might have looked worried. I had no intention of breaking confidentiality, but I hoped she would eventually tell Celeste everything.

I wasn't counting on it, though.

Celeste surprised me again. "Don't worry, she's told me everything—or at least what she says is everything. Including how she helped Danny find me. And even if she's held something back, I'd never ask you about it."

Celeste paused, then said in a rush. "I just wanted to thank you. I think most people would have given up on me, and I know exactly how difficult Marie can be. Especially if she's trying to hide something she's feeling guilty about.

I don't know how you found me," and she put up her hand as I started to speak. "But I will be forever grateful. I need you to know that. And to know that I do understand exactly how hard this case must have been for you. And I don't mean just getting shot."

"You're welcome. I'm just glad we found you in—I mean I'm glad you're fine," I said, feeling awkward. "You must feel safer with Danny locked away."

She waved a thin hand, dismissing it. "He didn't hurt me that much, not like he could have. He just wanted the life he thought he was meant to have. His father damaged him so badly, he managed to cripple both Danny's sense of self and his judgment of others. Danny needed a princess, and he was trying to turn me into one."

She grinned at me, and her face came alive. "It didn't work. I'm nobody's ivory tower princess. He couldn't break me, or twist me to his image of who I should be. No matter what he tried. I wouldn't wish an experience like that on anyone, but it was strangely empowering."

"I'm amazed you've come through it so well."

She smiled at that. "Funny, that's what everyone says. Right before they very tactfully suggest I consider counseling."

She looked across the desk at me. "You might understand, though. I survived growing up in Brenton, survived living with my aunt. I'm not as malleable or as breakable as people seem to assume."

I nodded. I did understand. Or at least I thought I did.

Celeste wasn't finished. "It would have been worse for me, I think," she said thoughtfully, "if I hadn't understood Danny so well. We both came from Brenton, after all, and I think he was just trying to put things back to a time when he'd felt happy and secure. He was always a loner, and I suspect he's a computer genius, which makes it harder for him. I just hope there will be some way he can contribute and feel valued, even now."

I wouldn't be that forgiving, so I didn't say much.

It didn't seem to bother her. I think she'd just needed to tell me her story, because she didn't stay long after that.

Though she did say she'd be in touch. I hoped she meant it—I liked her and was intrigued by her outlook on life—in about equal measure. I wondered what Andrea would make of her.

My sister, on the other hand, is still not speaking to me. If I didn't feel so guilty, I'd be quite happy about that part. She can't blame me for stuff if she isn't talking to me.

Or at least, that's what I'd always thought. Apparently I was wrong.

Cory's pretty happy, though. Susanna agreed he could keep working for me, but under some very rigid guidelines. I got a copy of the e-mail laying them out—so there would be no misunderstandings.

And true to my promise to him, we went shopping. His new laptop is being delivered on Friday. I'm still swallowing hard over the cost.

But he earned it—or at least he will. He still owes me for about half of it.

He's really excited about that part, too. For some reason, he thinks it's really cool to be working for me.

I keep trying to point out that he's not actually working for me, that I'm contracting some particular tasks to him, but he's decided not to hear that part.

Marie's not much better. She's still determined to work for me, too.

I'm still telling her no, but she was sneaky enough to enlist Margaret Courtland, who is now really insistent that she see at least four new paintings from me by the end of the month.

That would be the paintings I've barely had a chance to work on since this all started.

I can't see how I can run my business and get any of them done in time. And I'm not willing to give up either one.

Which Marie knows.

I have a suspicion Margaret knows it too. She's too experienced to push an artist too hard, especially when she wants something.

I sighed, poured another cup of coffee. I needed to go for a run, but the doc said not until next week. And apparently stinging nettle and paint is a bad combination, too.

Which was why I was stuck in my office, staring out at a spring day that looked more like November. I wandered over to the window, watched it rain, and brooded.

It wasn't even as if Marie needed the money she'd earn working for me.

My gamble in telling Kathleen about the two sisters had paid off. She'd immediately signed them on as clients, with a hefty advance against the value of their mother's works.

And she'd known exactly how to manipulate the buzz to turn

one high-priced artist into two high-priced artists. It helped that since both artists are dead, there would be no new works.

And that Anthea Swan's already limited body of work had just shrunk by approximately a tenth.

It also helped that the critics could now analyze both artists and their work in the context of the ongoing nature versus nurture discussion. To quote one critic "this casts a new light on the evolution of women artists at a seminal point in art history."

Of course, that article was followed by a blog that took exactly the opposite view. There was more, but I'd only skimmed it.

Long story short—Celeste and Marie wouldn't have to worry about money for a long time. Probably ever.

It would take quite a while for the lawyers to work through what part of Anthea's estate actually belonged to her sister, and hence to Celeste and Marie. But the paintings Eleanor had done that Bet had rescued were going to auction. And even at the proposed bid prices, Celeste and Marie were going to clean up.

So Marie wanting to work for me made no sense. She could afford to go to New York or Paris and study art immediately. She, of course, saw it differently.

"Nope," she said when I broached the subject. "I figure it would have taken me a few years to earn that money. I'd have worked days, taken courses at night. I'm still going to do that."

"But why, when you don't need to?"

She gave me a look I couldn't read. "I figure I owe you those years."

"You've paid me for the work I did."

I still couldn't believe the size of the check I'd just deposited. I'd have argued harder, except I knew she could afford it.

And I had earned it, every penny of it, for the annoyance factor alone. If I never had another client like Marie, it would be too soon.

And now she wanted me to hire her? Not happening.

"I paid you for helping me find, and rescue, Celeste. Which is what I hired you for. But finding out that my Mom had been an artist? Finding all those paintings? And building her reputation at the same time? I owe you big." A pause.

She stared at the floor for a minute, then looked up. Her eyes were shiny. "We both do, but me? I never knew my Mom, and the kind of artist my aunt was?"

She shook her head. "I didn't want anything to do with that. But now, knowing my Mom was an artist too, and a different kind of artist?"

She seemed to run out of words, spread her hands wide.

"I'm an artist too," I said. "It needed to be done."

She swallowed hard. "Yeah, I know. And that's why."

"Why what?"

"Why I'm going to work for you. You need to get those paintings done. And without someone to help you, you won't."

"But…"

She grinned, piercings glinting at me. "You might as well give up now. I'm pretty persistent when I'm right."

Maybe. But I've always considered stubbornness to be one of my better qualities.

No way was Marie going to work for me.

———

"SO WHEN DOES SHE START?" Nick asked me two days later.

It was a fresh, sunny day and we were both sprawled in the grass overlooking the ocean. "Monday."

He grinned. "You don't sound very happy about it."

Nope. Even my post-run high couldn't overcome how disgruntled I felt about my new assistant.

Not to mention that Marie had now unequivocally proven she could out-stubborn me. That was a bad sign for our working relationship.

"It's only for a few months, till after my show," I told him.

"I thought Marie had a longer time frame in mind."

Like I was going to put up with her for three years. "She did.

But once the show's done, it's time for her to focus on her own artistic career."

"Rather than yours?"

I grinned at him. "Yup. Rather than mine."

"And how do you think that argument will work for you?"

"P. I. work can be pretty boring. Especially when compared to painting in New York. Or Paris. And I don't think discipline is Marie's strong point."

He gave a snort of laughter. "Probably not. Pretty sneaky."

"Yup." And proud of it.

"I like that in a woman."

"Uh huh. Enough resting, you. I'll race you back."

"You are remembering my legs are longer?"

But I was already running.

ACKNOWLEDGMENTS

Writing is a solitary pursuit, but I'm blessed to be part of a larger community of writers, both in person and online, without whom finishing books would be even more challenging.

Many thanks to all those writers who were part of my journey with this book, including Bobbi Randall, Roberta Rich, Sandy Constable, Carla Lewis, Colleen Cross, Kelly Morisseau as well as all those blogging writers who seem to have just the right words of wisdom when I most need it.

Thanks also to Bobbi Randall for feedback on the beta version. Special thanks go to Linda Roggeveen for an amazing copy edit. Any errors or omissions are, of course, mine.

9 781988 037189